MURDER ON MONDAY

Recent Titles by Ann Purser

MIXED DOUBLES
NEW EVERY MORNING
ORPHAN LAMB
PASTURES NEW
SPINSTER OF THIS PARISH
THY NEIGHBOUR'S WIFE

MURDER ON MONDAY

Ann Purser

This first world edition published in Great Britain 2002 by
SEVERN HOUSE PUBLISHERS LTD of
9–15 High Street, Sutton, Surrey SM1 1DF.
This first world edition published in the USA 2002 by
SEVERN HOUSE PUBLISHERS INC of
595 Madison Avenue, New York, N.Y. 10022.

British Library Cataloguing in Publication Data

Purser, Ann, 1933-
    Murder on Monday
    1. Country life - England - Fiction
    2. Detective and mystery stories
    I. Title
    823.9'14 [F]

    ISBN 0-7278-5860-2

Typeset by Palimpsest Book Production Ltd.,
Polmont, Stirlingshire, Scotland.
Printed and bound in Great Britain by
MPG Books Ltd., Bodmin, Cornwall.

Sic transit Gloria mundi

In the damp, raw cold of a winter's evening, the women sat in rows in Long Farnden village hall, not listening to an elderly Land Girl's memories of 'Life on the Farm During The War'. Most of them had switched off soon after she began, when it became clear there were to be no memories of passion in the pigsty or tumbles in the hay. Soon they were thinking of other things, of husbands, lovers . . . husbands' lovers.

In the village hall kitchen, a gloomy room smelling of drains and unemptied rubbish bins, Miss Gloria Hathaway, small and trim and used to being obeyed, cursed and wrestled in vain with the control dial on a rumbling, rocking tea urn, full of boiling rusty water. It was her turn to make tea and she had laid out the cups and saucers, plates of cakes, sugar bowl and milk jug. Everything was ready, and now this wretched woman would not stop. She could hear her voice droning on about unwilling tractors and rampaging bulls, and tried again to calm the angry beast in front of her. The kitchen was full of steam and she could hardly see the numbers of the dial. In any case, it didn't matter. Even 'off' made no difference. The thing was out of control and she backed away from it.

She didn't hear or see the door out into the night open quietly behind her and the black shape slip into the kitchen. She pushed back her sandy hair from her damp face and turned around to go for help. Blasted thing! Typical of that lot in there . . . Then she saw the black shape coming towards her, arms outstretched as if to embrace her, eyes glittering through the steam. She gasped and stepped back, caught between two horrors. 'No!' she choked. 'What . . . ?' But before she could finish her sentence, the black-gloved hands had her by the throat and ineptly strangled . . .

1

'Any questions, anybody?' asked Mrs Evangeline Baer, as the Land Girl finally came to a halt. The women knew better than to ask, and Mrs Baer continued quickly, 'Has someone told Miss Hathaway we're ready for tea?'

But Gloria Hathaway had missed her cue, and after the women went into the kitchen to see why, things were never the same again.

One

Lois Meade walked angrily along the frosty pavement of Byron Way on the Churchill Estate, relieved that her house was now in sight. It would be quiet and deserted, and she could have a coffee and wind down. With the children all at school and husband Derek at work, she wouldn't have to explain about the flat tyre and her humiliating struggle, and the long walk up from the garage in Tresham. She passed by where her in-laws used to live, and thanked God old Mrs M could no longer rush out and drag her in for tea and criticism.

The Meades had been a bit above Lois's family socially. At least, that is what Derek's mother had thought. Derek's father had his own electrician's business, which Derek subsequently took over. Lois's parents were backstreet Tresham folk – her father had been in the same shoe factory all his working life – and were respectable enough. They had one child, Lois Jennifer, who, despite doting parents and a happy home, or perhaps because of them, had been a rebel from the start. In playschool, she had been withdrawn after she'd kicked a little boy in the face, despite her protestations that he'd stuck his tongue out at her. And by the time she was a teenager, tall and already beautiful in a dark, skinny way, with a lively brain but an absolute determination not to use it on school work, she was in constant trouble. She smoked at thirteen – always plenty of fags around at home – and had not bothered to conceal it. She had experimented with alcohol and rejected it only because she did not like the taste, and was not averse to a little light shoplifting in Woolworths. Lois grew up with the wrong friends and quite often on the wrong side of the law.

It was all mild stuff with never any more serious results than a severe caution from kindly policemen, but her mother, who could be formidable when required, eventually faced Lois with an ultimatum: either she changed her ways, or it was a job in Woolworths (this appealed to Lois's sense of humour) with no prospects. Lois's mother had a friend who could work it, so she'd better decide. A dead end job, or a new leaf; that was the choice. Lois chose the dead end job because she knew that it was the wrong choice, and there she had met Derek Meade. He had collided with her on a crowded Saturday and it was lust at first sight. Added to that, she made him laugh a lot, and had clearly never heard that the customer was always right.

Lois and Derek had started off their married life in Byron Way and Lois had matured, finally, under Derek's benign influence. He had not tried to change her because he loved her as she was – stroppy, fierce and strong-minded. But after three children had come along, a delight in motherhood and a latent sense of responsibility had brought out the best in Lois. To her great surprise, she found she loved babies in just the same soppy way she'd despised in others.

Derek's mother had been thrilled with her first grandchild, Josie, pleased that the second was a boy, Douglas, but when the third, Jamie, arrived, she'd fled back to Ireland, from where she sent postcards, hoping everything was well with them and looking forward to seeing them soon. Lois had not minded. Her own mother lived close by, and in her unfussed, straightforward way had helped out wherever needed. She took the boys to school, long after they considered it necessary, brought them home again, and was always there. Josie, Lois's only girl, came and went with her mates on the estate, but occasionally dropped in on her grandmother to shelter from her mother's wrath and listen to tales of Lois's own dodgy adolescence.

Derek's father had set him a good example, and he was never short of a job. He covered a wide area in and around town, and claimed he had found Lois's job for her. When Jamie had started school, she had announced that she'd be going out cleaning. 'It's all I know,' she'd said practically. 'And we could do with the money.' The kids had frowned on this, mainly because of the loss of status with their friends.

'They'll say you're a skivvy,' Josie had said.

4

'So?' replied Lois.

But she had relented and said she wouldn't work in Tresham but look for jobs outside the town, in the villages.

'Think of the petrol money!' Derek had said. 'Hardly worth it . . .'

In the end, it was Derek who solved the problem. He'd been rewiring an old house in Long Farnden, six miles from town, and been asked by the owner, Mrs Baer, if he knew of a cleaner. Evangeline Baer ran an art gallery in the converted barn at the rear of the house, and as it prospered she had less and less time for keeping her house as pristinely clean as she liked. Lois had suited her well and she had recommended her to friends in the village.

Now all Lois's mornings were taken up with Long Farnden houses, and on Derek's advice she had added the petrol money on to her rate of pay. On her first morning with each new employer she explained that she treated her cleaning as a business. 'You'll find me reliable and trustworthy,' she announced. 'And I shall expect the same in return. Money regularly each week, and cash, please.' One or two of them raised their eyebrows, but finding her as good as her word, they toed the line. When they met at local gatherings, they talked of Lois with respect and some awe.

'We're all a bit frightened of her!' said Evangeline Baer to the doctor's wife, and she wasn't joking.

Lois knew this, of course, and had no compunction in summarily leaving one job where she'd had to wait weeks for her money. She enjoyed her business, including one unexpected aspect which she found a great source of amusement and interest. She had her own unique position in the village: a close and intimate knowledge of five of its houses and their owners. Her declared policy was not to gossip, but this did not mean that she was an unwilling recipient of all kinds of juicy items. As she said to Derek, she knew more than ever appeared in the parish magazine, or on the noticeboard outside the village hall.

A family with three growing kids is expensive, and when Lois started with Mrs Baer, it had been hard for the Meades to find the money to buy the battered old Vauxhall Astra for

Lois to drive to work. But with a bit of help from Lois's mother, they'd managed it, and up to today she had been travelling without mishap.

Today she'd had her first flat tyre. She had felt the steering become heavy and suddenly the car had veered towards the kerb. The entrance to a free car park was fifty yards further on, and she'd bumped along slowly, turned in and stopped in a corner space away from the road. The front nearside tyre was completely flat and beginning to rip apart where she had driven it on the rim. 'Sod it,' she'd said loudly, and a little old man, struggling into a vehicle adapted for disability, had turned and looked at her and smiled.

'I'd help you, duck,' he'd said, 'but I ain't quite up to it now.'

She had sighed, assured him she'd be fine, and set about finding the spare tyre. An hour later, her hands covered with grease and dirt, Lois had had to admit defeat. She had failed at the first hurdle, unable to move the nuts that held the wheel. She'd phoned Derek on his mobile, and he'd told her to get help.

He was twenty miles away and in the middle of a job that couldn't be left. 'Get Fred from the garage opposite,' he'd said. But it was Fred's day off, and she'd been told to leave it there and they'd see to it when they had time.

'Yes, it would be today,' they'd said, but couldn't tell exactly when. She'd set off on the long walk home.

Now she approached her front door and noticed with alarm that it was ajar. She stepped inside the kitchen warily and saw Josie perched on the edge of the table, reading a magazine.

'What are you doing home?' she said, and was unconvinced by her explanation of a free afternoon from school. Lois was a parent governor at the local school and was well aware that she of all people should be able to put a stop to truancy in her own family. 'How did you get in, then?' she said.

'Gran let me in,' was Josie's reply. 'She was coming this way to see her friend along the road.'

'Huh,' said Lois, and reached for the kettle.

Josie was fourteen and already attractive in an adult way. Her soft, thick hair hung straight and long and shone from constant brushing. She was dark, like Lois, with the same brown, gold-flecked eyes. But she had spots, and suffered.

'Did you get that stuff?' she said.

'What stuff?' said Lois.

'The spot stuff! Oh God, I suppose you forgot!'

'Don't swear,' said Lois mechanically, stirring the tea bag round in her cup. One law for her and another for her children, Derek often reminded her. 'And no, I didn't forget. It's in that bag, and it'll cost you a week's baby-sitting money. I don't know why you bother, Josie. All kids get spots at your age.' She was cold, tired and irritable, and even as she said it she knew she was being unfair. Spots had been the end of the world for her, too, at Josie's age.

'You're late, anyway,' said Josie, and Lois softened and told her about the flat tyre and the long walk. Then there was another thing that had delayed her, and she hesitated. Josie persisted. 'What else, then? Shouldn't have taken you this long.'

'Blimey!' said Lois. 'What is this? The Spanish Inquisition, or what? Well, if you must know, I went to the cop shop, seeing as I was passing . . .'

Josie looked at her in alarm. On the Churchill Estate, anything to do with the police meant trouble. 'What's up, then?' she said.

'Nothing,' said Lois. 'Just went to ask something. Here, give us the milk . . . it'll be off by the time you've finished twiddling it about.'

The visit to the police station had not been a sudden impulse. Lois had been feeling restless lately. Her cleaning business was fine and the money regular, but she thought about things on her journeys to and from Long Farnden. Several times over the last few weeks she had remembered her father's words. He'd always said she'd regret her wasted schooldays, and she had jeered. 'A good brain's a gift,' he'd said. 'Reckon it's a sort of sin to waste it.' She had recoiled from this hangover from her father's chapel-going youth, and dismissed him out of hand. For God's sake, she had a whole life in front of her!

But now, with all the talk around of education later in life, she'd wondered. She had brought up the idea of evening classes in a conversation with her mother, who had said firmly that she thought Lois had enough on her plate for the moment, what with Derek and the kids. Lois had thought some more. Back to school? It'd be like surrender, wouldn't it? No, not really me, Lois had chuckled. I can read and write and that'll have to be enough.

Then, just by chance, she'd seen the notice in the *Tresham Town Crier*:

LOOKING FOR SOMETHING SPECIAL TO DO?
Why not consider becoming a Special Constable?

Lois had read that racial or ethnic origin, age, sex, marital status or disability, were no bar to entry and had decided to find out more. 'British, Irish or Commonwealth Citizen' – nobody more British than her. 'Able to give up at least four hours per week'. Not a lot, that. A bit of reorganizing with Mum and Derek and should be a doddle. She thought of her own previous encounters with the police – a long time ago now, but still clear in her mind – and smiled. It'd be the other side of the fence, but none the worse for that.

'I went about a job,' said Lois to Josie.

'Thought you said you wouldn't clean near home,' she said suspiciously.

'Not cleaning,' answered Lois.

'Well, go on,' said Josie, 'tell all. You up for Chief Inspector, then?'

'Clever!' said Lois with a smile. 'No, I went to find out about being a Special.' She handed over a shiny leaflet she'd been given.

Josie looked at it in silence, and then exploded. 'Oh my God!' she shouted. 'That's rich! Our Mum in the cops!'

'No,' said Lois calmly. 'Not a regular policewoman – a Special Constable. It's different.'

But Josie couldn't see the difference, and slammed out of the room, yelling from half-way up the stairs, 'Just wait 'til Dad finds out!'

Ah yes, thought Lois. There is that.

Two

Telling Derek was not going to be easy. Lois would have to choose the right moment, and then he would take some persuading. He was very old-fashioned in some ways, and Byron Way had never, so far as she knew, produced a woman Special. She thought about it on and off the next day and then, late on Sunday evening, decided the time had come.

Lois grinned to herself as she topped up the bathwater from the hot tap with her big toe. Fancy me, she thought, thinking of going over to the enemy! The nail polish on her toe was peeling, and she picked at it, sending blood-like slivers floating off on to the surface. She'd not bothered to take it off properly at the end of the summer, and now picked away until it had all gone. Ugh! She pulled out the plug quickly, before Derek should come in and be put off the plans she had for him.

'Derek?' Lois stretched out on the bed in what she hoped was a languorous pose.

'Yep, that's me,' said Derek amiably. He had won his darts match at the pub and had celebrated accordingly. Now he turned to look at Lois, and said, 'For God's sake, woman, get under the covers! You'll catch y'death.'

Lois sighed. So much for seduction. She slid under the duvet and smiled sweetly at him.

'Bugger it!' he said. 'Forgot to have a pee.' He disappeared off to the bathroom, stumbling on Lois's wet towel and cursing loudly. When he came back, Lois welcomed him with long arms and a warm body.

'Derek,' she said again.

'Me darlin'!' he said boozily.

'Um,' whispered Lois, 'I was thinking of training to be a Special. What d'you think?'

9

'You're special enough already,' he mumbled, turning towards her. Before things got beyond sensible conversation, Lois said quickly, 'No, a Special Constable . . . you know . . .'

'A *what*?' said Derek, rearing up over her.

'Well, a kind of spare-time job, uniform and that . . .' Lois squirmed a little, trying to release her trapped arm. She then giggled, knowing she'd get nowhere tonight. Might as well enjoy defeat.

Derek's head swam. He wished he hadn't had that last pint. With a big effort, he brought up before his eyes his late father's list of recommended ways of dealing with stroppy women. He selected the words 'a good seeing-to', and got on with it.

The next morning, Derek was quiet at the breakfast table. The children had all gone off to school with Lois's mother, and now Lois looked at him tentatively. 'Shouldn't you be gone by now?' she said. He swallowed a crust of toast, washed it down with the last mouthful of tea, and swivelled round on his chair to look at her.

'Got to talk, haven't we,' he said.

'Well, yes, but not right now,' said Lois firmly. 'It's Mrs Rix, Mondays, and she gets snotty if I'm late.'

'Never mind Mrs Rix. Cleanin' help is not that easy to find. Now you just sit down here and tell me what you're up to.' He was proud of Lois, but sometimes found it hard to assert his head-of-the-house position when she was in this mood.

Lois knew she needed Derek on her side, so fetched the shiny brochure and handed it to him. 'This'll tell you,' she said. 'I've more or less decided, but I'd like you to agree.'

'Well, thanks very much. Very honoured,' said Derek. He opened the brochure and looked at the photographs of attractive men and women in police uniform helping grateful people out of a number of difficult situations. Two of them, one a policewoman, were sorting out a fight between two hefty youngsters. 'Here!' said Derek, alarmed. 'I don't want you getting into no fights! We need you in one piece here at home. Fine mess we'd be in if you got beaten up!'

'Mum'd help,' said Lois. 'She's come round to the idea.'

'Told her before me, as usual?' Derek thought of making something serious of it, but realized his best course of action was compliance. Lois wouldn't like the job. Not with the police! No, better go along with it for the moment. 'Not much good my objecting, then, is it?' he said. Lois bent over and kissed him enthusiastically, and he grabbed her round the waist. 'Time for a quick one, then?' he said. 'Or shall I get arrested?'

Mrs Rix, Mondays, was waiting for Lois on the doorstep of her foursquare Edwardian redbrick house in Little Farnden. They were two of a kind, Lois had decided, Mrs Rix and her house. Secure and dependable and pleasant enough, provided you did not overstep the mark. Mrs Rix's husband was the local GP and the house had an appropriately reassuring air. Although Dr Rix was in partnership with other doctors at the medical centre in Tresham, he maintained the old tradition of a village surgery in his house, reserving a small room as consulting room, with an even smaller room for waiting patients. There was seldom a queue and the older people appreciated not having to travel into Tresham on the bus to see the doctor.

Mrs Rix ran a neat and orderly house, with a regular routine. Lois never moved the ornaments from their ordained places, never pinched off dead heads of flowers that might be saved for seeds. In some of her other houses Lois was encouraged to make suggestions of all kinds, but not here.

Dr Rix was approaching retirement, but still carried out his duties as doctor and chairman of the parish council with dedication, kindness and warmth. When he first came to the village as a handsome, newly-married young man, he had been shy, and the nearest he came to joking with patients was a pat on the head for a six-year-old malingerer with a jovial 'I expect you're longing to get back to school!' But his confidence had grown, and now he was an indispensable institution in the village. They knew they'd never get another like Dr Rix.

When Lois opened the latched gate and saw Mary Rix waiting for her, she knew the doctor would already have beaten a hasty retreat into his study and immersed himself in *The Times*. He couldn't bear the whirlwind upset of Lois days; the roaring of the old Hoover, her opening of windows

11

even in the depths of winter, her involuntary bursts of song in a loud and tuneless voice.

'Morning, Lois,' said Mary Rix, with only a small smile. 'We were beginning to think you were ill?'

Lois shook her head. 'Have I ever let you down, Mrs Rix?' she said. 'I'd always let you know if I couldn't come. No, Derek and me had something urgent to discuss.' She made it sound like a matter of life and death, and Mary Rix's irritation turned to sympathy, as Lois had intended.

'If there's anything we can do to help . . .'

Lois nodded at Mary, and took off her coat, collecting cleaning things from the cupboard. 'Doctor in his study?' she said. Mrs Rix nodded. 'He'll be gone shortly, though. Another call from Miss Hathaway . . . a creaking door if there ever was one!'

It was so unusual for Mrs Rix to say anything at all about the doctor's patients that Lois turned to look at her in surprise.

Mrs Rix's face was set hard, and she banged the cutlery drawer shut with a rattle. 'Right!' she said. 'I must get going, Lois. It'll be coffee break before we know it.'

Lois headed for the doctor's study thoughtfully. She'd seen Miss Hathaway outside the village shop on her way to work and she'd looked fine to Lois. Smarter than usual, with her hair done in a new way. Lois shrugged. There were plenty of ailments not visible to the naked eye and Gloria Hathaway was probably one of those who kept a medical dictionary by the bed. She paused, and then knocked at the study door.

'I shall be on my way, then,' said Andrew Rix, smiling at Lois, and touching her arm gently as he moved towards the door. 'Give you a clear field, my dear,' he added. Lois had a soft spot for the doctor. He always treated her with unfailing courtesy and this was a scarce quality in Lois's world.

Gloria Hathaway's cottage was like a tea-cosy: thatched roof, diamond-paned windows, criss-crossing beams, hollyhocks in summer, holly berries in winter, and a crazy-paving path up which Dr Rix now strode in the damp November air. He was still a fit, strong figure, never giving way to the self-doctoring temptation of his profession at times of stress. Dear Mary was his medicine! The perfect wife, he often told her, but knew from her expression that she still thought herself otherwise.

Miss Hathaway's door opened a few inches and her small, freckled face looked out. She glanced beyond the doctor and saw her neighbour, the community nurse, hovering on the footpath between their gardens. 'Ah, Doctor,' she said. 'You're early . . .'

'It's a Lois day,' he explained, and as she opened the door wider, he stepped inside.

Three

L ois had filled in the blue card with her name, address and telephone number, but hadn't ticked the box asking for a Special to visit. She could just see the boys scowling in the kitchen while she gave a cup of tea to the enemy. No, better to keep it as separate from home as possible. She would wait to be summoned to the station.

'Very good!' laughed Derek, when she explained it to him. '*Summoned* to the station . . . yo ho . . . very good!'

'All right, all right,' said Lois, 'it's not that funny.'

'What time's your train, Mum?' said Josie. 'See? station . . . get it?' she explained to Douglas and Jamie. Jamie still didn't get it.

'Oh yeah,' shrugged Douglas, refusing to be amused. 'Don't matter what she says, it's the cops. You want to watch out, Josie Meade,' he added maliciously, 'else they'll be checking on your school bag . . .' He made a swift exit upstairs then, too swift for Josie to follow.

'What did he mean, Josie?' said Lois sharply, and stepped forward to look for herself, but Josie nipped smartly out of the door and through the gate.

'Anyway,' said Derek, as if nothing had happened, 'it says here you can go to an Open Evening – gives a phone number of the Specials Project Officer – blimey, what're you gettin' yourself into, Lois?'

Jamie had picked up another leaflet and wouldn't give it back. Lois reached out to cuff him lightly round the ear. 'Watch it, Mum!' he yelled. 'Says here you got to be calm and restrained . . . and only apply force when necessary . . .'

'I'll teach you what's necessary, young man,' said Lois, as

14

he ducked. She sank down on to a chair and looked at Derek. 'Shall I give up now?' she said.

'Give up what?' said her mother's voice, and she appeared in the kitchen, a big stately woman, hatted and gloved, her specs glinting in the light. Before waiting for an answer, she continued, 'Come along you lot,' and like an experienced sheep dog, she rounded up the boys and all were gone.

'Time for me to go, too,' said Lois, clearing away the breakfast remains.

Derek was still absorbed by the leaflet. 'I've got an idea,' he said. 'I could join too, then we could be like Dempsey and Makepeace.'

'More like Morecambe and Wise,' said Lois. 'Anyway, I haven't decided . . . not finally.'

'Hey, wait a minute!' said Derek urgently. 'Says here Specials are volunteers and don't get paid!'

''Course they don't, if they're volunteers,' said Lois breezily, and ran upstairs to tidy the kids' beds before she left for Professor Barratt, Tuesdays.

Professor M.J. Barratt, MA, PhD, had lived in Long Farnden for only a couple of years. 'Though it seems like more!', said his wife Rachel, often. She was a friendly soul, anxious to be loved, and an embarrassment to her two teenage daughters. Malcolm Barratt had given up the Chair in Law at the University of Hull at an earlier age than was customary. He awoke one sunny autumn morning, when the trees were fiery reds and golds, and the world seemed to stretch away from the close confines of the university, full of mystery and promise. He knew quite suddenly that it was time to move on. Rachel was not pleased. She loved the academic world, though, as she said loudly and with a self-deprecatory laugh, she was no academic herself. But she felt the reflected glory of the professor's wife and liked the social life with other wives who were willing to talk about subjects of interest to Rachel. She was horrified at the thought of moving house, putting their trust in a new school for the girls, and the idea of starting out again in a strange and different community filled her with apprehension and reluctance.

Malcolm, however, was adamant. Over the years he had grown used to turning a deaf ear when Rachel began any protest or disagreement with the words 'I don't wish to argue, Malcolm, but . . .' By the time she had made herself miserable at the unlikely possibility of finding a niche as pleasant as her present one, he was already planning the kind of house they would need for his future life. Plenty of room, a study for himself on the top floor, well away from the girls' incessant pop music and Rachel's voluble friends, big garden for him to subdue, and, most important of all, situated in a village with a life of its own, but near enough to a motorway and a quick means of exit to the rest of the world. Rachel was still stressing the danger of moving the girls' schooling at this time of their education, as he stood up to find the road map of the Midlands and prepared to draw a circle, radius forty miles, where they could begin to house hunt.

By a process of elimination, they made a list of six villages, and set off for an estate agent. The right house, with most of the requirements fulfilled, turned up in Long Farnden. 'Long Farnden it is, then!' said Malcolm delightedly, and with the good luck that had accompanied him throughout life, it proved to be exactly the right house, in the high street of Long Farnden, near the fast-growing town of Tresham, East Midlands.

It had gone more smoothly than Rachel would have thought possible. Malcolm was a new man, fired with the thought of the intoxicating freedom he would experience as a freelance consultant and future author of a succession of authoritative books on his special interest, sexually motivated crimes of murder. Rachel kept this as quiet as possible in the village, wishing in her heart that it had been, say, Contract Law that had inspired Malcolm to great heights.

The first person to call, once the two large removal vans had been emptied and driven away, had been Mrs Mary Rix, wife of the doctor, who walked up the driveway bearing six new-laid eggs and a smile of official welcome. They learned from her that the village was very friendly, full of activity for all tastes, and, of course, known as 'Farnden' without the 'Long' to 'villagers and the *cognoscenti.*'

'*Lex loci,*' Malcolm had replied, with a flourish, and Rachel had sighed. She did hope Malcolm was not going to scupper a likely entry into Farnden society by showing off. But all this was now in the past, and the Barratts had settled down into Farnden life, become involved in village affairs, the parish council, and the playing fields committee. They felt they belonged, and would have been hurt if they'd heard themselves still referred to by the long-term inhabitants as 'the newcomers in the high street.'

Lois had been a blessing to Rachel. Recommended by Mary Rix, she had fitted in well, adjusting herself to Rachel's way of running her house, and adept at avoiding Malcolm in dark corners. From Lois's point of view, the Barratts were no trouble. A newish house, always tidy and neat, and her money always ready in an envelope tucked behind the kitchen radio. She wasn't sure that they would stay in Farnden, but they seemed settled enough. She knew Mary Rix and Evangeline Baer were both regular visitors, and that even Gloria Hathaway had fluttered her way up to the front door once or twice, passing Lois on her way out. Shame she chose the very days when Rachel Barratt had gone up to London to meet her aged mother for lunch. Still, Lois was sure Prof Malc would have been kind to her, solitary soul that she was.

Malcolm had quickly opened up the attics to make himself an airy space more suited to an artist than a law professor. He had a long workroom, lined with bookshelves filled to overflowing, a large desk for his computer and accessories, and a neat corner devoted to his sound system and large collection of Early Music CDs. There were two small rooms off this study – one with a double divan where he could rest his large frame when he had a knotty problem to unravel, and the other a starkly white shower-room and lavatory.

'Self-contained,' he said proudly, when showing friends around. 'You could be up to all kinds of mischief up here, and nobody would know.' He'd said that to Lois, and she'd given him her best icy look.

This morning, Lois began as usual by cleaning in the attic study. Malcolm welcomed her in and chatted as she worked, getting in her way and puffing out pipe-smoke which seemed to follow her wherever she went. This Tuesday morning, he was particularly talkative. A weekend bonfire party on the playing fields had got out of hand, and, as Malcolm said, 'four or five yobs ran amok'. At first, the crowd had been tolerant and good-humoured and the vicar, the Reverend Peter White (Lois's Thursdays), had appealed to their better natures. Fruitlessly, as it turned out, since the rioters had then nicked a box of sparklers, lit them all at once, and thrown them, fizzing and spitting, into a group of children.

'Were they hurt?' asked Lois, startled into standing still for a minute.

Malcolm shook his head. 'Not seriously,' he said, 'but they had burns and were treated for shock. Lucky thing that Janice Britton was there, and caught one of the young sods. Took him off to the police station double quick.'

'Ah,' Lois said, 'is that . . . er . . . the Janice who is a Special Constable, by any chance?'

'Right as always, Lois,' said Malcolm. 'Tough as old boots, she is.'

'Needs to be,' said Lois, and bent down to plug in the Hoover. Glancing sideways, she saw the eminent Professor picking up a paperclip from under his desk, ogling across at her upturned backside at the same time. Sneaky bugger, thought Lois. He doesn't give up. She switched on the Hoover and roared it as close as she dared to Malcolm's feet. 'Excuse me!' she yelled, and he had no alternative but to get out of her way.

Half an hour later, Rachel appeared at the door of the bedroom where Lois was changing sheets. 'Coffee's ready,' she said. She could never persuade Lois to sit down with her in the kitchen, like her daily had done in Hull. It had been the perfect way of picking up the local gossip. Now she had to follow Lois around the house, receiving the odd snippet of information as and when Lois felt like delivering it.

'Thanks,' said Lois. 'I'll come and get it. Oh, and Mrs Barratt . . .' Rachel stopped at the head of the stairs, looking back hopefully. 'This Janice, who's a Special Constable . . . d'you happen to know where she lives?'

'In the council houses,' said Rachel swiftly. 'Why, Lois? Surely she doesn't need a cleaner in that little box of a house?'

Lois shook her head, but said nothing more. Let her wonder. Council houses indeed. Lois's had been a council house, and she and Derek were now proud owners. Lots of people on the Churchill owned their houses and had built extensions and porches and put in modern bathrooms. Little box! Rachel 'Posh' Barratt should have seen the house where Lois grew up. Two up, two down, and few mod cons.

The coffee steamed on the big pine table, and Lois was very tempted to sink down on to a cushioned chair for five minutes. But this was against the self-imposed rules of her job. Never think yourself a friend of your employer, as they mostly think differently. Rachel sat at the table, leafing through a women's magazine and eating home-made biscuits. Poor woman, thought Lois. What a life. She felt momentarily sorry for her, not having a job or a life of her own, always second fiddle to those snotty girls or randy Malcolm upstairs.

'Have you heard?' she said, relenting a little. 'Seems Miss Hathaway isn't well . . . mind you, she looked all right to me in the shop yesterday. Doctor was on his way, though. Nothing serious, I hope . . .' She took up her coffee and went quickly back upstairs before Rachel could require more speculation on what this could mean.

Four

Evenings at 18 Byron Way were as peaceful as in any family of five. If Derek was not working late, he had his tea with the rest of the family, and later on, after a wash and change, set off for an hour or so at the Dog and Duck down on the Ringford Road. Lois washed up, made an heroic effort to get the boys and Josie to do their homework, watched television and waited for Derek to come home and give her the news from the pub. The house was quiet by midnight.

This evening the routine was broken by Josie announcing she wanted to go to a disco that night at The Hut, a youth group organised by the local happy-clappy church and patronised by the estate's teenagers when they had nothing better to do. Its reputation was of a respectable, but boring effort on the part of crusading adults to counter teenage crime on the estate, and so thought by Lois and Derek to be safe enough for Josie.

Now Derek looked up at the clock, and said, 'She's late.'

'Only half an hour,' said Lois. 'They'll be back in a minute.'

Derek shook his head. 'She was told to be in by ten. If she can't do what she's told, she's not going no more.' He got up from his chair and reached for his coat. 'Better go and look for her,' he said, frowning at Lois, who was sitting at the table biting the end of a pen and poring over police forms.

'She'll be with the others,' she said. 'Safety in numbers.'

Derek shook his head. 'There's no safety anywhere these days,' he said. 'I'm goin' to have a look down the road.'

He was half out of the front door when he heard Lois shout, 'Hey! Wait a minute – there's somebody round the back!'

Derek rushed into the kitchen, and wrenched open the back door, shouting, 'Who the hell is that?'

Lois pushed past him and peered out into the darkness. She heard Josie's giggle. 'S'me, Dad – me and Melvyn.'

'Who the bloody hell is Melvyn!' said Derek, pulling his daughter into the kitchen. Whoever Melvyn was, he'd vanished into the darkness, and Josie giggled some more before sliding gently on to the floor. 'Well, now,' said Derek, 'and what've we got here!'

The sickly smell of cheap wine wafted under Lois's nose as she bent over a smiling but unconscious Josie.

'Don't be like that, Derek,' she said. 'There's always going to be a first time. Give me a hand, and we'll get her upstairs to bed.'

'You're very calm about all this,' puffed Derek accusingly, as they struggled up the narrow stairs. 'She's only bloody fourteen!'

Lois heaved Josie on to her bed, and began to undress her. 'Never been fourteen?' she replied, and followed it up with a swift chaser. 'And anyway, you're not much of an example. Remember last Saturday week? Josie woken up by you tryin' to jump into your pyjamas?'

Derek stumped downstairs muttering, and when Lois finally sat down heavily next to him, he said sternly, 'She wasn't at The Hut, that's for sure. They're very strict about no alcohol. She's only a kid, Lois.' He looked at the papers still strewn over the table. 'Are you sure you're goin' to have time to see to the kids properly, clean other people's houses every day, *and* join the cops as well?'

Lois leaned back against the cushions and closed her eyes. She was quiet for a minute, then said slowly, 'Dunno. Worth a try, maybe. Find out more about it. I don't have to decide right now, do I? By the way,' she added, 'better put a bowl by Josie's bed when we go up.'

Wednesday, and it was Lois's day at the small redbrick cottage of Long Farnden's community nurse, Gillian Surfleet. Lacking the outward charm of Miss Hathaway's thatched teacosy next door, it was nevertheless warm and comfortable, filled with knick-knacks and souvenirs from grateful patients. Lois liked this job best of all, because Nurse Surfleet was seldom there, being out on her rounds in neighbouring villages, and enabling Lois to get on without interruption. When she was at home, Lois was glad to see her, though ten minutes' conversation with Gillian was like a pep talk from the games teacher at school. Nurse Surfleet was brisk and optimistic, and had no time for what she frequently referred to as 'the miseries'. Lois wondered how this went down with the clinically depressed, and could imagine herself in such circumstances telling her to sod off. Typical nurse, she supposed. And yet Lois had seen a warm side to her. Once, when there'd been a ding-dong over the fence with Gloria Hathaway, she'd seen Gillian Surfleet in tears. She'd quickly recovered when she remembered Lois was there, but it had been a pathetic sight. Women living on their own, Lois had thought. Nobody to confide in. Although apparently very popular in the village, in the same way as her colleague Dr Rix, Nurse Surfleet seemed to have few real friends, and Lois, breaking her own rules, always sat down for coffee with her if she was not out on her rounds.

Gillian's neighbour, Gloria Hathaway, was one of the few people who could upset her. Lois had witnessed more than the one sharp conversation over the garden fence, but found Gillian unwilling to talk about it. 'Gloria's a bit difficult, Lois,' she had said shortly. 'Can be a misery, but a nice woman at heart. Most people are, you know.' Lois reflected that she'd seen little of Miss Hathaway's good heart. She was apparently a keen gardener, always bent double with a border fork and a galvanised bucket for the weeds, though the garden had a neglected air. She never looked up as Lois walked down the path, though once or twice Lois had glanced back and caught Miss Hathaway staring unsmiling in her direction.

'Saw your friend, Gloria,' she said now, 'cutting down some dead stuff in the garden, and not a hair out of place!'

'You'd never catch Gloria in dirty trousers,' Nurse Surfleet said flatly, and swiftly changed the subject. 'Help yourself to biscuits, my dear. I'm off to an old lady at Ringford Lodge. Nasty case of 'flu, and dangerous at her age. See you next week, perhaps.' She was off at a cracking pace out of the little gate onto the footpath and away down to her car, but Lois noticed that she looked furtively into the garden next door.

Lois had half an hour left and found she'd finished the routine work, so collected up some of the brass knick-knacks, spread old newspapers over the table and began cleaning. She hated this job. The cleaning fluid had a powerful smell that made her feel dizzy. Still, the result was worth it. Shining brass that flickered in the firelight certainly added a cosy feel to the place. Must comfort Gillian Surfleet in her long, lonely evenings. Lois rubbed away at the tarnished metal, reflecting that the woman was probably not lonely at all. Only too glad of a bit of peace and quiet in front of the telly after a day listening to moans and groans.

It was quiet in the cottage. Sometimes Lois put on the radio and listened to music. She never did in the doctor's house, even when they were out. But here it was all right, so long as she remembered to put it back to Radio Four before she left. This morning, though, she didn't mind the quiet. Derek had made a scene at breakfast time, determined not to let Josie off lightly, and Lois was glad of the time to think about it. He was right, of course, but she remembered her own youth and knew that coming down on her like a ton of bricks was the surest way to encourage her to do it again.

A loud rattle in the backyard startled her, and she rushed out to see a scrawny ginger cat leaping away over the coal bunker. 'Get off!' she yelled after it, and turned to go back in. A movement in the garden next door caught her eye, and she saw the tail end of a figure in a greenish jacket disappearing into Miss Hathaway's front porch, under a rose-covered trellis that was a picture in summer. The ginger cat saw its opportunity and slipped in after it. Funny, she thought, I could have sworn that was Prof Barratt's old Barbour jacket . . . still got that oily stain on the sleeve . . . ah well, there's plenty of Barbours about in this village. Like horses, she said to herself. More horses than people in Farnden, and Barbours to go with them, women as well as men . . . Probably Rachel Barratt borrowed it to go round bothering people. Not enough to do, that woman. Rachel was scared of horses, she'd admitted to Lois, but liked to be thought of as one of the set.

She returned to the table and finished off the brass. I hope that lasts for a few weeks, she thought, sneezing, as she washed the dirty dusters. Her thoughts wandered on inconsequentially as she took the dusters out to the washing line. No sign of anyone now in Gloria's garden – she wondered if it had been the Prof, and if so, what was he up to? From what Gillian Surfleet had said, her neighbour didn't socialise much in the village, being very choosy about her friends.

Ah well, none of her business. She hurried round now, anxious to finish and be off. She had planned to drop in on that woman the Prof had mentioned – Janice Britton, the Special Constable. If she was at home, that is, and willing to talk to Lois for a few minutes.

Janice Britton glanced out of her window, and saw Lois walking up the path. She knew who she was, having seen her around, in and out of various houses in the village. A nice woman, she'd thought, and attractive. Always smiled, if they met in the shop. She went to open the door.

'Excuse me,' said Lois, 'sorry to interrupt . . .'

'I'm not busy,' replied Janet. 'Do you want to come in?' She was used to hearing tales of woe, marriages degenerating into violence, youngsters off the rails, drugs found in school bags.

'Just wondered if I could have a quick word with you about being a Special,' said Lois, standing awkwardly in the middle of the room. Janice persuaded her to sit down, and soon had Lois talking about her own life, her teenage daughter and young sons, and her own ambitions. It made a change from the usual appeals for help.

'It's not all that glamorous, you know,' she said, noting Lois's dark good looks and her natural grace even in working clothes. 'Some people think it's all smart uniforms and flirting with the blokes. But it's not like that at all, as you can imagine.' She started with the success stories; reuniting lost children with their mothers, settling differences in a street punch-up, helping old ladies across the street. Then moved on to the tragedies, failures and disappointments that figured largely in her work. She told her of extricating a middle-aged postwoman from under lorry wheels, letters spilled all over the road and the bicycle and postwoman mangled into a twisted heap. She described her feelings when a fourteen-year-old girl, who'd taken an overdose, died in spite of all the help that could be given. At this, she noticed Lois's face lose colour, and recalled her mention of Josie. She wondered whether Lois's real reason for wanting to find out about being a Special was a fear that her daughter might be in trouble. But she knew better than to pry, and quickly moved on again to the long hours when boredom was the greatest hazard, like the time when she'd been on a five-hour vigil in an empty car park, waiting for action, and nothing had happened.

After Lois had gone, Janice cleared away coffee mugs and prepared for duty. Had she answered the questions honestly? Had she herself really known what she was getting into at the beginning? The truth was, you never knew from one day to the next what would happen. That was part of the attraction, she supposed. And she could not imagine anything more boring than cleaning other people's houses. She had said as much to Lois, but later had reason to eat her words.

Josie arrived back from school looking pale and tired. She had insisted on going that morning, partly to get away from her ranting father. As Lois had watched her walking off down the road in her school uniform, long thin legs wobbling on clumpy heels, head down against the bright sun, she'd almost cried. Such a little girl, really. If only they wouldn't grow up.

Josie sat down wearily at the kitchen table and looked up at Lois. Her eyes were deeply shadowed, her pale face showing up the freckles that peppered her nose and cheeks. 'Cuppa tea goin'?' she said bravely.

'Headache?' said Lois gently. Josie nodded, and bit her lip. Lois put her arms around her and rocked her quietly to and fro. 'It's all right, baby,' she said. 'Just so long as you've learnt . . .'

Much later, when Josie and all the others were in bed,

Derek and Lois did what they'd never done before; they looked carefully through Josie's school bag, putting everything back in its place. They found nothing – nothing but innocence – and were reassured.

Five

The post came early on the Churchill Estate. The postman went round as quickly as possible, occasionally throwing a bundle of post into an unlocked door, avoiding, with a skill learned of bitter experience, dangerous Alsatians and Jack Russell terriers. He stopped for two cups of tea only, one with old Fred, his uncle, and the other with Lois's next-door neighbour, a youngish, flashy-looking blonde with no kids and a succession of 'friends' who came and went at all hours of night and day.

'We'd get *our* letters a lot earlier if Postman Pat had more sense than to join the queue at Marge's,' Derek said, running a hand through his thick fair hair, and giving Lois a peck on the cheek. 'Be back a bit late,' he said, and was gone.

Lois was on the way out when Pat O'Henry came smiling up the path. 'One for you, Lois,' he said with a smirk. 'Police . . . what you bin' up to now?'

'Bugger off,' said Lois, snatching the letter from him and retreating into the house. She ripped open the envelope and found what she had hoped for. There were a couple of vacancies in Tresham for Specials, and she was given an appointment for interview next week. 'Derek!' she yelled, and then remembered she was alone in the house. Excitement rising inside her, she tucked the letter behind the clock in the kitchen and went off to work.

Thursday was Lois's day for the Reverend Peter White, bachelor, and inevitably suspected by most of Farnden of being gay. Lois, however, knew otherwise. She had found the magazines by mistake, thinking she would give the laundry basket in his bedroom a good turnout and wash some of the grubby socks that had lurked at the bottom for as long as she

27

could remember. And then, underneath them all, she'd seen a picture in glorious colour of a plump, pink, naked female on all fours, pneumatic boobs dangling like udders, with a dog biscuit between her regular white teeth, and a tartan lead clipped neatly round her neck. Oh, my God! she'd muttered, and sifted through the small pile, all of the same genre, before putting them back as she found them. Kinky he may be, she'd said often enough since, but gay he is not. She'd never told how she knew, though, and never would.

You've got to feel sorry for the silly fool, she said to herself as she dusted round the laundry basket and saw again the tell-tale magazines through the wickerwork. Anybody who has to rely on that muck for getting it up is in a bad way.

'Lois?' It was him, the Reverend, calling her for coffee. He was another who would have liked her to sit down and have a chat. 'I promise not to try and convert you,' he'd said playfully one morning. 'Just keep me company for a few minutes.'

Why not? Lois had thought. He's probably lonely. Even a suspect bachelor vicar is put on a pedestal and finds it difficult to make real friends. But Lois had reminded herself of her rules, and said she'd never get through if she stopped, and had left him sadly stirring his coffee.

This morning, however, she needed to tell someone her news. 'Do sit down, Lois,' he said, as always. He was tall and thin. Everything about him was thin: thin, mousy hair, thin beaky nose, thin lips and thin, scrawny neck, with a prominent Adam's apple that moved up and down like a frog swallowed by a snake. In the pulpit it was hypnotic, and many a good Farnden church-goer had been kept awake during the sermon watching its efforts to escape. His fingers, wrapped around the coffee mug for warmth, were long and thin with chewed nails. His eyes, pale behind thick glasses, were shifty, never focussing on anything for longer than a few seconds.

Not a happy man, thought Lois this morning, as – to the Reverend's great surprise – she sank down onto a kitchen chair and accepted his offer of a coffee before she began her work.

The kitchen was cold, its early morning warmth having vanished quickly; the central heating programmed for economy.

The vicarage was modern, built when the old one was sold for a large sum of money to a rich couple reputed to have won the lottery. (All newcomers who paid fancy prices for old village houses were unreliably reported as having won the lottery.) Peter White was the first to occupy the new vicarage, and found it small, anonymous, and either freezing cold or overwhelmingly hot. It was nothing like he'd imagined when he applied for the job. No oak-panelled study, no large kitchen with a comfortable old cook providing plain but delicious meals, no elegant drawing-room where he could entertain the gentry. In other words, it was what the Church Commissioners, in their lack of wisdom, thought suitable for a modern man of God. Parochial church council meetings in his study were a fuggy squash, making the already prickly members even more argumentative and un-Christian. The garden was much too small for the summer fête. He'd never tried inviting gentry for a cocktail, as the sitting room overlooked the sewage works, and even when the fast-growing fir trees had burgeoned into a dense, high hedge and he could no longer see it, there was no time of the year when he could not smell it.

'Wind's in this direction this morning,' said Lois, sniffing.

Peter – he had asked everyone to call him by his Christian name, but none did – nodded sadly. 'Did I ever tell you how Maisie fell—'

Lois quickly interrupted to say, yes, he had told her, several times. It had been a gruesome story. One awful afternoon Peter White's ancient cairn terrier, Maisie, had got out through a broken fence and wandered into the sewage beds. She'd mistaken the greenish crust, always present on the village's excrement, for a grassy place to roll, and would have met a disgusting death by drowning had not Miss Hathaway been passing along the nearby footpath and climbed in to the rescue. Maisie had run into the house, shaken herself vigorously, and Miss Hathaway and the vicar had taken it in turns to shower off the evil-smelling mess. For Peter, there had been a glimpse of a surprisingly generously endowed Gloria Hathaway reaching for a towel. She had gone home in borrowed trousers and jersey, all of which had made the

29

occasion even more memorable for Peter. These last details he omitted when telling the story, of course.

Reminded of Miss Hathaway, Lois said, 'Do vicars still call on the sick?' Miss H. was the churchy sort, surely? Ever since she'd discovered the magazines, she'd had a contrary respect for Peter White. His particular frailty had made him more of person, more like the rest, and because of that, more approachable.

Peter White looked round nervously, as if a queue of the halt and the lame was forming at his door. 'Ah yes . . . Miss Hathaway,' answered the vicar. 'Just a little out of sorts, it seems. I called this week after noticing she was not at Evensong, and was assured that it is nothing serious. I must go again, though, to make sure.'

'Yes, I should,' said Lois firmly. As she took her coat from the cloakroom, she took a look at the untidy array of dingy coats and jackets. She could spare the time to put them straight, maybe suggest taking one or two to the charity shop. She sighed. Poor man needed a good woman, but who would even look at him in his present state? She began to sort through, and found a greenish-black cloak that needed a couple of buttons, an old tweed jacket that smelt of dog, and a scruffy Barbour with none of its waterproof quality left. She would take these three, anyway. Then she noticed the dark stain, spread across the sleeve of the Barbour, and was reminded of Gloria Hathaway's visitor. She sniffed at it curiously. Mmm . . . not sewage, thank heavens. Must have been him, then, though it *had* looked more like the bulky professor. She bundled up the coats, checked that it was all right to take them, and was told that he needed the Barbour. The others she could take. With a cheery, 'Bye! See you next week!', Lois left the vicarage, unaware of the pale face of Peter White at his bedroom window, clutching his Barbour and watching her. It was not until half way home that she remembered she had not told him about being a Special, after all.

Six

L ois turned up early for her interview at the police station. She had negotiated the heavy entrance doors, the
dark lobby, the queue for attention from briskly efficient
women behind the glassed-in reception. Bullet-proof, no doubt,
thought Lois. They dealt smoothly with an anxious social
worker and a girl who bit her fingernails feverishly whilst
trying unsuccessfully to quieten her crying baby. The baby
was well wrapped against the cold wind outside, but it was
tiny, and the girl looked too young, too much of an amateur.
Lois tried smiling at the girl but received a cold stare in
return. She imagined a grim scenario, single mother, no
money, damp lonely flat, no luxuries and scarcely enough
food. Lois remembered her own loving mother who stepped
in and helped at any time, and resolved that Josie would never
find herself here like that poor kid.

Finally a side door opened, and a dark-haired man in
uniform – casual jersey over shirt and tie, but clearly uniform
– approached her. 'Sorry you've had to wait,' he said, smiling.
'In here, please.' He strode off down a corridor and unlocked
a door, leading her into a room with no windows, furnished
sparsely with a table and two chairs.

'Where's the spotlight?' said Lois. A nervous attempt at a
joke, ignored by the policeman who pointed to a chair and
said politely that he was Police Constable Keith Simpson. He
said he was deputed to give her some first-hand information
about being a Special, because he'd started as one himself,
before deciding to make the police his career. Now he was a
community policeman. 'The bobby on the beat,' he said, smiling, adding that his 'patch' included Long Farnden, where he'd
noticed from her application she had several cleaning jobs.

'I'll have to watch it, then,' said Lois lightly, but he didn't find that funny. She thought he looked a bit of prat.

'So you want to be a Special?' he said. He reminded her of her old geography teacher, who'd had a knack of making even the most straightforward question sound portentous. However, Lois hadn't lost her skills with geography teachers, and said, 'Yep. That's why I'm here. I've read the stuff, and I'd like to do something worthwhile for the community.'

Keith Simpson was no fool and he recognised the quote from the brochure. Nettled, he glanced down at the details she had sent in, personal and family details, and said, 'Well, Mrs Meade, I should have thought looking after three kids, a husband and doing cleaning jobs five mornings a week was a worthwhile enough life! And –' he added, peering at her application – 'a parent governor, too. We know that's quite time-consuming. Where are you going to find the extra time?'

Lois had thought of this one. 'I've worked it out carefully,' she said firmly, 'and my mum is willing to fill in at any time.'

'Lucky you! But how old is your mum? Still active enough, is she?' he said, smiling again.

Lois was not sure whether the smile was friendly, or one of pity. 'She's sixty-four,' she said, 'and young with it.'

Now PC Simpson laughed. 'I believe you,' he said. He looked down again at her papers. 'But have you really thought it through? At least a hundred hours a year, and while you're training, another hundred on top of that?'

After a fractional hesitation, Lois nodded again. Why was he making such a thing of it? She'd always been able to do anything she'd set her mind to. Now he was rising to his feet. He was tall and loomed over her in his dark jersey.

'I'll just get my colleague,' he said. 'I'd like to bring her in on this.'

A plump, middle-aged policewoman came in and, after hearing Lois's circumstances, said that her first reaction was to advise Lois to wait for a few years until the children were more independent, pointing out that young kids must come first in a family's priorities. Lois thought of protesting that her kids

32

were fine, thanks very much, but the policewoman spoke with a finality that was not to be challenged.

Lois frowned and stood up, pushing her chair back with a rasping sound. She ignored their mutterings about talking some more about it, and interrupted harshly. 'I'll be off, then,' she said. 'Seems I've wasted your time . . . and mine,' she added.

PC Simpson opened the door for her and escorted her back to reception, walking fast to keep up with her. 'See you again one day, I hope,' he said kindly. Lois choked back an inappropriate reply and pushed her way out through the heavy station doors. The world continued to go by; cars in both directions on the dual-carriageway, children with swimming things on their way to the municipal baths next door to the police station, a drunk shouting at passers-by on the pavement opposite. She walked back to the multi-storey car park and was furious to find hot tears of disappointment and frustration running down her cheeks as she climbed into her car.

By the time she reached home, the family were all gathered, waiting for her. Her mother, who sat at the kitchen table with Lois's largest teapot at the ready, took one quick glance at Lois's face, and said, 'Don't say anything, dear. Josie, get some fresh milk,' she added, and began to pour.

'Where's Derek?' said Lois, suddenly needing his comforting hug.

'Upstairs,' said her mother. 'He'll be down in a minute.' As she spoke, Lois could hear Derek's footsteps on the stairs.

He came straight over and put his arms tight around her. 'Don't say nuthin',' he said. 'It was the way you opened the door. Here, Douglas,' he added, 'get the you-know-what.'

'But—' said Douglas.

'But nuthin' – just get it.' Douglas disappeared and came back holding a large bottle. Lois saw that it was champagne, and began to laugh. Derek said, 'That's more like it,' and opened the bottle with a satisfactory crack. He poured out the fizzing liquid into glasses Josie had set out on a tray, and handed one to Lois. 'My Lords, Ladies and Gentlemen!' he began, and Josie giggled. 'A toast! A toast to our Mum. We don't want no cops in this house, do we, kids?' Even Jamie had a taste, and then Derek refilled Lois's glass and her Mum's, saying it was the best day's work Lois had ever done. 'God, the relief,' he said, pretending to mop his brow. He looked at the champagne speculatively. 'Not bad,' he pronounced, 'but give us a pint of Best any time. Now,' he said. 'What's for tea?'

'I'll see to it,' said Lois, 'else I'll not be wanted here, either.'

Later that evening, when Derek was ready for the pub, she helped him on with his jacket – not a Barbour, of course, but a cheaper imitation. It reminded her of Long Farnden, the Vicar and the Prof, and Gloria Hathaway. She remembered that the Prof was usually very careful about his clothes. Probably wasn't him, then. 'Here!' she said, peering closer. 'You've got some, too!'

'Some what?' said Derek. He hoped his stomach could take a pint or two on top of all that champagne. Lois certainly wasn't making sense.

'This mark, look . . .' She rubbed at it with her hand.

'Oh, that,' he said. 'It's a working jacket, that, so what d'you expect? Bye, love.'

'Don't be late,' said Lois, kissing his cheek. 'Not likely,' said Derek, and disappeared into the night.

Seven

The long, narrow street that gave Long Farnden its name had become a muddy track as the Reverend Peter White stepped like a miserably-hunched stork, standing first on one leg and then the other, trying to avoid the heaps of dung and straw which had fallen off a muck trailer travelling at speed through the village that morning. The heavy, incessant rain had leached greenish streams from the mounds, and it was difficult to avoid squelching into it in his old, leaky black shoes.

Vocation? he said to himself. Is this what I was called to endure? A dreary, self-absorbed village in the Midlands, populated with a few real rural oafs who have been here for generations and think they own the church and the right to dictate its progress, and a growing intake of urban idiots who have convinced themselves that they are living the rural idyll they read about in the Sunday supplements: 'Arabella's all-white garden!' 'Timothy weaves an arbour from the living willow!' 'Charles's wild-flower meadow!' Weedy field, more like, with thistles and nettles taking over, strong and persistent, resisting even the predations of 'Jemima's darling rescue donkey, George'. Vicious brute. It had nearly taken his fingers off last time he offered it a Polo mint.

No, theirs wasn't country life. Real country life was that of the few small farmers who remained to fight their corner in a world of huge, landowning conglomerates, arable technocrats, and contract farmers who hired out themselves and their giant, foundation-shaking, verge-destroying machines, to disturb the village at all hours of night and day.

So thought Peter White as he gave up all hope of dry feet, and splashed dismally through wet and weather towards Gloria Hathaway's cottage. He tapped lightly on her door and, seeing a light behind her leaded diamond panes, knew that she was at home. The door opened fractionally, and her small, frowning face appeared. Without make-up and her metal-rimmed glasses, she was a soft, watercolour version of her usual self. Pale eyes, pale lashes, pale skin revealed at the open neck of a pale pink dressing gown.

'Ah, vicar . . .' she said, in a cool voice.

'How are you, Gloria?' Peter began, shaking dripping hair from his eyes. She opened the door a little wider, and he could see a bright fire of logs in the grate. Small lamps gave a rosy glow to the room, and he longed to burst in and settle himself in all that warmth and comfort.

Gloria Hathaway looked him up and down and said with a touch of humour, 'I'm all right, but how are you? You look like a drowned rat . . . better come on in. You won't catch anything. That is if you don't mind my state of undress . . .' she added in a neutral voice. She indicated the dressing gown and fluffy slippers, which he shrugged away with a grand, worldly gesture, and entered Rose Cottage with grateful alacrity.

'You'd better take off your filthy shoes.' Gloria indicated his sodden, mud-caked feet, and he quickly removed the offending shoes, trying unsuccessfully to conceal the large holes in his socks.

'Enough potatoes there to boil for dinner!' said Gloria, eyeing the socks speculatively. She fetched her work-basket. 'Sit down and take them off. I'll mend them, and then we can dry them by the fire.' She sounded unusually motherly, and he sighed deeply. He thought of his own mother and remembered a warm bed, hot drinks, a night-light, and a bosomy pillow for his head.

'Oh, please, no, no . . . they'll only be just as wet again by the time I get home. No, no . . . don't worry about me. You're the invalid, Gloria. I should be waiting on *you*.'

Gloria allowed herself a wry smile, and sat down opposite him in a low armchair. Her dressing gown fell apart at the knees, revealing sturdy, shapely legs, and he had trouble dragging his eyes away. She was aware of this, and was slow in hiding away temptation.

Peter White gathered his wits with some difficulty and

chatted in his light voice about village matters, which he hoped might interest her. The project to make new kneeler covers for the church was not progressing as quickly as he had hoped. She said some critical things about certain members of the congregation, and promised to speed up her sewing so that she might manage two kneelers by the spring, when they were due to be unveiled and blessed with a special service. He told her of the disgusting state of the street, and the dawn chorus of starlings under his roof which woke him every morning. He did not tell of his desperate efforts to go back to sleep before he should weaken and open the laundry basket.

She finished one sock, and then disappeared to make coffee. He looked happily around the room. Small paintings of children, charming children dressed in Kate Greenaway bonnets and boots, were arranged neatly either side of the window. A watercolour of Farnden church and its surrounding yews hung over the fireplace, and as Gloria returned with the coffee he asked who had painted it. 'An old friend,' she said briskly. 'It was a present . . . did him a favour once . . .'

'Let me help,' said Peter White, his pale face colouring and his manner suddenly rather agitated. He leapt up to take the tray from her, lavish in his appreciation of the steaming coffee, the jug of cream and slices of shortbread in triangular segments on a rose-splashed plate.

Gloria smiled, abandoned the old friend, and obligingly changed the subject to the difficulty of turning-out shortbread without cracking it into small shards. She settled him again by the fire, and he toasted his bare feet whilst she sewed quickly and efficiently, finally hanging his slightly smelly socks by the fire to dry.

'I have some you can borrow,' she said, and added with a catch in her voice, 'they were my father's, and nearly new. I couldn't bear to throw them away, though they are much too big for me.' She smiled bravely then, through a hint of tears, and Peter thought how vulnerable she looked, her expression softened and her cheeks warmed by the cheerful fire. Here was one of his parishioners who merited his continuing protection and care.

When he could no longer ignore her glances at her watch and

heavy hints of things she must be getting on with, he stepped out again into the persistent rain and lightly touched her hand with his lips. 'Thank you so much for the coffee and socks! And do take care, my dear. You are much needed in this parish,' he said with emphasis, as she slowly took away her hand and shut the door without a sound. Halfway down the path, a loud, deep cough, seeming to come from an open bedroom window, caused him to turn his head. So she wasn't completely better, he worried, and made a mental note to mention it to Dr Rix.

Eight

Dr Rix, present chairman of Farnden Parish Council, sat in his study sorting papers for tomorrow's meeting. He had occupied the chair for fifteen years, and when his wife accused him of wasting his time on trivial, parochial matters, he consoled himself by thinking of things that had been achieved or resolved since he was first elected: a waste bin in the recreation ground, a seat on the green in memory of an old inhabitant, young trees now well established on the small hill that ran up to the village. No matter that he had thought they were poplars, and they'd turned out to be hawthorn. They were extremely pretty in the spring and reminded him of his childhood in the Sussex countryside.

After a more or less idyllic childhood, he had completed his medical training at Barts in London, and there he had met his wife, a smart young secretary working in hospital administration. Her parents had lived in Finchley and he'd been dazzled by their obvious wealth and comfortable way of living. Not that his own parents were poor. There had been no struggle to put him through college, nothing like that, but their Sussex village house was modest, and their everyday lives were humdrum and pleasant. One family car, a cleaning woman once a week, no help with the garden, which, anyway, was his father's passion. It had been expected of him to follow his father's profession and he had been glad to agree. He had always admired his father, and thought that nothing could be as useful as the work he did.

Mary had belonged to a different world altogether. Money was of primary importance, and everything measured by it. Her parents talked of little else, Andrew Rix quickly discovered. They gloated over bargains they had won, prided themselves

39

on getting value for money, watched with anxiety the rise and fall of stocks and shares. They knew where they could find the cheapest petrol, track down cut-price food on Saturday afternoons, find for Mary and Andrew the best quality furniture marked down because of 'invisible' blemishes.

It had soon occurred to Andrew Rix that his own parents were well aware of these things, too, but would have thought it bad form to bring the subject of money into social discourse. Although he tired of this endless preoccupation with money, he had fallen deeply in love with Mary, with her liveliness, her ready good humour, and her sparkle and enthusiasm for life. She, in her turn, loved Andrew for his steady judgement and reliability, and his lack of interest in money. He and she were delighted with each other, and a quick courtship and glamorous wedding followed. Their early days of marriage were heavily subsidised by Mary's parents, and Andrew was not so happy about that. Gradually, though, the handouts tailed off, and they managed well on his income as a family doctor in a country practice. Their only abiding sadness was that they had no children.

When they had arrived in Long Farnden, they endured the usual year or so of suspicion and unfriendliness from the village. After that it was generally accepted that Dr Rix and his wife were a good thing, and he was elected to the parish council, giving him contact with the local people in a different way from in his consulting room. He was good at making friends and, with very few enemies, had in due course been elected chairman. Now he had promised Mary he would resign from the chairmanship at the next annual meeting. He realized he would miss the pleasant feeling of being held responsible for the well-being, in however insignificant a way, of his small community.

There were plenty of contenders for the job, of course. Evangeline Baer from the gallery fancied herself a good organizer, and let it be known that she considered running the small parish of Farnden as a doddle to someone of her experience. Maybe she was right, the doctor thought. There were certainly more cars parked outside her house these days. Another thing to be brought up at tomorrow's meeting. Some thought the corner too dangerous for parking, and they might review the placing of double yellow lines.

Then the professor, Malcolm Barratt, was clearly looking for another chair to inhabit. Organizing departments was his speciality, he reminded the doctor every time they met in the pub. A quick half pint was the doctor's usual, but if buttonholed by Malcolm Barratt he stood no chance of a swift escape. The professor had time on his hands, Andrew Rix reckoned, and now Malcolm had been elected to the council he had already begun to suggest radical plans for village reorganization.

The vicar, of course, came to parish council meetings as a traditional courtesy, though he was not a member, but Nurse Surfleet was a legitimate contender, a capable woman and not without ambition. Andrew Rix was well aware of the respect she commanded in the village. She had no family of her own to care for, but regarded the whole of Farnden as hers to cherish and protect. A splendid woman, but had she the necessary experience of handling the outside world: the planners, speculative builders, social engineers with bright ideas and very little practical knowledge?

Anyway, the chair was not in his gift. He would resign, and there would be a democratic election amongst the parish councillors. Dr Rix folded his morning paper, took his hat from the hall, and shouted his usual farewell to Mary in the kitchen. As he shut the door, he heard her shout a reminder that she would be out that evening, and he carried on. It was Open Minds, and he'd not forgotten. Now he was late, and still had to call in to see Gloria Hathaway. Peter White had said Gloria was still not completely right, and he wanted to check on her. So many bugs about . . . He coughed deeply as the cold air caught him.

The village street was empty, except for one car slowing down, and he saw it was Lois, turning into the gallery. She waved, and he raised his hat. Charming girl, he thought. What would we all do without her? She looks after us all so well. Perhaps it is time for Gloria to have a bit of help in the house? Maybe Lois has a free hour or two.

Lois had waved at the doctor, but her thoughts had nothing at

41

all to do with her responsibilities in Farnden. She was thinking about Christmas. Only eight weeks to go, and the pressure was on. She pulled on the handbrake with a rasp. Derek was forever yelling at her to release it first, but she liked the ratchety sound and ignored him. It was a small revolt, but one in which she persisted.

Eight weeks only, and nothing done. She did all the shopping for the family and her mother cooked the Christmas dinner. The cake and the pudding were made weeks before. One day she won't be there, and I shall have to do it all myself, Lois thought, as she parked her car outside the gallery. Evangeline never minded that. In fact, she encouraged it. People will think we have customers, and that encourages more to come in, she'd said. Lois, still thinking of her mother, reminded herself that she always shopped for all the presents, including from her mother to the family, and that would save Mother's feet. The thought of all that shopping depressed Lois further, and she began to wonder if that smug policewoman hadn't had a point.

'Morning, Lois,' said Evangeline Baer. 'I'm sure you remembered to wipe your feet. Dreadfully muddy in the village . . . muck-spreading everywhere and not just in the fields!' Evangeline laughed heartily, and Lois bridled. She had already taken off her outside shoes and put on slippers, something she did every week at the Baers', knowing Evangeline's obsession with cleanliness.

'Look at my feet, Mrs Baer,' she said, holding up one leg. 'Slippers on and not a speck, as you can plainly see.' On the whole, Lois and Evangeline rubbed along. Lois respected her foibles, as she did those of her other clients, and also recognised that Mrs Baer had a lot to put up with with that husband of hers.

Evangeline would have been surprised that Lois thought this of Dallas. She was sourly aware that everyone else they knew looked on him as the perfect husband, regular in his habits, faithful, as far as they knew, and fully in tune with his wife's neat and tidy preoccupations.

Lois had observed that perfection was not always a good

thing. Her Derek left stubble shavings on the bathroom basin, drawers half-open, stumped through the house in boots covered in oil from the car. She yelled at him, of course. But when he'd gone on his own to visit his sick mother in Ireland, his absence had struck her forcibly. She had missed him, stubble, grease and all. 'It's all part of him, isn't it?' she had said to her mother. 'That's my Derek.'

Her mother had surprisingly agreed. 'What I missed most about your Dad, when he went,' she had said, 'was suddenly having clean ashtrays everywhere.' Lois had nodded.

'Forty a day . . . bound to make a mess,' she agreed.

Dallas smoked, which was his one transgression. Lois dusted the big sitting room and emptied last night's ashtray. Apart from this, she sometimes wondered why they wanted her at all. A slight film of dust each week, a few screwed up pieces of paper in the waste bins, the floors to wash and polish; all could have been done by Evangeline in a couple of hours.

Still, Mrs Baer was a businesswoman, Lois reminded herself, as she watched Evangeline walking swiftly across the yard to greet customers in the gallery. Business was good lately, Lois had noticed, and she'd thought of looking in herself for Christmas presents, though she suspected everything would be too arty-crafty and expensive for her lot.

Just as she reached out to dust the telephone, it began to ring, startling her. Evangeline had forgotten to switch it through to the gallery so Lois lifted the receiver. 'The Baers' residence,' she said smoothly. 'Can I help you?' Not just any old cleaning woman, see. A woman's thin voice said she was sorry – she had dialled the wrong number – and the line went dead. Funny . . . sounded like Miss Hathaway, thought Lois. Still, she probably wanted the doctor or the vicar. Poorly again, I expect.

When Evangeline came back into the house, grinning with triumph at having sold a pricey painting, Lois told her about the call. 'Silly creature,' said Evangeline dismissively. 'Needs a man, that Gloria.'

'Hasn't she got one?' said Lois, not really concentrating.

Mrs Baer's reaction was swift. 'Of course not, Lois!' she snapped. 'And I'd be glad if you would refrain from spreading rumours of that sort. Extremely dangerous and stupid! . . .

and for goodness sake sit down and eat that biscuit if you must – crumbs everywhere!' Before Lois could recover from this onslaught, Evangeline had gone upstairs, and could be heard stamping about on the polished boards of her bedroom above.

Lois finished her work, washed her hands and pulled on her coat. 'I'm off now, then,' she shouted up the stairs, picking up the envelope with her money. She hesitated, and then as she heard Evangeline making her way out of her bedroom, she continued, 'I'd just like to say, Mrs Baer,' she added with emphasis, 'that I'm not used to being spoken to like you did, nor accused of dangerous gossip. I don't know anything about Miss Hathaway, and what I said was a perfectly innocent question. There was no cause for you to react like you did.'

She waited and watched as Evangeline turned to face her and all her anger evaporated. 'I'm sorry, Lois,' she said, sighing. 'My fault. Apology accepted?' Lois nodded but did not smile. As she left, she looked back and was mortified to see Evangeline wiping her hand across her eyes.

The weekend was always the gallery's busiest time, and the following Monday saw Evangeline sitting there in the half-darkness, the lamp on her desk the only source of light, counting the takings and doing her weekly accounts. She enjoyed this. After the tension of persuading customers to buy things in no way essential to their lives, playing them like wriggling fish on the end of a line and occasionally landing a really difficult one, Evangeline loved to sit in the silence of the gallery totting up columns, calculating percentages and writing neatly in small columns. The total was more than satisfactory on the sales side, and she shut her account book with a snap. Excellent, she thought. It is all going very well, and if Dallas should ever leave me, I shall have a nice little business to support me. Heavens! What on earth had put that into her mind? She locked the gallery door and walked back to the house. Nothing on the calendar for the rest of the day. She decided to go into Tresham and spend a modest amount of her profits on new shoes. Perhaps she was looking a bit shabby these days, never thinking of anything but art and artists and not enough about her husband and her marriage. New make-up too, she thought. All the old stuff had hardened and dried up with lack of use. With this resolve, she changed into a smart skirt and jacket, and set off for town.

'Last Open Minds meeting before Christmas,' said Evangeline to Dallas, as they finished supper that evening. 'Shame I have to go out, with that new arts programme starting.' She had put on the new shoes and made up her face with care. Dallas appeared not to have noticed.

'I'll record it for you.' Dallas got up from the table and sorted through a pile of videos. 'Nine o'clock, is it? Better set the timer.'

'But you'll be here, won't you,' said Evangeline sharply.

'Might go down the pub,' he replied. 'Half promised old Malcolm I'd see him there, though the prospect doesn't fill me with total ecstasy. In training for champ BOF, our Malcolm.'

'I don't know what you mean,' replied Evangeline irritably. He might have made a comment about the lipstick, surely. She hadn't worn any for such a long time and he must have noticed.

'Boring Old Fart,' said Dallas, beginning to laugh nastily. 'Thought everyone knew that, especially you and your artyfarty friends. Just their sort of patronising code.'

Evangeline flushed. In the beginning, she'd known very little about art of any kind, but was curious and friendly, and had soon enlisted the help of an experienced watercolour painter, a successful potter, and several jewellery designers, just out of college and only too pleased to show off their newly-acquired knowledge. She'd delighted in their friendship and had tried having them to dinner. Not all at once, of course, but mixed up with locals. It had been a dismal failure, not least because of Dallas's persistent mockery of everything 'hand-bodged'.

'No need to be unpleasant,' said Evangeline. 'You may very well be glad of my success with the gallery one day. No job is safe now, not even yours . . . and don't forget to empty that ashtray before you go out,' she added. Always a winner, she thought, as she saw Dallas's furious face.

But he had the last word, as usual. 'Has the cold wind made

your lips sore, dear?' he said with thinly-disguised malice. 'Better put some Nivea on before you go out.'

In the coolness generated by this conversation, she went upstairs to get her coat, wishing she could stay at home and dissuade Dallas from going to the pub. Oh well, Open Minds had been her own idea. She'd thought it would be a useful adjunct to the gallery, bringing in the new villagers with wider interests than the old rural families. It had started out well. They'd tried to avoid speakers of the flower-arranging and icing-your-Christmas-cake variety, but gradually the emphasis had changed, and she'd grudgingly given in to home-grown holiday slides from Marbella and a man who'd devoted his life to growing ever-fancier fuchsias.

The raw wind sent shivers through Evangeline as she hurried down the street to the village hall. Her ears hurt, and she thought longingly of the soft, hand-woven scarves she had for sale in the gallery. She had decided early on not to buy everything she fancied just because she'd get it at cost. 'There go the profits,' she'd said to Dallas, who'd tried to persuade her to have a bracelet she coveted.

Evangeline turned into the village hall porch, festooned with Christmas paintings from the playgroup, and saw Miss Hathaway standing precariously on a chair. Gloria Hathaway was the Open Minds treasurer, in charge of all things financial, and now here she was furiously pushing fifty-pence pieces into the electricity meter. She rapped out that she'd meant to be down earlier to warm up the hall, but a telephone call had delayed her.

'We'll just keep our coats on for a bit,' said Evangeline. It was time the village began to think about a new community hall. She knew Malcolm Barratt had suggested it, but had so far come up against a brick wall of old guard resistance. She turned, hoping the temperature would improve by the time the speaker arrived, when the door opened and a sturdy elderly lady with short silver-grey hair and a tanned, outdoor face, marched in.

'Evening,' she said briskly. 'I'm Joan Page – Land Girl,' she added.

'Ah yes, I'm Mrs Baer,' replied Evangeline, stretching out a welcoming hand. 'So you were a Land Girl during the War? We are all very much looking forward to hearing of your experiences . . . seems so long ago now, doesn't it?'

'Only yesterday to me, Mrs Baer,' said Miss Page, who'd been polishing up her memory for the benefit of such gatherings for years now. 'Very cold in here, isn't it?' she added critically.

Evangeline bridled. 'Yes it is, I'm afraid. Still, you must have grown used to the cold, digging cabbages in frozen fields and things,' she said brightly as she led her speaker to her seat.

Nine

Rachel Barratt's scream filled the steamy kitchen and echoed back into the hall. She went on screaming and terror spread rapidly around the women. With a scraping of chairs and gasps of horror, the Open Minds group rushed towards the kitchen door. 'Wait,' shouted Mary Rix, who had learned from her husband that hysteria could be catching. 'Quiet, everybody,' she said. 'It's probably a dead mouse . . . you know our Rachel . . .'

But it wasn't a dead mouse. It was a dead Gloria Hathaway, and her slim, neatly-dressed body lay propped up against the sink unit, her head lolling like a rag doll. Her skirt had been pulled down discreetly over her knees and her hands were lapped carefully one over the other.

'She's holding something,' whispered Rachel Barratt, trying very hard to pull herself together after a brisk shake from Mary Rix. She looked more closely, stepping forward tentatively as though Gloria might suddenly awake and castigate them all. 'It's a teaspoon,' she said, beginning to sob again.

'It's a village hall teaspoon,' added Evangeline, as if this made it far worse.

'Don't touch it,' said Mary Rix. No one moved. 'Now then, Rachel,' she continued, 'perhaps you'd use that mobile phone of yours and dial 999. Best coming from you, as you found her.' She pushed the women back into the hall, and nodded to Evangeline. 'Better wind up the meeting,' she said, 'though everyone must stay here until the police arrive.'

It was then they realized that Joan Page, heroine of the wartime farmyard, had gone. 'Huh!' said Evangeline. 'Doesn't surprise me. Anyway, I've got her particulars, so she needn't have panicked. Now,' she added firmly, 'if you could all sit down we have a wait on our hands, so perhaps someone would volunteer to make the tea?' The urn was still bubbling ferociously, but amidst fearful looks towards the kitchen, no one volunteered.

'It was horrible,' said Mary Rix to Andrew, much later, as they sat in front of a dying fire in the sitting room. 'And worst of all was having to be cool and take charge. Usual thing, doctor's wife, she'll know what to do. Well, I did my best, but felt very tempted to run off like that tedious Land Girl.' She looked at Andrew and wondered if he had heard a word she'd said. He could have been a bit more supportive, she thought, looking at him closely. After all, unlike many doctors' wives, she was not a nurse, and was now feeling cold and shaky. But Andrew had slumped in his chair, eyes vacant and fixed on a spot somewhere around the middle of the hearthrug. He seemed deaf to all that Mary had to say.

She had tried calling him earlier from the village hall on Rachel's mobile, but there had been no answer. Still, he'd said something about going to the pub to talk parish council business ahead of the meeting tomorrow. When he finally turned up, long after the police and ambulance, and after poor Gloria's stiffening body had been taken away, he had the same absent look, as if he'd been in a land of ice and snow and hadn't thawed out yet. It was a raw night, of course. Mary's thoughts were not coherent and to her own amazement, she began to giggle. 'It'll be very cold for Gloria Hathaway in that mortuary,' she spluttered, and then laughed louder.

At last Andrew looked at her, properly looked, directly into her wild eyes. 'Stop it!' he said sharply. 'Stop it at once, Mary.' And in just the same way that she had curbed Rachel's screams with a shake, Andrew slapped her across the cheek. She was sober at once, enough to register that the slap seemed unnecessarily hard. How dare he? 'You'd better go to bed, try to get some sleep,' he said, without apology. 'I expect there'll be more questions tomorrow.' The police had concentrated on getting down the facts – names, addresses, times and so on. Tomorrow and the next day, and the next, and for many more days, they would be interviewing the entire village. In a place as small as Farnden, almost everyone would have some connection with Miss Gloria Hathaway.

Andrew was still sitting stiffly on the sofa, and Mary got up and walked towards the door. She hesitated, and turned to look at him. Hardly a rock to lean on. 'How can I sleep, Andrew?' she said bitterly. 'How can any of us sleep?'

His answer was shocking to her. 'Oh, God forgive me . . .' he muttered. 'Oh, poor little Gloria . . .' And he began to cry silently, his broad shoulders shaking as dreadful, racking sobs consumed him.

In the Barratt house, Rachel lay silent and very wide awake next to Malcolm, listening to his steady breathing. 'You awake?' she said softly.

'Yep,' said Malcolm. 'And so is most of the village, I expect,' he added. He turned and took Rachel into his arms. 'What on earth's been going on?' he said. 'Why should anyone wish to harm that woman?' Rachel moved closer to him, trying to gain comfort from his warm body.

She kept thinking of Gloria laid out, stiff and cold and . . . well, dead. 'None of us knew her very well,' she said.

'Not much to know, I reckon,' he said. 'Kept herself to herself, didn't she?'

'I often wondered how she lived . . . I mean, what she did for money,' said Rachel, and felt Malcolm twitch. He always twitched when his mind was working overtime.

'Private means, probably,' he said. 'Anyway, let's try and get her out of our minds and sleep for a bit. Busy day tomorrow, no doubt, and it's a Lois day. She'll want to know all the details.'

'Maybe,' said Rachel, 'though she's not much of a gossip. Never wants to swap news with me, anyway.'

'Thank God for that,' said Malcolm, and Rachel heard him mutter something. 'What did you say?' she asked.

'*Sic transit Gloria mundi*,' he repeated, and to her amazement, gave a snort of laughter. Then he disentangled himself, turned over and in minutes loud snores reverberated round the room.

I'd hardly call *her* the glory of this world! thought Rachel, but she's certainly passed away. She nudged him, but he continued to snore. Irritation made her nudge him harder. She knew a real snore from a false one. Then a thought struck her; suppose the murder had something to do with sex. It would be right up Malcolm's alley then. His speciality in the academic world. No doubt he'd be in there like a shot, assisting the police with their enquiries. As she drifted off into a troubled sleep, her last waking thought was of Gloria and sex. Gloria and sex? That tight, secretive face? Those net curtains and locked doors? Oh well, anything was possible.

Peter White sat and shivered in his cheerless kitchen, vainly trying to warm his hands on a mug of lukewarm Bovril. He'd been sitting there for some time, trying to think rationally about the dreadful events of the evening. He'd been summoned to the village hall as an afterthought. Well, he was used to that. It had been Rachel Barratt who called, saying she thought some of the women were so upset they could do with as much help as could be mustered. He was last on the list, of course, and had gone along, pale and apprehensive, and done what he could. Which, he accused himself, was very little. The police seemed to find him a nuisance, an irrelevance, and the Detective Inspector actually suggested it might be better if he returned home.

'Just confuses things, you see, sir,' he'd said, quite respectfully, but firmly. And anyway, most of the women's husbands had arrived and were holding their hands. The Farnden grapevine had wasted no time, and by morning there were few of its inhabitants who could not imagine Gloria Hathaway, dead as mutton, lying shockingly naked on a marble slab.

'Oh, dear God,' prayed Peter White, now doubled over with his head resting on the cold kitchen table. 'Dear God, give her rest and peace and let me, your servant, come to your judgement in due humility.'

But not, he added to himself, as he fell into an uncomfortable doze, not yet.

He awoke the next morning with a stiff neck and an appalling headache. A sharp knocking brought him to his feet and he stumbled towards the door. 'Reverend White! Are you there?' It was Lois's voice, anxious and loud.

He let her in, explaining that he'd bolted and barred the doors because of the dreadful murder. Then he filled her in with as much detail as he thought appropriate. He frowned and looked at her curiously, his thoughts coming back into order. 'But it's not my day for you,' he said. 'Shouldn't you be at the Barratts?'

Lois nodded. 'Couldn't get any reply. All the curtains still drawn, and they're bolted up just like you. Nobody in the street and the shop blinds still down. It's like a morgue,' she added, and then wished she hadn't. Peter White's face crumpled and with a sound like a chicken being strangled, he rushed upstairs.

Lois finally got some sense from Nurse Surfleet, who was up and dressed, and very wide awake indeed. 'Come in, my dear,' she said. 'Come in and have a cup of tea. You'll find no one astir in the village! Tongues exhausted as well as bodies.'

The bare bones of the previous evening's events shocked Lois nearly as much as the villagers themselves. 'Poor old thing!' she said. 'She'd certainly got on the wrong side of somebody! Still, she was a bit of a mystery, wasn't she . . .'

'She wasn't that old, about the same age as you, Lois,' said Gillian Surfleet, as they sat at her kitchen table drinking hot tea. 'I sometimes saw her first thing in the morning, in the bathroom with the windows wide open, as if she didn't care who saw her. She was in good shape, you know, Lois. A good body for someone of thirty-eight.' The word 'body' seemed suddenly loud, and assumed gigantic importance in the little kitchen.

Both women were silent for a minute or so, and then Lois said, 'Had she got any blokes?'

'Lovers, do you mean?' said Gillian, with a small hesitation. 'Not to my knowledge. Mind you, only someone around here all day long would notice if men came and went. I'm out on my rounds such a lot. And then again, it's only that bathroom window that's overlooked, and only by me. And I've got better things to do . . .'

Lois had heard a hint or two that Nurse Surfleet leaned a little towards her own sex, but she'd always dismissed it as malicious nonsense. 'I reckon I can tell,' she'd said to Derek. 'You get to recognise a sort of glint in the eye.'

'Fancy you, then, does she?' Derek had teased her.

Lois had been defensive, said that she knew very well how to put off any advances of that sort. Now she looked at Nurse Surfleet sitting there in the kitchen, her solid body well controlled, her considerable bosom propped up on her folded arms, and could see no glint. No, it was more likely she'd been one of those whose career had come first and then, when she put her mind to men and marriage, thought it was too late. The most she got now was probably being grabbed by the lecherous old codgers in the senile ward at Tresham General.

'Didn't she have any mates, you know, girls together and all that?'

'Didn't seem to,' said Gillian Surfleet dismissively. 'She'd go away occasionally and ask if I'd keep an eye on the house. She trusted me, of course. Very cosy inside that cottage, Lois.'

Lois nodded encouragingly. 'Go on, then,' she said, her curiosity now thoroughly awake.

'Like a fill-up, dear?' said Nurse Surfleet irritatingly.

They had second cups, but Gillian Surfleet was saying no more on the subject. Soon she stood up, brisk as ever. 'Now, we'd better get moving,' she said, making it quite clear that their chat was at an end. 'Those Barratts must be up by now,' she added, 'so I'll see you tomorrow, my dear.' Lois put on her coat, said thanks for the tea, and walked off down the street towards the Barratts' house, her thoughts churning. She passed Gloria Hathaway's gate and looked up towards the cottage. The curtains were drawn and a policeman stood outside, not exactly on sentry-duty, but keeping a sharp look-out. Lois stared and saw that it was the constable who'd given her the heave-ho. She felt anger rising again. Smug prat! She quickened her step, not looking at him. Then she changed her mind. He was like an Aunt Sally, a sitting target. 'Hiya!' she shouted, smiling broadly. 'Caught any good crooks lately?'

He pretended not to hear her, and she walked on, feeling a great deal better. After all, if they *had* taken her on, *she* might have been stuck outside Miss Hathaway's front door, whilst excitement was developing behind lace curtains and in private conversations. As it was, she had the perfect job for picking up information here and there, a word overheard, a quarrel with too much said in anger. These were the everyday occurrences of her work here in Farnden, and she suddenly realized that with the murder of poor old Gloria she had a unique opportunity for a bit of detective work of her own. No reason why I shouldn't, she told herself. Seems a shame not to take the chance. In truth, she knew that it was a chance for getting one-up on Keith Simpson and that policewoman . . . and the entire police force. Her anger was surfacing again, and was still bubbling when Malcolm Barratt greeted her with a glance at his watch.

'No need to check on the time, Professor,' she said, stepping into the hall. 'I was here on time, but you were all asleep . . . or something. Bolted and barred. Had to go all round the village before I could find out what was going on.'

Malcolm subsided like a pricked balloon, and stood aside. 'You'll have heard, then,' he said mildly.

'Yep,' said Lois shortly. 'And no doubt I shall hear some more. Meanwhile, I'll make a start, if you don't mind.'

Now Rachel emerged, looking pale. 'Morning Lois,' she said. 'Would you mind doing the breakfast things? We're a bit behind schedule . . .' She tailed off, looking at Malcolm for guidance. He took her arm and they wandered into the sitting room, looking lost. Lois began clearing the table, happy to be in the kitchen. It was as good a place as any to pick up scraps of conversation. Then she could follow the Professor when he went to his study. Chat him up a bit . . . but not too much! Don't want to end up like old Gloria . . . victim of a sex maniac! Her mood improving rapidly, Lois tackled the kitchen with a will.

'Would you mind not whistling, Lois,' said Rachel, emerging from the sitting room. 'My head's splitting . . . and so is Malcolm's. Thank you,' she added with an effort as Lois grudgingly stopped. 'And if you could keep the vacuuming to a minimum today, we'd both be grateful.'

Great, thought Lois. I shall hear everything they say. And I'm just part of the wallpaper to them.

Ten

Lois's noisy car heater broke down halfway home, and with her mind still taken up with Gloria Hathaway, it was some time before she realized that the fan was blowing freezing cold air into her face and around her icy feet. By the time she reached home, she was shivering and her hands were stiff with cold. Even so, she noticed the holly wreath on the door, cheerful with its gilded fir cones and bow of scarlet ribbon. Nice of Derek to think of that! As she put her key in the lock, she realized the door was open, and going through to the kitchen she saw Josie.

'What are you doing here? Skiving again? Or are you ill?'

Josie smiled placatingly at her and explained she had the afternoon off. 'Teachers' meeting,' she said, and Lois decided to give her the benefit of the doubt. Josie noticed her mother's blue hands, filled the kettle and took out two mugs. 'Did you see the holly wreath?' she said. It seemed Derek had not been the benefactor. 'It was Melvyn,' Josie said, desperately casual. 'He gave it to me after school this morning. Said his brother bought two by mistake, and did we want one.'

'How much?' said Lois swiftly.

'Nothin'. It was a present. Melvyn said to tell you and Dad he was sorry about that time when I came home a bit rocky.'

'He could've waited with you and said he was sorry,' said Lois. 'Instead of scarpering like that. Who is he, anyway? Does he live round here?'

Josie shook her head. 'Dunno where he lives,' she said. 'Don't know him all that well, really. He goes around with the crowd. Oh, and Mum . . .'

Here it comes, thought Lois. Nothing's for nothing. 'Well?'

'There's this Christmas Disco at the club . . .'

'Club!' said Lois. 'What club?'

'It's where the crowd goes – all except me,' said Josie. 'Melvyn said he'd look after me, and—'

Lois interrupted her. 'Just who is this crowd? And how old are they? And will Melvyn whatever his name is look after you like he did last time? No, Josie. This is a definite *no!*' Lois knew she was being unreasonable, and should allow Josie more time to explain, but all the morning's tension in Farnden still clung to her, and her first thought was that if such a gruesome thing could happen there, who knows what might go on in some disreputable club in town?

'I shall ask Dad, then,' said Josie, close to tears. 'At least he'll listen. You've never got time for any of us, with your rotten cleaning and special cops, and . . . and . . .' She rushed out of the room, banging doors on her way up to her bedroom, where she cried angrily, loud enough for her mother to hear in the kitchen below.

It was not the first time the kids had made this accusation, but the cleaning jobs were a necessity to make ends meet with a growing family. Lois's ambition to be a Special had not been in any way a necessity, of course. Not only was there no money in it, but it would probably have cost her in the end. It had been for Lois alone, something that she wanted for herself to prove that she could do it, something that took her away from everlasting cleaning up after other people. Selfish, really, some would say. Kids expect you to be there, to listen, to put them first. If you have them, this is what you have to do, thought Lois. After all, look at me, still taking for granted that my mother will be there when I want her, put us and our needs before hers.

Lois rinsed out the cups in the sink and put them upside down on the drainer, noticing that tea stains had turned the unglazed edges dark, tobacco brown. They need a good scrub, she thought, but did not attempt to do it. She could not get Gloria out of her mind. Who would want to kill a pathetic creature like that? Ignoring the slowly diminishing sobs from upstairs, she rummaged in the kitchen drawer for an unused notebook she had put in there weeks ago. A few pages for each of her clients, she thought. That should organize the evidence enough for a start.

Barratt – Rachel and Malcolm, she wrote. *Day One*. She then added snippets of their conversation over coffee and the fact that they had both looked so shell-shocked. She noted down Rachel's presence at the village hall, safely seated with the other women, at the time of the crime. Also Mary Rix. But Malcolm Barratt? Where had he been? Something to check. She turned to the back of the book and wrote down *Alibis*, then a list of the names of her clients.

'But it could be *anybody* in Farnden, not just one of your people,' objected Derek, when he came in for lunch. He'd looked stunned at the news about Gloria Hathaway, but collected himself quickly. 'Could've bin' me, or you . . .' he'd said, with a weak smile.

'Or the Pope!' said Lois crossly. 'I've got to start some-where,' she added, and resolved not to tell Derek any more about it. He was clearly not taking her seriously. And anyway, where had he been when Gloria snuffed it?

'Right here, with you and the kids, you dope. For God's sake, Lois, this is getting ridiculous.' Lois thought otherwise, but decided to drop the subject.

A pile of ironing took her attention for most of the afternoon. She usually listened to the afternoon play while she ironed, but Josie had pop music going full blast in her room, triumphant because Derek had said he'd think about her going to the club. He hadn't looked at Lois, knowing her view, but asked Josie more questions to which she had given very vague answers. He'd dodged out, back to work, before Lois could tackle him on the subject, and now Josie had taken his 'think about it' as a yes.

Picking up a school shirt and starting on the collar, Lois looked at the radio, thought of telling Josie to turn down the music, but decided against it. I'll just let my thoughts wander, see where they take me. What do I know about the late Gloria Hathaway? She cast her mind back over the time she'd been working in Farnden, and realized that Gloria had surfaced in one way or another quite often. There had been the time she had banged on the doctor's door halfway through the morning, crying and carrying on, saying she was seriously ill and nobody believed her. Lois had let her in, shown her into the surgery and called the doctor from upstairs. He hadn't looked too pleased, but had gone in to see Gloria, shutting the door firmly behind him. The crying and shouting soon ceased, and Lois, dusting the picture frames in the hall outside the surgery door, had heard their voices murmuring. Gloria had emerged a while later, eyes red and cheeks tear-stained, and had marched out, head in the air, away down the path. The doctor and Mrs Rix had had words then, though Lois had caught only a few accusations and sharp advice from Mary that the doctor should treat the silly woman like everyone else. Lois distinctly remembered her saying, 'The more you let her get away with, the more she'll take!' The doctor had slammed out of the house himself after that, and Lois had remembered this particularly, because he was usually such a gentle soul.

Lois folded the shirt neatly, and took a second one from the pile, reminding herself that all doctors have difficult patients, ones who take up far more time than they are entitled to. Still, the doctor had seemed very angry.

And what else? Lois did a mental walk up Farnden High Street and into the gallery. Any connection between Gloria and the gallery? No, she'd never been near, not while Lois had been around. You'd expect her to be the arty-crafty type, but nothing had ever appeared with Gloria Hathaway's name on it. Mind you, Evangeline was very particular. She could easily have turned down Gloria's artistic efforts, and then . . . ah, hang on, there *had* been something . . . Lois ran the iron swiftly over the shirt front to finish it off, and took a third from the pile.

It had been the week Evangeline was away in Devon collecting paintings and pottery for the gallery. Dallas had had time off and was filling in for his wife. So far, he told Lois, he'd sold nothing. 'She'll be pleased,' he'd said, explaining that Evangeline loved to think nobody else had her gift for bringing off a sale. 'You'll see,' he'd added, 'if I sell a picture for four hundred, she'll be livid.' Lois had thought privately that he was just being nasty, but said nothing. The gallery bell had rung then, and he'd gone off to look after the customer. It had been Gloria Hathaway, and she wasn't buying but selling. She'd had a clutch of little watercolours of children, carefully done, and nicely framed, but not, Dallas told Lois on his return, Evangeline's cup of tea. 'Shame, really,' he'd added. 'She looked so disappointed. Said she had some prints we might be interested in, so I said I'd call in and take a look this afternoon. I might surprise Evangeline with my enthusiasm for the job!' Lois couldn't remember any more about this occasion, except that when Evangeline returned, there'd been an icy atmosphere in the house for a week or two.

At last the pile was finished, and she struggled up the narrow stairs with the basket all but toppling over.

'Mum!' shouted Josie from behind her closed door.

'What?' said Lois flatly, unforgiving.

'Forgot to tell you,' Josie said, opening her door and trying a tentative smile. 'Somebody phoned for you before you came in. Name was Keith something . . . can't remember the other name. Said he'd ring back later. Sounded quite nice . . . you got a fancy man, then, Mum?'

Lois ignored this. Keith? It rang no bells, and she had to content herself with waiting for the telephone to ring.

'Lois Meade?'

'Yes? Who's that?' She knew, of course, straightaway recognising the voice.

'This is the police – Keith Simpson. We met—'

'I remember, only too well,' said Lois.

'Ah, good!' said Keith. 'Well, as you know, I'm a police constable and cover Long Farnden, where you work . . .' Oh yes, Bobby on the Beat. Lois did not feel in any way chummy towards Keith Simpson. She answered his next questions unhelpfully in muttered monosyllables. It seemed that Keith had been chatting to the Detective Inspector – Hunter Cowgill – yes, it was a good name for a detective. She must have heard of him? No? Well, he was a legend in the criminal fraternity.

'Which I am not part of,' said Lois sharply.

'I told him,' Keith pressed on, regardless of Lois's hostility, 'that you cleaned in several houses in Farnden, and might be worth talking to. So he said I could make a start on that . . . with your co-operation, that is,' he added hastily.

Lois was very surprised. Blimey, they'd cottoned on to that

one pretty quickly. Her opinion of Keith Simpson modified a little. As for Hunter Cowgill – God, what a name! – she had no intention of fraternising with legends of any kind. Still, if she could be useful to them, then they could be useful to her. And she'd be in control, with no duty to tell them anything . . . or just as much as she chose.

'Hello? You still there, Lois?'

'Yeah, I'm still here. I'm thinking. I'm not sure what you mean by co-operation,' replied Lois slowly. Keith began to give her a lengthy explanation, but she cut in suddenly. 'Don't bother with all that,' she said. 'Tell you what. How about an exchange of info?' That sounded good, she thought. Very cool and professional.

'Well, we'll see about that,' said Keith soothingly. 'But a dialogue would be very helpful, Lois.'

'Mrs Meade,' said Lois.

Keith cleared his throat. 'Yes, well,' he said patiently, 'would you be able to come down to the station?'

Lois's laugh was bitter. 'Good Lord, no,' she said. 'Um, how about at Janice Britton's, in Farnden? She was very nice to me . . .' She paused to let that sink in. '. . . and three heads are better than two,' she added. Then she rang off, pleased with how things were going.

Eleven

The Reverend Peter White awoke as usual to the whistlings and splutterings of starlings under the vicarage roof and for a moment thought quite optimistically of a hot cup of tea, half an hour with the morning paper, and then a stroll round the parish to show his face to an indifferent community. Then he remembered. Gloria Hathaway was dead, murdered by an unknown hand, and he was just as much implicated as any other person in the village. And it was a Lois day.

He pushed back the bedcovers and reached for his dressing gown. It was thin, old and too short to cover his spindly legs. He caught sight of himself in the long mirror in the wardrobe door and shuddered. The very model of a sex maniac, he thought to himself. The thought that Gloria might have been the victim of a jealous lover, crazed by rejection and frustration, would occur to more than one person, he was sure, and he had a mental picture of Gloria in the shower, breasts swinging as she washed off the slurry from the sewage works, from which she had bravely dragged poor Maisie. Well, who knows what a man may do in a moment of blind rage? And then not be able to recall the dreadful crime afterwards, going about his business as if nothing had happened? Poor little Gloria, he thought, shivering as he had a quick clean-up with a cold flannel. He pulled on greyish-white, sagging underpants and a vest that had ceased to be thermal long ago. He hesitated, then clumsily knelt on the rug by his bed to say a lengthy prayer, ending with 'May God preserve her soul . . . and that of anyone else in need of preservation.' This last supplication he added quickly, with a shiver.

Lois's knocking sent him scuttling downstairs to open the door. 'Late up again, I'm afraid, Lois!' he apologised. 'But come in, my dear, come in. Would you like a nice cup of tea to warm you up? Just going to make a pot, and some toast. Breakfast for two – what do you say?'

Lois shook her head, as she had so many times before. 'No thanks, Vicar,' she said. 'I'll have a cup later on, but I'd like to get started now, if you don't mind. And excuse me for saying so, but it's time that dressing gown went in the bin. There's sales on in Tresham and you could get a nice warm one for next-to-nothing.' She collected dusters, cleaner, a brush and dustpan, and headed for the stairs. 'Oh, and by the way,' she added, turning to catch him squinting worriedly at himself in the spotted mirror by the sink. 'Would it be all right if I go ten minutes early? I'll make it up next week. Family business, I'm afraid. Our Josie being a bit of a worry . . . More important than the Great Farnden Murder Mystery!' This jokey remark was not as casual as it sounded. Lois had planned it on the way over, thinking it might jolt something useful out of the vicar.

She was gratified by Peter White's reaction. He whipped round and glared at her. 'Kindly watch your tongue!' he said in a voice she had never heard before. 'I need hardly remind you that poor Miss Hathaway's death is a very serious business and not one to joke about. I am surprised at you, Lois, and disappointed. And no, you may not go early. I have to go out, and I am also expecting a telephone message. I told the caller that you would be here until twelve o'clock.'

It was on the tip of Lois's tongue to tell him exactly where to go, but she remembered in time that she needed all the contacts in Farnden she could get. So she shrugged, said that maybe if the call came through before ten to twelve, she could go anyway, and stomped off up the stairs, pondering this aggressive side of Peter White, hitherto unrevealed.

Peter White did not have to go out at all, but now he had to think of something. I could call on the doctor, he improvised, or see how Nurse Surfleet is getting on with the numerous policemen who have plodded up her neighbour's path. Yes, that was it. He'd try a little counselling of parishioners, though on second thoughts he had distinct qualms about starting with Nurse Surfleet. She was quite likely to dismiss him briskly, or

– even worse – turn the tables and worm out of him some of his darkest hidden secrets. She was known for being a sympathetic listener. No, perhaps not Gillian Surfleet. Rachel Barratt, then? She had found the body, so they said. Yes, she was a nice woman, anxious to please and keen to take her place in the village. Yes, he would drop in on Rachel Barratt, and hope that rather dreadful husband of hers was not at home.

He finished dressing and went down to make breakfast. The bread stuck in the toaster, and he extricated the burnt offering, buttered it as best he could, and washed it down with scalding tea. Lois was vacuuming fiercely overhead, and he had to go halfway up the stairs before he could make her hear his voice. 'I'm off now, Lois,' he said coldly. 'I can't say when I'll be back, but your money is in the usual place. And there's a pad and pencil by the telephone for that message.' And without saying goodbye, he took his coat and slammed the front door behind him. Murder Mystery indeed, he muttered to himself.

'There'll be plenty of that going on,' he added, as he saw a police car parked outside Doctor Rix's house. He turned into the Barratts' and saw with relief that Malcolm's car was not there. 'Good morning, my dear,' he said, as Rachel opened the door. 'Might I come in for a minute or two, just for a little chat?'

'No, sorry,' said Rachel Barratt flatly. 'I've got a sore throat and I'm going back to bed.' And she shut the door firmly in his face.

No respect for the cloth, thought Peter White sadly, though it was most unlike Mrs Barratt to be impolite, especially to a person such as himself with his position in the village. He hurried off down the drive towards the doctor's house, remembered the police car, and swerved off towards the shop. He needed some potatoes. At least they couldn't slam the door on him in the shop. Then the Tresham bus cruised down the street, and as it stopped by the pub, Peter White, on an impulse, boarded it. What am I doing? he thought, as he fumbled for change. Oh well, perhaps the Lord has a plan for me this morning. I might as well follow Him wherever He takes me. Peter White was not being entirely honest with himself. He knew exactly where he would end up in Tresham, and it was not a place likely to be frequented by his dear Lord, or anyone else he knew, with luck.

Lois had finished her usual jobs in the vicarage in record time, finding that without Peter White's constant and well-meaning interruptions, she could move much faster. She looked around, still quite determined to leave early. The mysterious caller had still not telephoned. Lois frowned. She guessed the vicar had invented his appointment and the telephone call too, and couldn't think what had put him in such a bad mood. She reflected that in his capacity as moral leader of the village, he might well feel an extra burden of guilt that he had not been able to help Gloria Hathaway, maybe even prevent her dreadful death. Pity he wasn't a Catholic. Catholic priests knew all about everybody, didn't they, from the confessional? Lois had fancied becoming a Catholic, reckoning they had it easy. All they had to do was confess their sins, get absolution, and then go off and do the same things all over again.

She decided to turn out the kitchen cupboards and throw out anything beyond its sell-by date. Lois wrinkled her nose at the stale smell as she opened a door. Vicar always smelt a bit, too, she reflected. Wonder what's his sell-by date? She opened the window and grinned at the thought. Still, if he'd spend a bit of money on himself, clothes, barber, some good food, he could be much improved. Well, perhaps not greatly, but certainly he could look a lot more wholesome, more fanciable. Why hadn't he got a wife? Not gay, she knew that. A lot of women would like to be married to a vicar . . . social position and all that. Perhaps he was one of those men who were neither one thing nor the other, like neutered tomcats. Lois thought of the laundry basket upstairs and knew that he certainly had yearnings for something, even if it was a touch kinky. Wouldn't be the first, but it could end in tears, especially with a vicar! *News Of The World*, and all that.

'Oh, my God!' Lois sat back on a chair, struck by the dreadful thought. It could have been him. Nobody thought anything of it when he went calling on single women. She herself had sent him off to see Gloria Hathaway when she'd been ill. He'd had the perfect opportunity to plan it all, to ask Gloria if she was going to Open Minds, to discover that she was doing teas, to appear at the back door of the village hall without alarming her . . . oh yes, it would have been so easy.

A shoal of unused small pots of herbs suddenly cascaded down from the cupboard, bursting open and scattering dry green specks all over the floor, making her jump. 'Damn!' said Lois. She fetched the broom and began to sweep for the second time.

It's certainly possible, her thoughts continued along this unattractive track. No doubt that he could have done it. He had every chance and nobody to check on him at home. But why? Did Gloria know some secret of his that he wanted passionately to conceal? Hopeless love, was that it? Lois consigned all the herbs to the bin, and followed them with half-empty pots of jam, grey with mould, and cereal packets with a few stale flakes rattling around. Ugh! She washed out the top cupboards, dried them and put the few remaining pots and jars back neatly.

Now the bottom cupboards. She glanced at the kitchen clock and saw that she still had half an hour to go. No telephone call yet, but Lois had given up expecting it. The next cupboard contained a tangle of saucepans with greasy bases, lids with dried potato stuck to the rims, all in a heap with cake tins, rusty from the damp and never used. A strange four-legged device that looked like something Nurse Surfleet would use in dire circumstances, turned out to be a juicer from the ark, with lemon pips still clinging to its smelly interior. Lois reached deep into the cupboard and her hand met something cold and hairy. She gasped involuntarily, recoiling with a shudder. Get on with it, gel, she told herself and pulled it out with the handle of the broom. It was a rat, very dead, decomposed beyond putrefaction and light as a feather on the dustpan.

Quite enough for one day, Lois decided, and, tipping the rat into the bin with all the other rubbish, she rinsed the grubby pans quickly, washed out the cupboard with bleach and replaced everything in some kind of order. It was a quarter to twelve and she had promised to be home early to talk to Derek over lunch about Josie, the club, and Melvyn.

In the empty vicarage, the telephone was silent. It was a cold, unfriendly silence, unbroken until Peter White returned alone to his unwelcoming house, whistling sadly to himself.

Twelve

M elvyn and Josie walked slowly, holding hands, along the edge of the muddy canal which wound its way round the backs of warehouses and deserted industrial sites in Tresham. 'You should be in school,' he said, but without much conviction. 'What did you tell them this time?'

'Said I had to go to the dentist,' said Josie, giving his hand a squeeze. 'They never ask for a note or nothin'. I reckon you could bunk off most days and nobody'd care.'

'Don't be stupid,' said Melvin, turning to face her and frowning down into her smiling face. 'Bunkin' off most days'd be pushing it. If you're up to something, don't push it. That's what me and the lads say, and it's right.'

Josie knew who the lads were and they frightened her. They were in reality a sad little gang of school-leavers with no prospects, no jobs to go to, spurning further education as fit only for nerds, and prowled about the town wasting their last year of school as lawlessly as they could without being caught. Most of them were suspended from school and should have attended special classes at the community centre, but none of them went, and nobody checked. Melvyn was not one of them, but used them when he needed to, and they were flattered by his apparent enjoyment of their company.

Josie stood on her toes and kissed Melvyn's frowning face. 'OK, OK,' she said. 'I'll watch it. Anyway, where shall we go, now I've got the time off?' She didn't much care where they went, so long as she was with Melvyn.

'Want me to show you a secret place?' he said, and grinned.

The factory had been a flourishing business for years, but had failed to compete with the growing number of cheap furniture supermarkets in the area. After a brief struggle,

67

the end had come, bankruptcy declared, and the gates had shut for the last time. The building dated from a time when canal traffic had been an accepted form of transport, and its rear walls bordered the towpath. Now Melvyn led Josie by the hand through a half-open doorway and into a storeroom deep inside the building. Here stood the melancholy remains of a once healthy factory: chairs with broken legs, an oval mirror broken into shards of splintered glass, a rickety bed complete with dirty mattress pushed into one corner. Empty beer cans and used syringes crushed under fleeing feet were evidence of visitors Josie preferred not to think about. She realized with sudden panic that Melvyn was leading her through the detritus to the uninviting bed in the corner.

'I could get done for this, you know,' he said tentatively, bending to kiss her.

'Sod you!' yelled Josie, pulling away from him. '*I'm* not getting done! Let me go!' But she had no cause for alarm. Melvyn released her at once, and watched her run off with the hint of a smile on his face.

'Well, I don't like it. She's too young to go down to that club,' said Lois. 'It's for adults and I should think they've got an age limit anyway.' She and Derek had eaten fish and chips straight from the paper.

'Wipe your hands, gel,' said Derek as Lois handed him an apple. 'Everything'll taste fishy.'

'Don't change the subject,' said Lois, rinsing her hands under the tap. 'Why did you say we'd think about it? And after I'd said she couldn't? Honestly, Derek, sometimes I think you do it just to annoy. As if I hadn't got enough to worry about, what with the boys, and Mum, and Christmas, and . . . and . . .'

'. . . and Josie,' said Derek.

'And Josie,' Lois nodded, and put her arms round Derek's neck.

'Ere, none of that!' he said. 'That won't change me mind. I only told her I'd think about it, anyway.' They sat in silence for a minute and then Derek said, 'Perhaps we should find out a bit more about this Melvyn first? Would that make you happier?'

'Depends what we find out,' said Lois grudgingly. But she recognised a climb-down when she saw one, and agreed that they'd do a bit of ferreting about and see what emerged. 'Don't even know his surname,' she said. There was a silence, and then she had a bright idea. 'I could ask the postman,' she suggested. 'Not much he doesn't know.'

Derek nodded, and stood up, stretching and smiling. 'Got to get going,' he said. 'And isn't it time you got out the notebook and jotted down today's developments in the case of the strangled spinster . . . ?'

Lois moved towards him, but he was faster on his feet. He turned at the gate and waved. You could say this for Derek, thought Lois with a reluctant smile, he certainly knew when his number was up.

Lois spent a long time with her notebook. Peter White had acted very strangely this morning, very out of character. He'd been jumpy and irritable with her before he went out, which was something she could not remember happening before.

P. White very edgy, she wrote. *Where was he going? Not his usual visiting day, did not mention any names. Mysterious telephone caller? Did not call. Blackmail? P.White knows something.* Had Lois seen Peter White boarding the Tresham bus when his car stood in the drive, her curiosity would have been doubled. As it was, she added a couple of notes about the state of his bedroom, and the fact that though she tipped out his laundry basket to get some smelly socks from deep inside, there was now no trace of the girlie magazines.

By the time Josie wandered in, out of breath and shoulders slumped, Lois had finished her notes and had her arms full of dirty washing. 'What's up, Josie?' she said at once, seeing her downcast face. 'That Sharon again?' Josie had been the butt of a cruel, plain girl in her class all the way up the school. But the bullying seemed to have died down in the past year and Josie had seemed happier.

Josie shook her head. 'Nope,' she said. 'Just a bit of a headache, that's all.' She sat down at the kitchen table and put her head in her hands.

'I'll get you an aspirin.' Lois dried her hands and ran some water in a glass. 'Here,' she said. 'Swallow it down and I'll make a nice cup of tea.'

To her amazement, Josie began to cry. 'Bloody cup of tea,' she snuffled through her fingers. 'That's your answer for everything!'

Lois stared at her, anxiety rising, and walked over to put her arms around Josie's shoulders. 'Hey, come on . . . what's the trouble? You'd better tell me. Nobody else at home, so we shan't be interrupted for once.'

The story came out gradually, in bits and pieces, and when Josie described the old furniture factory and the dirty bed in the corner, Lois's heart was thumping in terror. 'Who was this boy?' she shouted.

Josie looked at her fearfully. 'Nobody you know,' she said.

'Not that bloody Melvyn?'

'No,' Josie lied quickly. 'Just a boy from town. Anyway,' she continued, crying so messily now that it was difficult to make out what she was saying. 'He never done it.'

'Never done *what*!' said Lois, trying to keep control.

'Oh, you know, Mum. It. Seems he was planning to, but he let me go and I got out. I know a quick way home, through that alley between them old houses . . .' She petered out, sniffing and wiping her nose with the back of her hand. Lois silently handed her a tissue and sat down at the table opposite her.

'Josie,' she said, calming down and speaking gently, 'I think we need to talk. With Dad, and that. You've been missing school a lot, haven't you.' She didn't wait for a reply. 'And all this going around with boys older than you and talking of clubbing and dancing, and being out all hours. You're still a child, Josie, and our responsibility. Now –' she added, standing up briskly – 'I shall put the kettle on and make a cup of tea, whether you like it or not, because I need one. No more talk until your Dad gets home and you'd better go and wash your face. Go on, up you go.'

Left alone in the kitchen, Lois felt her maternal omnipotence slipping away. Always able to console, to kiss and make it better, to find solutions to all childish problems, now she felt out of her depth. Her little Josie in that disgusting place, with some strange boy who'd nearly taken away her childhood for ever. Thinking back to her own teenage years was no help. She'd just been lucky. Oh, my God, how was she going to find the right words to tell Derek? She made two mugs of tea and sat at the table, waiting for Josie to come down.

'Mum?' Lois looked up, and there was Josie, her face washed and with no make-up, her hair tied back in a ponytail, changed into a white T-shirt and jeans, looking for all the world like the ideal teenager. 'Mum,' Josie said again. 'Can I say something before Dad gets home?'

Lois nodded. 'Drink your tea before it gets cold,' she said.

Josie sat down opposite her, and smiled wanly. 'Look, Mum,' she said. 'Things have changed a bit since you were young.' Lois began to splutter, but Josie asked if she could please finish what she wanted to say. 'Most of the girls in my class have done it and there's only me and one or two others who haven't. I'm the odd one out, Mum.'

'At *fourteen?*' said Lois incredulously.

'Oh, Mum, where've you bin'?' Josie laughed now and choked, trying to drink tea at the same time. Lois said nothing more and sat and listened while Josie brought her up to date. One of her schoolmates, said Josie, had left to have a baby. 'She was really pleased,' said Josie. 'To get out of school and have somethin' to love. Didn't get much at home.'

'Ah, come off it,' said Lois at last. 'You've been watching too much telly. Somethin' to love? Love hasn't anything to do with it, so don't try that one.'

Josie shrugged. 'It ain't all sex, Mum,' she said wisely. 'Some girls just like the cuddling bit. Still –' she added with a dismissive shrug of her shoulders – 'if you're not even going to try an' understand . . .'

'No, no, go on, tell me everything, the whole sordid lot,' said Lois. 'I need to know it all when I tell your Dad.'

'Must you?' said Josie.

Lois frowned at her. 'What do you mean?' Surely Josie knew that Derek and she had no secrets.

Josie struggled on. 'Must you tell Dad? After all, nothing happened. I was dead scared and no bugger is goin' to get me in there again. No harm done.'

'Don't swear,' said Lois automatically. She was silent for a minute, and then said, 'Well, I suppose we could leave it. Let the heat go out of it. I'll think about it. Let you know. But for Christ's sake, Josie, be more sensible in future. Seems you know quite enough to be able to see trouble coming.'

Neither talked for a few minutes, then Josie got to her feet. 'Need any help?' she said sweetly. 'Ironing, shopping, or anything?'

'Never mind that,' said Lois. 'And this clinches that clubbing business, my girl! So don't even think of it. And as for Melvyn . . . You don't fool me all the time, you know. If we hear you've been with him anywhere at any time, it'll be real trouble. And no more missing school. I shall know, Josie, you can be sure of that. Plenty of spies around here, who'd be only too pleased to let me know.'

That night, unable to sleep, Lois woke Derek and told him the whole story. He was so quiet she thought he'd gone back to sleep and hadn't heard her. But he moved suddenly, put his arms round her and stroked her hair. 'You done well, gel,' he said. 'Nothing more to be done, for the present. But if we hear of anything else, by God, I'll skin that bloody Melvyn alive.' Reassured, Lois drifted off to sleep and dreamed that Josie was lying dead in Gloria Hathaway's cottage, her thumb in her mouth and clutching her old teddy bear.

Thirteen

Lois met the postman on her way out next morning, late for the Baers' and well aware that Evangeline would deliver a well-worded rocket. 'Hey!' she called, as she watched him disappearing up her neighbour's path. 'Can I have a word?'

Yes, he knew the lad she meant. He lived in one of the back streets of town, where red-brick terraces had survived from the days when Tresham had been a busy railway junction and industrial town. Yes, he said again, curious now, the family seemed all right, several kids, all boys, quite a bit younger than Melvyn. He'd been on that round for a while, and the mother had always given him cups of tea on cold mornings and a drink and a mince-pie at Christmas. Nice woman, worked hard with all those kids. Never saw the father. Melvyn was the quiet one, he remembered. The others were always yelling and fighting, like kids will, but Melvyn didn't. Clever at school, if he had the right one, and he was sure he had. Yep, tall and thin, with reddish hair and dark eyes, a bit more about him than most.

'Thanks,' said Lois. 'I knew you'd be the one to ask.'

'Your Josie fancy him, then?' said the postman with a grin. Lois pretended not to have heard, and got into her car. It wouldn't start first time, and by the time she got going, her neighbour's door had shut firmly behind the postman and the frosty street was quiet.

Evangeline Baer was ready for her. 'This is unlike you, Lois,' she said. 'I was relying on you being here on time. I have to go over to Ringford to pick up some stuff from a young potter just moved in there. Very nice, it is. Good shapes and glazes.'

What is she on about? thought Lois, and said, 'No, it isn't like me, and I have a good reason for being late. Anyway, you

73

could have gone. I've got the key you gave me. And you know I'll make up the time. Or you can dock my pay.'

'Don't be silly, Lois,' said Evangeline mildly, and quaked when she saw Lois bridle. Lord knows I can't do without her, she thought, and said tentatively that she'd be grateful if Lois could do an extra half-hour anyway, with pay, to help her unload the pottery.

'Sorry, can't do that,' said Lois. 'Got a meeting with the police.' That'll fix her, she said under her breath, and disappeared upstairs.

Lois had arranged to meet Janice Britton and PC Simpson at Janice's house in Farnden, after she'd finished at the Baers'. She was apprehensive and excited at the same time. Her notebook was half-full of snippets of events and information she had remembered, and she hadn't yet decided just how much she was going to share with the others. She had to admit she was nervous in case they laughed.

When, however, she knocked at Janice's door and was ushered in to her small front room to meet Keith Simpson again, she saw their faces and remembered with a jolt that this was not a game. Murder was the worst crime in the book and it was quite likely that someone she knew had done it.

'The difficult thing, in a way,' said Janice, 'is that the poor woman had no relatives we can trace. None living, anyway. If she was in trouble – and she most likely was – she'd got nobody to turn to.'

'Except Doctor Rix,' said Lois, without thinking. She was remembering those frequent telephone calls, the out-of-hours consultations in the surgery. 'And the vicar, of course, Reverend White,' she added. 'Vicars are supposed to help people in trouble, aren't they? And then there's her neighbour, Nurse Surfleet. She's always helping people. Loads of people in this village would've helped . . .' She tailed off, looking at their patient faces.

'If she'd asked,' said Janice, humbly aware that Lois had left her off the list. 'From what I knew of her, she kept herself very much to herself. Anti-people, in a lot of ways. Gillian Surfleet tried, and sometimes it was all right and other times she got the bum's rush. She could be very rude, could Gloria Hathaway.'

'Anyway,' said Keith, sitting up straight, 'we'd better do this in some sort of order. Can you make notes, Janice, and I'll ask Lois some straight questions. We don't want to ramble about too much . . . if you don't mind?' he added quickly, seeing Lois's face. He was well aware that if the Inspector considered Lois to be potentially useful, he would take on dealings with her himself.

'See what you can get out of the woman,' Cowgill had said. 'Let her think we're sharing information, if she wants to play detective. String her along a bit, but don't tell her anything.' Keith reflected that he hadn't got anything of real interest to share anyway, and could not resist a small smile. If DI Cowgill thought he could handle Lois, good luck to him!

'Firstly, how does your week go, Lois?' said Keith, in his best official voice.

'Monday, Rixes; Tuesday, Barratts; Wednesday, Nurse Surfleet; Thursday, the vicar, Peter White; and Friday the Baers. Three hours at each, starting at 9 o'clock.'

'Excellent,' said Keith, and Janice's pen moved rapidly across her notebook. 'All the facts, and in good order. If only all witnesses were as orderly.'

'I'm not a witness,' said Lois flatly. 'I didn't see who killed Gloria Hathaway. I wasn't even at that meeting. Not for the likes of me, you know. Open Minds is for those with minds, and cleaners don't have minds.'

'Come off it, Lois,' said Keith reprovingly. 'That kind of comment is of no use to a police enquiry. Just stick to answering my questions with the facts.'

'Oh, shut up!' said Lois, losing patience. 'I agreed to come here to exchange some information, and that's what we'll do.' Janice Britton nodded vigorously, smiling sympathetically. Lois continued firmly, 'So what have you got so far? Not a lot, is my guess.'

Keith put down his papers and Janice her notebook, and all three relaxed. Keith started again. 'We've taken statements from every woman who was at the meeting, and corroborating statements from their families; times they set off, came back, whether they went on their own to the meeting, or joined up with friends, that sort of thing. Nothing untoward there.'

'The speaker that night was an old woman, wasn't she?' said Lois. Keith then assured her that they had followed her up and she'd been there in front of twenty pairs of eyes, whilst in the next room poor Gloria had met her terrified end.

'Didn't they hear anything?' Janice asked this obvious question, because it seemed strange that in a roomful of women listening politely to a quiet-voiced,elderly Land Girl, no sounds of alarm or struggle had been heard.

Keith shook his head. 'Some of them said there was the usual rumble from the urn. Seems it's an ancient old crate of a thing, difficult to control. They get it up to boiling, then leave it on low until they make the tea. But it goes on rumbling and bubbling, so they say. Fills the kitchen with steam.'

'What?' said Lois, looking up sharply.

'*What* what?' said Keith, startled.

'What's that you said about the steam?'

'Fills the kitchen, they said. Especially on cold nights. Nothing remarkable about that, is there, Lois?' Keith was dangerously near his patronising tone again, and Lois frowned.

'Nothin' at all,' she said. 'Except she wouldn't've seen him – or her – coming, would she. Not if the steam was thick.'

'Ah,' said Keith. Janice began jotting in her notebook again.

'So who else've you talked to, apart from the women and their families?' Lois was beginning to feel much more confident. She saw that already she knew a lot more than they did, all in all. Not much they could add, she suspected, but it was worth going on with it for a bit.

Keith felt uncomfortable. Tables seemed to have been turned on him in some way, and he answered Lois reluctantly. 'We are taking a list of village residents one by one,' he said. 'Street by street. Amazing what turns up, with patient investigation.'

'Meanwhile,' said Janice treacherously, 'the murderer may well have been busy covering his tracks.'

'Could be in Australia by now,' said Lois, and burst out laughing. 'Oh, come on, Keith,' she added. 'Anything juicy emerged yet?'

'Well,' he answered huffily, racking his brains for something Lois would consider juicy. 'It may be nothing to do with the

76

murder, but one of the neighbours saw someone walking up the footpath that goes behind Miss Hathaway's and Nurse Surfleet's cottages, but just assumed it was one of the women going to Open Minds.

'Where does the footpath end up?' said Lois. 'I know it goes along the back of the gardens.'

'At the village hall,' said Keith, and shifted a little in his seat. 'But it doesn't have any lighting, so the neighbour couldn't say who it was.'

'Well,' said Lois. 'It might be interesting, or, as you say, it could just be one of the Open Minds women . . . though wouldn't they think twice about going along there in the pitch dark?'

They had a cup of coffee then, and Keith asked Lois several times if she had noticed anything odd going on in the houses she cleaned, or had overheard any worrying conversations. But Lois side-stepped his questions, revealing nothing of much use.

Finally Keith rose. 'Well, better be getting back to the station,' he said, 'I must report back to DI Cowgill. Anyway, thank you, Lois,' he said. 'You have been most helpful.' He wasn't quite sure about this, particularly when it actually came down to anything new he could tell the Inspector.

She glared at him. 'Oh, I dunno. None of us knows who did it, do they? Could've been Dr Rix, or Prof Godwin . . . or then again, the Reverend . . . or Mr Baer . . . or even Nurse Surfleet, when you think how strong she has to be in her job . . .'

Janice was smiling broadly, and even Keith began to laugh. 'All right, all right,' he said. 'Anyway, let's all keep in touch. Sharing info can only be a good thing, don't you agree, Lois?'

She nodded, but had doubts about just how much she would share with Police Constable Keith Simpson, or, indeed, how much he was willing or able to tell her.

It was Derek's idea to have a family Christmas shopping trip to the new mall outside town. It was a mammoth building, all plate glass and Corinthian pillars, and was already very popular. The official opening had been in September, but Lois and family had not yet seen it. 'Just a temptation to spend more money than you've got,' Lois had said when Josie and the boys had pursued a sustained campaign. All their friends had been, they said. They were the only ones who hadn't.

'It's got birds flying about, Mum, and real trees,' said Jamie, as if this nod towards rurality would convince her. 'Real birds, pretty ones.'

Lois had laughed. 'With real bird shit all over the place, I suppose,' she said. 'Better take hats,' she added, when Derek finally persuaded her.

Saturday was probably the worst day to go, but it was the only one they could manage as a family, and as they drove round and round in convoy, nose to tail, looking for a parking space, Lois's heart sank. Douglas and the others were packed into the back of Derek's van, and she and Josie squashed together on the bench seat in front. It was raining steadily outside, and the windows had steamed up, the demister unable to cope.

'Look! There's a place!' said Douglas.

'Disabled space,' said Derek.

'Oh, for God's sake, just drive into it,' said Lois in desperation. 'Ten to one nobody'll check. We shall never get in there if we don't park soon.' She felt sick in the airless van, but Derek shook his head and drove on until they finally saw someone leaving and moved in quickly. Lois opened the door and struggled out. She drew in deep gulps of wet, fume-laden air, and then helped gather the rest together.

An hour later, Lois had to admit that it was not nearly so bad as she had expected. She and Josie had gone off on their own, while Derek and the boys had headed for the sports shops. In the large central hall it was spacious and, though packed with hundreds of shoppers and sightseers, it seemed airy and light. A magical Christmas display had been set up and queues had formed for a small train which crawled its way in and out of small houses in a scaled-down Swiss village, snow-covered and glittering in the lights, with animated characters from favourite children's stories waving and bowing in their mechanically good-humoured way.

'Come on, Josie,' said Lois, dragging her away. 'You're too old for that! Let's get a cup of tea and rest our feet.'

They'd done most of the shopping on their list, and needed a break.

As they turned to walk away from the crowds, Lois heard Josie gasp, and then a voice said, 'Hi, there, Josie! Fancy seeing you here. How're y'doing?' Josie had stopped dead and her cheeks were fiery.

'Hello,' said Lois, collecting her wits. 'Who's this then, Josie?' She did not recognize the lad, but a moment later she knew.

'Mum – this is Melvyn.'

'Yes,' said Lois. 'So it is. Well, Melvyn, I won't say nice to meet you. But since we have met, you'd better come and have a cup of tea with us. A chat might be a good idea.'

Melvyn, not in the least daunted, smiled in return, winked at Josie, and followed meekly behind as they headed for a café with chairs set out on a stone terrace surrounded by Italianate box hedges.

'Well, where the hell were *you*, then?' said Lois sharply as she and Josie finally found Derek, Douglas and Jamie looking wistfully at an unbelievably shiny Porsche parked at the edge of the square; first prize in a nationwide charity raffle.

'What's up?' said Derek. 'You look a bit flushed the pair of you? Bin' sampling some festive spirit?'

He laughed at this, but realized his mistake when Lois took his arm and squeezed until it hurt. 'We've just had a cup of tea,' she said. '*And* we had company.'

Josie grinned at her father, not in the least embarrassed now. The truth was that Melvyn had been charming and Lois had found it hard to know how to tackle him. He was really very mature for his age, she had thought. But the minute Melvyn had said goodbye and disappeared into the crowds, Lois's strong misgivings had returned. He was too smooth, too old and too smart to be anywhere near her fourteen-year-old, let alone taking her into deserted factories intent on seduction. She had failed, she knew, to give him any sort of warning. She'd fallen too easily under his spell. My God, he sure knew what he was about.

Derek clammed up when she told him, shepherded them out of the mall and into the car park. It took a long time to find the van, and when they did, it sprouted a notice neatly folded into a plastic bag to keep it dry. A parking ticket. They'd run out of time. All they needed, thought Lois, as she watched Derek, unsmiling and worried, push the notice into his pocket. They drove home in silence, except for Josie, whose soft humming irritated Lois so much that she exploded and threatened to shove her out so she'd have to make her own way home.

Later in the evening, when only Derek and Lois were left watching television in silence, the subject was finally approached. Derek switched off mid-programme and said, 'Not watching this, are you?'

Lois shook her head. 'Can't concentrate,' she said.

'Me neither,' said Derek. 'Cup of tea?'

They sat side by side on the sofa and talked. 'He comes over really nice,' said Lois. 'If only we didn't know what we know.'

'You didn't say anything, then . . . nothin' about that factory business?'

Lois shook her head. 'Nope,' she said. 'I must've been mad. But it just didn't seem right, what with Josie sitting there trembling, worrying what was going to happen. I mean, I couldn't say outright that he was a dirty little sod and had better leave our Josie alone else her father'd chew his balls off, could I?'

The ghost of a smile crossed Derek's face. 'Don't see why not,' he muttered. 'Anyway, now we know what we're up against. Maybe you did the right thing. Y'know, keep it all out in the open, not drive it underground and that. Could be the best thing in the end.'

'Mmm,' said Lois. 'Let's hope so.'

Fourteen

Small flecks of wet snow settled on Lois's windscreen as she drove into Farnden and parked outside Nurse Surfleet's cottage. It wasn't so cold now the snow had started, but Lois was apprehensive about her return journey. The clouds hung low and heavy, and were an ominous yellowish-grey colour. She clicked open the gate and walked up the garden path, glancing across at Gloria Hathaway's blind little house, with its curtains drawn and remnants of unwanted junk mail blowing untidily about the dismal garden.

'Morning, Gillian,' said Lois, as she approached Nurse Surfleet's front door.

Nurse Surfleet was just on her way out and held the door open for Lois as she walked past. 'Morning, Lois,' she said. 'Looks like some serious snow on the way. Got to go over to Ringford again this morning. Old Ellen Biggs is worrying me a bit. Not improving, and tries to look after herself, you know. Might have to get her into the Red House for a bit of respite. Poor old thing, very independent . . . Mind you, she's got good friends.'

'Shall I carry on as usual, then?' said Lois, her half-formed plan adjusting in her head as she talked. It must be possible, she thought, to get in there somehow. No police on duty this morning, no officious Keith Simpson barring the way. An idea occurred to her, and she called Gillian Surfleet back just as she was opening the garden gate. 'I've forgotten my keys,' she said. 'Sorry!'

Lois waited while Gillian Surfleet came back up the path, into the house and rummaged through the rows of keys, mostly obsolete, on her board in the kitchen. 'Here,' she said. 'Here's a spare back door key. Use that and return it next week. And do be careful with them, Lois. I was never nervous in this village . . . until . . . well, you know,' she finished, giving herself a shake. She looked again at the board, muttered that she really must sort them out and throw some away. 'There's Gloria's spares there,' she said, just as Lois had hoped. 'Better give those to the police some time,' she remarked as she looked at the clock. 'Oh Lord, I'm late! Old Ellen'll be watching out when she should be in bed. Thanks in advance, Lois. See you next week . . . bye!'

It was too easy. Nothing is that easy, Lois realized later, but now she just sighed with relief as Gloria's back door opened smoothly without a sound. A smell of damp and undisturbed air greeted her. The kitchen was tidy, but it was a final, depressed kind of tidiness, with no one to put on the kettle, run the tap, open the cupboards and the fridge or turn on the cooker. Lois wrinkled her nose at the unpleasant smell and walked on tiptoe through to the living room. Don't know why I'm being so quiet, she thought. Gloria's beyond hearing anything anymore. She began to whistle, to banish the shivers that had begun to run through her. It wasn't just the cold – though it was very cold – no, there was something else, something that always takes up residence in an empty house. Lois couldn't put her finger on it, but decided to have a quick look round, then scarper.

The cottage was small, but had a decent-sized living room. Lois nosed around and the first thing that caught her eye was Gloria's sewing box half-open, with cotton and silks spilled on to the floor. A cup with mouldy coffee dregs stood on the small table by the diamond-paned window. Everything else looked dusty but ordinary. Nothing remotely out of the ordinary. She debated whether to go upstairs. Might not get another chance. She went swiftly up the narrow staircase and into what was obviously Gloria's bedroom. Lois gasped in surprise. My God, this was the secret life of Gloria Hathaway, no mistake! A huge bed, an elaborate dressing table, curlicues on the bedhead, silky drapes and frilled sheets, and a pile of dolls, with ringlets and frills. They seemed to be staring at Lois, and she shivered. A spider crawled over one of the china faces, and Lois backed away. God, they were sinister! Lois sniffed.

82

The damp, decaying smell was up here, too. It was all over the house. Lois felt a strong desire to run, but forced herself to turn back into the room. She stretched out a hand to take a book from the bedside table, but before she could look at it, she heard a sound from downstairs, and froze. Her heart thumped wildly, and she looked around hopelessly for a way out. Heavy footsteps, making no effort to be quiet, began to mount the stairs, and Lois shoved her fist into her mouth to stifle a scream.

'Well, well,' said PC Keith Simpson, 'and what 'ave we 'ere, Mrs Meade? Doing a spot of private investigation, are we?'

His mock copper voice broke the spell of terror, and Lois sat down heavily on a silky, padded stool. 'Blimey, you nearly gave me a heart attack!' she said. 'Just give me a minute, and I'll explain,' she added, panting heavily.

It took some explaining. Keith Simpson was not stupid and he did not believe her story about hearing a cat calling piteously to be let out. He knew Nurse Surfleet had keys, and he had meant to collect them, so he had no trouble in working out how Lois had gained entry. 'What *you* don't know,' he said smugly to Lois, 'is that we check this place every day, and it's just your bad luck we coincided. Still, lucky it was me and not one of the others. I'll let you off with a caution this time, provided you promise to let *me* know what you come up with. And no more trespassing. Better get back next door as quick as you can. We'll be in touch,' he said, as he held the bedroom door open for her. 'Notice anything here, by the way?' he added, but Lois shook her head.

Not so clever, Lois, she said to herself, as she went back through the kitchen and headed out to the path at the back of Miss Hathaway's cottage, thereby denying Keith the fun of watching her ignominious retreat through Gloria's front garden to the road.

Fifteen

M elvyn Hallhouse cycled home from school on the last day of term and parked his bike in the backyard of the house where he lived with his family. Home to my family, he said to himself. But it's not a family like young Josie and her lot; Douglas and Jamie looking so like their father that there was no mistaking their relationship. Melvyn didn't look like his mum or dad, or any of his brothers. They were all fostered, except him and he was adopted. Although there was affection from his mum shared out equally between them, he had never felt a real sense of family as other people knew it. Affection wasn't quite enough. There was always a fair hearing if you did something wrong or lied to Mum, but he couldn't remember a time when, like other mothers, she'd stormed off to school to tackle his teacher with arms akimbo, regardless of whether he had been right or wrong. Melvyn had come to the conclusion his family was different just because of his mum's even-handedness and fairness. It wasn't natural. His mates at school from an early age had been toughened up with a quick vent of temper from an angry mother. They knew when to dodge. But they also knew that their mothers were, when push came to shove, on their side. Melvyn was far from sure that he would always have his mum solidly behind him – he tried not to think about his dad at all.

He opened the back door and greeted his smiling mother. 'Hi,' he said, and gave her a peck on the cheek. If only he'd known how her heart lifted when he did that, how he was her first and her favourite, though of course it was against all the rules to show favouritism. He dumped his school bag, and changed quickly into clothes that transformed him from a schoolboy into the young man he nearly was. 'Can I just have

84

a sandwich, Ma?' he said. 'Got to get out early to meet Charlie. We're going up the centre to do a bit of late shopping.'

'Christmas shopping?' said his mother, taking out the loaf and thin slices of turkey that Melvyn liked.

Melvyn nodded. 'Make a start, anyway,' he said.

His mother pushed the pile of sandwiches down with the flat of her hand. 'Have you got enough money?'

'Yep, enough for now,' Melvyn said, stuffing his mouth full, and turning on the television.

Melvyn's mother wondered sometimes how Melvyn managed his money so well. All the boys had an allowance, of course, graded according to age. His father paid them all each week, handing out money over the table on Fridays as regular as clockwork. Occasionally his mother tried to discuss Melvyn's allowance with his father, anxious that he should measure up well against the other lads. Melvyn never complained and never asked to borrow a quid or two until next week. His father said he'd bloody well better *not* ask. He wasn't made of money.

It was crowded in the shopping centre, and although Melvyn and Charlie had made an arrangement to meet outside John Lewis, there was no sign of Charlie when Melvyn arrived. He stood for a while, watching the shoppers, the weary mothers and whining children, their pushchairs piled high with shopping in bright festive bags. Watching the mothers made him think of his own, his real mother. Well, she'd never had to cope with a pushchair, had she? He wondered if she'd bought a pushchair, then decided against keeping him and had handed him over complete with vehicle? One careful owner. He often tried to imagine how she must have felt when he was born. Young, alone and frightened? Had she wept when she gave him away? He hoped so.

'Wotcha mate!' It was Charlie, unrepentant for his tardiness and smiling broadly as usual. 'Ready for it?'

Melvyn nodded. 'Usual routine?' he said and Charlie laughed.

'Works every time, dunnit?'

They had their system worked out to a degree of fine timing

that would not have disgraced a professional team. First, saunter through the crowded streets, idly glancing into shop windows. Chat to each other, smiling. A well-behaved pair of lads – they even attracted the occasional approving glance from a passing grannie. Second, split up with a good-humoured fare-well. Then, with Charlie walking behind, but still near enough to see Melvyn, they would go into operation mode. Melvyn selected their victim, always one of the young mothers. 'They got their brains addled, see. Easy meat,' he said to Charlie. It was certainly easy enough to drop a coin just behind the chosen woman, tap her on the arm and say he'd just seen her drop it out of her purse. He'd stand and watch as she fumbled in her bag, opening her purse and allowing him to see whether it was going to be worth it when the time came. A few minutes interval, then he would motion Charlie forward, in advance of the woman and her load. Charlie would suddenly turn around, bump into the pushchair with exaggerated apologies and give Melvyn every chance to help himself to the purse and walk away – but not too quickly, so as not to arouse suspicion. Both would then vanish by a prearranged route and not meet up again until school the next day for the share-out. It was foolproof, provided you took care, said Melvyn, and Charlie, admiring his friend's coolness, agreed. He got his half of the proceeds, and told no one.

No trouble, thought Melvyn, as he sized up the woman in front. Well-dressed, kids in expensive gear and the pushchair the latest from Italy. Shoulder bag swinging free, with an open top. My God, they asked for it! He felt in his pocket for a twenty-pence coin.

It wasn't much of a haul, but as Melvyn cycled home, head down against the icy wind, he felt the usual pleasure at having got one up on the enemy.

Sixteen

When Lois arrived at the vicarage on Thursday morning, Peter White was just going out, though he said briefly that he would be back later. He had still not returned by the time she was ready to go, so she left him an acid little note. She would see him next week, she wrote, when perhaps he would have two weeks' money ready for her.

Then on Friday, when she had hoped Mrs Baer might be in a confiding mood and come up with something interesting, Evangeline had been busy all morning with customers, and had hardly spoken to her. Lois reflected that everyone in Long Farnden seemed to be in a bad mood with not a shred of Christmas spirit in sight. It's not as if they'd all been close friends of Gloria Hathaway, Lois thought to herself. Her death had been sad, of course, but they were all behaving as if they'd lost a close relative.

'It's because they're all possible murderers,' Derek had said with relish. She had told him that on Monday the Rixes had more or less ignored her and been unusually snappy with one another. 'Bet they've all got guilty consciences one way or another. After all, think about it, Lois. Dr Rix hears all the village secrets in his surgery, so he could be an evil blackmailer. Then that Barratt bloke thinks he's God's gift to women, so maybe he made a pass and she rejected him, and he was so mad he killed her? Same blackmailing opportunity for the vicar, and that Dallas Baer is a slippery one, you said. Maybe she owed him money, and he got fed up waiting?'

'You're talking about Gloria Hathaway, remember!' said Lois incredulously, wondering how Derek could invent such a ridiculous scenario. 'You forgot Nurse Surfleet,' she said acidly. 'What has the great brain dreamed up for her?'

Derek thought for a moment. 'Nosy neighbour,' he said. 'Old Gloria found out something in the nurse's past and threatened to talk. So, off goes the nurse with the surgical gloves on, straight for the windpipe.' He disappeared back into the house, laughing at Lois's face, but deciding that he had gone quite far enough.

Now it was Tuesday, Lois's day for the Barratts. As she drove over to Farnden, trying to ignore the rattle that seemed to come from directly under her feet, she reviewed the clues she had written in her black notebook and now knew by heart. She had discovered that if she read through her notes before going to bed, some new interpretation of things occurred to her when she woke up. Oddly assorted bits of information that had seemed unconnected formed a possible link. Scattered remarks, often in different houses on different days, considered together, pointed to some possible evidence. Trouble is, Lois considered, I never have time to think things through properly. There's always Derek, Josie and the boys and endless tidying up in Farnden houses. Still, she reminded herself, it's my job that gives me the chance to find out more than most, including the police, so I shouldn't grumble. I just need to concentrate, and not let my mind wander off to Josie and Melvyn, and why Derek hasn't got that dirty mark off the sleeve of his jacket. Better take it to the cleaners, she decided, and then laughed aloud at her next thought, Better not, might be destroying evidence!

Ridiculous or not, the thought came in useful, and as soon as she had hung up her coat and collected her cleaning things, she had a good look in the hall cupboard where the Barratts hung their coats. There it was, the professor's Barbour jacket, and it had quite clearly been cleaned. The ticket was still stuck to the lining with a safety pin, and an unmistakable smell of cleaner's fluid hung about it. So. He hadn't wasted much time, or maybe Rachel had taken it for him. Why so quickly after the police had announced their intention of revisiting all Farnden people who had any connection with that horrible evening's events? But then again, why not? He liked to look the part. Perhaps he needed to wear it to a lunch with county friends, or for going away for a weekend's hunting and shooting. Lois smiled to herself. Derek did a bit of shooting over the fields outside Tresham, but it was a different thing entirely.

Lois walked into an empty sitting room and called 'Cooee!' loudly. She had seen nobody since she arrived, and thought she'd better check for any extra instructions before making a start. No answer. She called again, and still there was silence. Funny, not like them to go out and leave the door open. It was so quiet in the house that she felt a shiver of apprehension. Should she look upstairs? Malcolm might be up in his eyrie, or whatever he called it, and not hear her. Halfway up, she heard a sound and stopped dead. It sounded like someone choking, and she called again, 'Mrs Barratt! Are you there?' A muffled sound now, coming from the main bedroom. Lois forgot caution and rushed up, opened the door and marched in. An unlovely sight confronted her. Rachel Barratt was sitting up in bed, a rumpled nightdress clutched round her, her hair tousled and her face blotched and swollen. She was gulping and choking, and tears streamed down her already soaked cheeks.

'Whatever is the matter?' said Lois sharply. She had no time for self-pity, and something told her that this was what she was confronted with. Rachel shook her head violently, indicating that her despair was beyond words. 'Oh, come on, Mrs Barratt, it can't be as bad as all that!' Lois was hearty, reassuring. 'Better be getting up,' she added. 'Else I shan't be able to do this room.' Again the shake of the head, and Lois gingerly sat down on the bed beside the weeping woman. 'Come on now,' she said, softening her tone with difficulty. 'Anything I can do to help?'

After a few minutes of silence, the gulps and sobs subsided and Rachel scrabbled under her pillow for a handkerchief, which she used to dab at her puffy eyes. 'Gone,' she said finally, and having managed the word, sat completely still, staring at Lois from blank eyes.

'Who's gone?' said Lois, though she knew. It must be Malcolm. Only Rachel's beloved spouse could have caused this depth of misery. Though everyone in the village knew that Prof Barratt was a vain and lecherous nuisance where women were concerned, they also knew that his wife either knew nothing about it, or had decided to pretend it wasn't happening. Not that Lois had ever heard anything serious about the Prof. It was all flirtation in the pub, groping at parties in dark corners, the car parked in field gateways on summer evenings. Nothing regular, no recognised mistress. It was nothing more than a silly middle-aged man unwilling to acknowledge the passing years.

'Who's gone?' repeated Lois, and this time Rachel focussed her eyes on Lois's enquiring face.

'Malcolm, of course,' she said, and then added in a stronger voice, 'The bugger's gone. Cleared out. Vamoosed.'

'You mean he's gone away?'

'For good, he said. And I told him good riddance, and then when I was sorry, it was too late. He'd thrown some things in a suitcase and driven off like a crazy man down the road. He even forgot to put his lights on . . .'

'Lucky there was nobody about,' said Lois, and then, inconsequentially. 'And he forgot to take his Barbour.'

Rachel said, as if there was nothing odd about Lois's question, 'Well, he wouldn't want that, would he?'

Lois got up. 'I'll make a drink,' she said. 'Then you can tell me more about it.' A sharp look from Rachel Barratt, now rapidly improving, brought her back to the status quo, the exact nature of the relationship between them. Master and servant, thought Lois. Still, worth pursuing Rachel while she was vulnerable. She might have something useful to say.

By the time she returned with mugs of strong coffee, Rachel was out of bed and sitting on a stool in her dressing gown, gazing at her ravaged face in the mirror. 'God, I look terrible,' she said, taking the coffee gratefully. 'Look, Lois,' she said, 'do you mind listening for a few minutes? I can't tell the girls – they're not here anyway – and I've got to talk to somebody.'

And I'm all there is, said Lois to herself. 'Yes, of course,' she reassured Rachel. 'Carry on. I can stay an extra half an hour today if necessary.'

The thought of paying Lois extra money for her sympathetic ear galvanised Rachel into action. She began to tell a tale of arguments and quarrelling, a big row about nothing at all, and then Malcolm storming out, shouting at the top of his voice. 'He could have woken all the neighbours,' said Rachel, as if, on reflection, this was the worst thing about the whole sordid business.

'But what exactly set off the row?' said Lois. Maybe if Rachel could tell her that, it might lead to something important. Any happening out of the ordinary routine of Farnden life was worth consideration. Maybe it wasn't just an erring husband. There was something about the way Rachel kept stopping mid-sentence, giving Lois sideways looks. She was covering up, Lois was sure of that. But what?

Rachel's next remarks, meant to be semi-humorous but not fooling Lois, took her by surprise. 'He wanted us to go away for a holiday, straight away, and for several weeks. To Russia, of all God-awful places! I said I couldn't, wouldn't and didn't want to go. And what about the girls? Things would have to be arranged, and why couldn't we go somewhere nice and warm? Not bloody Russia in the winter!'

So was Malcolm running away? And if so, from what? 'What did he say next?' prompted Lois keenly.

'He said if I wouldn't go, he'd go with someone else, and that was it. Holdall from the cupboard, all his clean underpants and socks, and several shirts . . . toilet things . . . and he was gone before I could think again. I don't think he wanted me to change my mind, Lois. It was like he had it all planned.'

This dramatic outpouring threatened to set her off again, so Lois quickly took the mugs, stood up and suggested a warm shower. 'Then you can get dressed and come down. I'll clear up the kitchen, and by then you'll have decided what to do. Mind you,' she added firmly, 'I know what I'd do.'

'What?'

'Nothing,' said Lois. 'He'll be back before you know it. Men always are.' Rachel looked doubtful, but disappeared into the shower obediently, leaving a trail of sodden tissues as she went.

Lois's house was also silent, but with a warm, welcoming silence, pleasantly scented with the smell of freesias. Derek had brought them home from some job he was doing at a big house in Round Ringford. 'Loads of 'em in the greenhouse,' he had said. 'And this kid – daughter of the house, I think – picked these and insisted I took them. Funny kid . . .'

'But didn't her mum or somebody say anything?' Lois had asked.

'Nope. Well, the mother's one them snotty-faced women who don't give nothing away. But she could hardly make a scene about a few flowers. You could see the kid was goin' to catch it, though, once I was out of the way.' Derek had chuckled at the memory. 'You take 'em and enjoy 'em, Lois,' he'd said. 'They could spare a few flowers for the deserving poor.'

Now Lois topped up the vase with water, breathed in the wonderful scent, and finally settled down at the kitchen table with her notebook. She had a good two hours before the rest of the family arrived and demanded her services, so she began by reading through once again what she had written.

Stained jackets – vicar, Barratt, (Derek!), Dr Rix. Well, there was something odd straight away. All the stains were in roughly the same place, and presumably made by something that cleaned out easily, as the Prof's now showed no trace of the mark. *Possibly off the underside of car? Check again on Thursday at the vicarage.* That would account for the similarity. But is it likely that all would have trouble with their cars in the same way? No, not really. *Empty nursery – Rixes' house.* Lois couldn't remember why she'd noted that, except that she found it creepy every time she passed the door. She wasn't allowed to clean it, and the one time she'd offered to vacuum through there, Mary Rix had made such a fuss that Lois had never mentioned it again. She knew it was still furnished as a baby's room. She'd seen Mrs Rix in there one day with the door open, holding a doll and staring out of the window, not hearing Lois approach. Lois had never seen such sadness on a woman's face and her heart turned over. But what had it to do with Gloria's death? Nothing, on the face of it, but there was something very funny going on there. *Possible trouble between doctor and wife? Old secrets still festering?* Lois smiled. That was a good word. Things rotting under the surface. Villages were like that, in Lois's considerable experience. All thatched cottages and roses round the door on the surface, but like a muck heap underneath.

There was quite a lot more, odd facts and snatches of conversation that she had noted down, and she realized she had amassed some useful inside information, some of which, in due course, she should probably pass on.

Lois looked up at the kitchen clock and was amazed to see that in ten minutes the first of her brood would be bursting through the door, hungry, irritable and overexcited by the approaching season of goodwill. She sighed. She loved Christmas when it came, but at this stage saw it more as the season of spending, drinking and eating enough to feed two starving families for weeks. Lois stood up, pushed her chair back, and closed her notebook. She put it back in its hiding place, pleased that she had several positive lines of enquiry to pursue. Got the jargon, Lois, she said to herself, and went to the freezer to see what she could rustle up for tea.

Seventeen

As Christmas approached, Keith Simpson decided it was time he had another word with Lois Meade before the school holidays and seasonal shutdown put her out of his reach for weeks. He was certain she was beavering away on her own, gathering information about the murder of Gloria Hathaway, and telling him as little as possible. In fact, telling him nothing. There was, of course, nothing to prevent her from her own investigations, but if he felt she was withholding vital information from the police, then he had every right to put on some pressure.

The morning he had caught her in Gloria Hathaway's house had been proof that she was still very curious. Her feeble excuse about a trapped cat had not fooled him for one minute. However, he'd judged it best to let her off the hook. Well, not exactly off the hook, but play out the line a bit, just to see what she would do next. Trouble was, she was elusive. He knew which houses she went to, but if he turned up asking for her that would give the game away and her clients would stop talking to her at once, suspecting her of colluding with the police. As for her own home, she'd agreed to co-operate with him and Janice Britton only if he promised not to come bothering her family. So far, her idea of co-operation had not amounted to much, and Hunter Cowgill was asking pointed questions. He seemed to be more interested in Lois's potential, rather than the information garnered from her so far, and Keith himself was still convinced she could be a valuable source if she chose.

He decided to take another turn around the Hathaway cottage and if he happened to see Lois in the village, well and good. All most irregular, he worried. Still, at the moment he had no option but to play it Lois's way, and keep his Inspector informed.

Lois unloaded Nurse Surfleet's clothes from her washing machine and glanced out of the window. High clouds and a fresh, cold wind. Rain had been forecast, but there was no sign of it yet. She fetched the peg bag and went out into the back yard, where she fixed the washing line and began to hang out the wet, cold clothes. The wind blew a pillowcase slapping against her face, and she swore, wishing she'd put them in the drier as usual. But, as her mother frequently reminded her, waste not, want not, and if the wind would dry the clothes, why waste money on electricity? Lost in such thoughts, Lois did not at first hear the faint knocking. It grew louder, and she turned around. It seemed to be coming from Gloria's cottage, and she peered up at the window where the sound came from. The window opened and she saw Keith Simpson beckoning to her and nodding fiercely. Blast! She'd been keeping out of his way, too busy with Christmas looming to have had time to think much about Gloria Hathaway. She turned away. Best to ignore him. She took the now empty basket and was about to return to the house, when a thought struck her. If she went over there now, it would be an opportunity, however constrained, to look around the cottage again. It might be her only chance.

She took a quick look around. Nobody on the footpath and Nurse Surfleet not due back until lunchtime. She put the clothes basket in the kitchen, locked the door, put the key in her pocket, then went through out to the path at the back of the cottages and into Gloria's back garden. Not a soul in the street and only Keith's car parked outside. Lois headed for the back door, which she saw stood ajar, and slipped inside.

'Up here, Lois,' said Keith's voice, and she climbed swiftly up the stairs.

As she reached the top, she said, 'This had better be something good, fetching me over from . . .' Her voice tailed away, as she saw a man who was not Keith Simpson sitting at Gloria's dressing table, his back to the mirror.

'Morning, Mrs Meade,' said Hunter Cowgill. 'Very nice of you to come over. We shan't keep you long.'

After Lois had recovered from the shock, and Keith had introduced his Detective Inspector, something like a conversation eventually got going. Lois was angry. She was angry about being tricked by Keith Simpson, she was angry with this cool, polite policeman for putting him up to it, and she was still very angry with the police in general for turning her down. Every time she saw a woman in police uniform she felt a stab of anger. It should have been her. Still, it was clear they wanted her now, but in a very different way.

'You've had an unusual arrangement,' said Hunter Cowgill mildly. He suggested that Keith should now go and keep a lookout downstairs.

Dismissed, thought Keith Simpson, and reluctantly withdrew. It had been his idea, after all.

'What arrangement?' said Lois. 'There wasn't any arrangement with Keith and Janice. It was just informal. I'd tell them if anything came my way, and they'd tell me any bits that might help me put things together. In any case, nothing much has happened lately, either way.'

'I know,' said Cowgill. 'That's why I'm here. I'd like you to step it up a bit. I can give you some lines to go on and you can feed back to me what you discover. You'd be recompensed of course.' He was not prepared for Lois's reaction, and recoiled.

'*What!*' she spat out. 'Me a bloody grass! You must be off your trolley, mister!'

'No, no,' said Hunter Cowgill. 'You've got it all wrong.' His patient voice was the final straw.

'Strikes me I've got it exactly right!' she yelled at him from halfway down the stairs.

At the foot, Keith stood, barring her way and looking very uncomfortable indeed. 'Hear him out, Lois,' he said pleadingly. 'It's not grassing, not like that at all.'

'It'd be something new, a try-out,' said Cowgill from Gloria's bedroom. 'At least listen to what I've got to say.'

Lois's face was scarlet and her heart thudding in her ears. What the hell would Derek say? She shook her head, and advanced towards Keith Simpson, who did not move.

'There could be another murder,' said the cool voice from

upstairs. 'Always a danger. We need to move on pretty fast now. Your help could be vital, Mrs Meade.'

For God's sake, thought Lois quickly. It's not my business. I don't even live here! But then, I have made it my business, my cleaning business, and that's why they want me. Duty? Is that what he's getting at? Oh, to hell with it. She turned around and went slowly back upstairs. 'Go on, then,' she said. 'Explain.'

Hunter Cowgill smiled then. 'No money, then,' he said. 'Nothing to do with grassing, something different. Just information. It'll be a bit one-sided, I'm afraid. Rules are rules. But I can guide you along lines of enquiry, help you put together what you know. You are interested in that, aren't you? And all under strict cover, of course. That's vital for both sides. You'd have to be aware of possible danger to yourself. I'm not saying it will come to anything, Mrs Meade,' he added. 'Considering your exceptional position in this village, it should, in my view, be given a try.'

There was a long silence while Lois thought about it. This was different from dealing with Keith Simpson. He was a lowly constable, and she felt quite at ease with him, and with Janice Britton. But this man was an inspector, a boss. Oh well, she thought finally, he's just a man, like all the rest, and she nodded. 'OK, give it a try,' she said, and sank down on to a frilled bedside chair.

'Good!' said Cowgill, sitting up straighter. 'Now, anything you want to tell me now? I expect you're anxious to get back as soon as possible.'

Lois frowned. Ah well, here goes. 'Did you know the Prof's done a bunk?' she said.

'We know he's away on business,' said Cowgill. 'Is there more? Gone to Russia, his wife says.'

Lois hesitated. Was this disloyalty? This was going to be difficult. Still, it could be important. 'More like buggering off, if you ask me,' she said. 'He's always been one to spread it about a bit. She was a mess when he went, but manages now, just about.'

'Another woman?' said Cowgill.

'She thinks so,' Lois replied. 'It could have something to do with your second round of questioning. That's what I thought, anyway. He's not actually gone off before. More the quick fumble before the wife sees – that kind of thing. Anyway, over to you. I shall no doubt hear more next week, if he's not already back.' She stood up. 'Got to go now, else the nurse'll be back. I'll pick a bit of holly in Gloria's garden on my way – a reason for being here . . .'

'Gloria's not going to need it, that's for sure,' said Hunter Cowgill, with a small smile that was quickly gone. 'Thanks, then, Mrs Meade. I'll be in touch.'

Keith was still at the foot of the stairs, but now stood to one side as Lois came down. 'Rat!' she said, as she passed him, and then, because his face fell like one of the boys in trouble, she added, 'You know what's out of kilter in that bedroom?' He shook his head. 'The bed,' she said. 'That horrible bed. And them dolls. Blimey, would *you* want to hop in there?' She was gratified at the embarrassment on Keith's face, and left the cottage, brushing past the trellis surrounding the front door as she escaped. She felt in a turmoil filled with such mixed feelings, which were relieved only by loud cursing when she pricked her hand on the vicious holly in Gloria's garden.

'Those are lovely berries!' said Gillian Surfleet, walking into her yard as Lois returned. 'What a good idea. Thank you!' she added, as Lois gingerly handed her the branches of holly. 'Poor old Gloria used to make a lot of Christmas, though she was always on her own . . . mostly . . .'

Lois looked at her closely. 'What do you mean, "mostly"?'

'Nothing, nothing,' Gillian said, shrugging. She took off her coat and put down her bag, full of supplies for the sick and convalescent in the surrounding villages.

Lois thought again how capable she looked, with her generous bosom and sturdy legs. I wouldn't mind being looked after by her. She wondered if Gloria had come to her for reassurance, spilling out her worries and disappointments. 'Gillian,' she said hesitantly. 'Gillian, did Miss Hathaway have admirers? You know, boyfriends of any sort? You'd be the one to see them going up and down the garden path.'

Gillian Surfleet looked away, shaking her head. 'Better

not ask me that, Lois,' she said. 'You know what they say: eavesdroppers never hear any good of themselves. And I can't deny I did hear some conversations through the garden hedge that wouldn't bear repeating to the wrong person.'

'Like the police?'

Again Gillian nodded. 'Best to keep things to yourself if you're not sure what they mean,' she said. 'It's against the rules of my job to gossip. You can just imagine how many secrets I'm privy to on my rounds.'

Well, you've told *me* something, thought Lois. So the sharp and solitary Gloria did have admirers or boyfriends or whatever. Men. Men used to go up and down her path and in and out of the little arched trellis. As Lois polished, she wondered where else the men went. Up the stairs and into the scented bedroom with the huge bed and its creepy pile of dolls? And which men?

Her work finished, Lois struggled into her coat. She had more layers than usual to keep out the cold, and felt like an overstuffed armchair with her scarlet scarf round her neck and thick knitted gloves. But it was still cold and the heater had finally packed up in her car. One thing, she said to herself as she drove slowly up Farnden main street, the murderer may not have gone up and down Gloria's path that night, but he certainly knew where she would be, where he could find her and finish her off in that violent way. Must have been easy. Lois shivered. Skinny woman like that, with a neck like a chicken. She peered round into the Barratts' to see if there were any signs of the Prof's return. There were no cars in the drive, and the windows looked blank and lifeless.

Lois changed gear with a clumsy grating sound and accelerated out of the village. The Prof was a strong man. She'd seen him in the garden heaving great rocks about when they were building that fancy pond. He'd wring the necks of those poor pheasants he went shooting without a qualm, she was sure. It was the obvious conclusion. But it was too obvious. Lois had read enough detective stories to know that the obvious suspect is never the guilty one. She wished she had asked Nurse Surfleet if she'd ever seen Professor Barratt knocking at Gloria's door. Still, she wouldn't have told Lois. Professional secrecy, and all that. Gloria Hathaway was hardly Malcolm's type, was he? Lois couldn't imagine what type would want to jump into that bed with Gloria Hathaway, poor stringy thing, with her gingery hair and freckled skin. But there was always someone, and the attraction could have been that Gloria was willing.

Swerving to avoid a roving dog brought her sharply back to the present. That Cowgill's got me thinking again, she realized, and felt suddenly happy. It was, after all, what she'd wanted. Put your brain to work, her dad had said so many times, and she hadn't. Well, now she was, and what the result would be was anyone's guess. At least I'll have had a go, she told herself, and turned into Byron Way with a flourish.

When she opened the door, she saw Derek sitting at the kitchen table, a mug of tea in his hand, his shoes off, reading the sports pages. 'Home early!' she said. 'What went wrong at the Hall?'

Derek shook his head. 'Nothing wrong – just finished the job. The lady of the house couldn't get rid of me fast enough. Maybe she thought I'd pinch some more freesias. Anyway, the kid came prancing in and asked if I'd like to look at her new pony and her mum came down like a ton of bricks. "The electrician has to be on his way," says she. "Thank you so much . . . send us your bill and if the work is satisfactory we shall no doubt have other things for you in the future." Satisfactory, my eye. She'll not get a better job done nowhere. Anyway, Lois, how was the nurse today?'

'Fine,' said Lois absently. 'Any tea left in the pot? Give us a cup then. I've got some thinking to do.'

Derek looked at her fondly. 'You're a wonder, gel,' he said. 'As if you hadn't got enough on your plate without playing policewoman. Here, let me take your coat off and you sit down and warm up first.' He stood behind her and helped her off with the duffel, turning to hang it up. 'Hello, what's that,' he said, running his hand over the sleeve of her jersey. 'Nasty mark on that,' he said. 'Hope it'll wash out.'

Lois was upstairs in a flash, pulling the jersey over her head and turning it round to look. She saw a dark stain at the top of the sleeve that had certainly not been there when she went out.

She sniffed at it and smelled creosote. Not an unpleasant smell, but she could not think for the life of her where it came from. She wondered whether to tell Derek about Hunter Cowgill, but decided not – not yet.

Rachel Barratt sat in her cheerful sitting room, the fire blazing and the television on. It was four-thirty in the afternoon and she had a full glass of white wine at her elbow and a half-empty box of chocolates on her lap. She felt very happy and when the doorbell rang she ignored it. Whoever it was could go away. The girls had broken up from school and were staying with their grandmother. Malcolm was presumably lost in the snowy deeps of Russia, and she was watching a sexy film which had just got to the good bit. She shifted round in her chair to get more comfortable and took another chocolate.

The doorbell rang again. Blast! 'Go away!' she shouted, and then gasped as a face appeared at the window. She rushed to the door then, and opened it quickly.

'Afternoon Madam,' said the tall man standing on the doorstep. 'Detective Inspector Cowgill . . . can I come in for a few minutes? One or two things I'd like to check with you.'

Eighteen

'**M**um!' It was Josie, followed by the boys. 'Mum! Dad!' Lois struggled awake, nudging Derek as she became aware of the little party standing at their bedroom door. She and Derek had been up until the small hours finishing the decorations and stacking the parcels under the shimmering Christmas tree. Now she sat up muzzily and saw Josie bearing a breakfast tray and a wide grin.

'Happy Christmas! Happy Christmas!' Jamie leapt on the bed and bounced up and down.

'Careful!' said Derek, rubbing his eyes. Douglas, in his position as eldest boy, pushed Jamie off the bed and made a grand gesture to Josie, indicating that she could now safely present the tray. On it, on the best china, were grapefruit, cereals, toast and marmalade, and Lois's cut-glass vase containing one greenish-white Christmas rose from the garden. 'Blimey! Must be expecting some good presents, this lot . . .'

Lois's lip quivered, and she grabbed Josie's hand. 'Thanks, love,' she said. 'What a great idea.' She turned to Derek. 'Shall I be mother?'

'Not again, I hope!' said Derek jovially, and reached for a cup of tea strong enough to take the back off his throat.

Lois's mother arrived early, bringing her share of the Christmas feast, and the two women worked most of the morning in the kitchen, filling the house with such good smells that a series of interruptions from the rest of family began, asking obvious questions about whether they could help and surely they should lay the table now?

It was the family tradition that presents were not opened until after dinner, and as there were so many, this went on more or less until bedtime. Occasionally they took a break, and one or another would stroll around the estate for a breath of fresh air and reassurance that the normal world was still out there. Nobody could eat Christmas cake at teatime, and Lois was just taking it back to the kitchen, saying they could have it later, when she saw a figure approaching the back door. Tall, head down, dressed carefully in neat jeans and jacket, Melvyn knocked diffidently at the door, at the same time peering anxiously through the window into the kitchen. Oh Lord, now what? Nobody ever called on Christmas Day. Families kept themselves to themselves on the estate. It was one of those accepted norms. None of your sherries for the locals before lunch that Lois's clients in Farnden seemed to think was necessary. She'd often pitied them for not being able to spend one whole day with their families and nobody else.

And now here was Melvyn, smiling pleadingly at her through the window. She opened the door. 'Happy Christmas, Mrs Meade,' said Melvyn. 'I was just passing and wondered if I could see Josie for a minute? Got something for her . . . just a little something,' he added, seeing Lois's face.

'You'd better come in,' Lois said grudgingly, standing back to let him step inside. He looked at the cake and said, 'That's a good'un, Mrs Meade!' Lois didn't reply, but walked ahead of him to the sitting room, where the usual quarrel about presents was in progress. As Melvyn followed her, there was a sudden silence, and Josie, crouched on the floor with a half-assembled construction toy, struggled to her feet, her face scarlet.

'Hi, Josie,' said Melvyn, his composure regained. 'Happy Christmas, Mr Meade and all . . .'

Nobody replied, and Derek got to his feet, scowling. 'What're you doing round here on Christmas Day?' he said.

'Got a present for Josie,' said Melvyn, unabashed. He fished in his jacket pocket and brought out a small, square package wrapped in glittery paper. 'Here,' he said. 'You said you liked them in that shop, so I got you one.'

Josie held out her hand, glancing fearfully at her father and took the package. 'Thanks,' she said, and smiled defiantly.

'Open it, then,' said Melvyn. It was as if they were the only two in the room, the rest struck dumb by some pantomime fairy godmother.

Derek had been doing some quick thinking, and suddenly spoke: 'Well then,' he said. 'What'll you have to drink, Melvyn? Mustn't forget the festive spirit, Lois,' he added with a meaningful look as he turned to the tray of bottles on the sideboard.

'Thanks,' said Melvyn, visibly relaxing. 'Got any cider, Mr Meade?'

'Move up,' said Douglas to Jamie and made a space on the sofa where Melvyn sat down smiling.

Josie nervously pulled at the wrappings of her parcel and finally produced a small, framed picture. 'Oh!' she said, colouring again. 'It's the one I liked!' Inside, behind the glass, was a tiny tableau of fabric mice, dressed in human clothes and busy about a minute kitchen. It was charming, and clearly expensive. 'You shouldn't have!' Josie exclaimed, and gave Melvyn an impulsive kiss on his cheek.

'That must have cost a bit,' said Lois, peering at the picture. 'It's really lovely, Melvyn.' She felt uneasy, and glanced across at Derek. She could see by his expression that he felt the same. Neither of them said anything much, but Lois's mother was full of praise and admiration.

'Lucky you,' she said to Josie, 'to have such a generous boyfriend!'

'She's too young for boyfriends,' said Derek jerkily.

'Melvyn's just one of the gang,' added Lois defensively. 'Now, shall we all have a game of cards? I expect you'll have to be getting back, Melvyn?'

But Melvyn had no intention of getting back. The usual traditional Christmas was in full swing in his house, with all the right trimmings, but here in this crowded semi on the Churchill Estate, he basked in the warmth that was missing back at home. Here, amongst the quarrelling and shouting, and gleeful boasting, the over-eating and drinking, was something special, and he stayed on obstinately, until it was dark and Jamie began to yawn and was packed off to bed.

Melvyn's Christmas visit caused a great deal of argument between Lois and Derek during the rest of the holidays, but both agreed that it was better to have him there where they could see what he was up to. Better than some dark corner of a derelict factory. It was not until the children were back at school that Lois had time to think again about Gloria Hathaway. There had been the usual round of treats for the boys – a visit to the cinema, a hugely expensive night at the pantomime in Tresham's Theatre Royal. Lois's mother had come too, and Derek had looked ruefully at the bill for the tickets. 'Could get you a new car for that, Lois,' he said. But it was traditional. They all had ice-creams in the interval, and Derek said thank God Christmas only came once a year.

And then it was all over. New Year was not made much of in the Meade household. Lois always said they had enough celebrating by the time the New Year came in, and she and Derek did not even stay up to watch the celebrations on the television. Derek was back at work, the children reluctantly returned to a new term, a sprinkling of new teachers and a new curriculum at school, and Lois went back to her weekly routine in Long Farnden and her curiosity about the increasingly interesting Gloria Hathaway. A fall of snow held her up, but the heavy old car pushed on slowly, and her thoughts returned to the puzzle before her.

Who was the real Gloria Hathaway? Lois was beginning to wonder. The early picture of a sharp, unfriendly spinster was beginning to change. The quiet ones were always the worst, her Dad used to say. Just what was she up to in her tea cosy cottage? And how did she live? Lois couldn't remember anyone saying she went out to work. Yet she had a new little car every two years and her furniture and clothes were all clearly good quality. Lois knew expensive clothes when she saw them. No sign of poverty, or even economy. The cottage was well maintained, paintwork good, clearly renewed regularly, and the thatch had been recently repaired. Lois was on her way to the vicarage, but she drove on as far as Gloria Hathaway's cottage and pulled up, staring at the pleasing picture of a thatched cottage under snow. The trellis porch with its now bare tangle of rose branches, sagged slightly under the weight. The wooden lattice showed darkly through the stark whiteness, and a small link connected up in Lois's brain. Creosote. She'd noticed spots of it on Gloria's otherwise immaculate front doorstep. The trellis had been treated very recently and it hugged the door so closely that it was impossible to step inside without brushing against it. And thereby stain one's jersey, thought Lois excitedly – and one's Barbour too, especially if you were a big man, pushing his way in.

She turned around and accelerated down the street, skidded alarmingly by the village shop, and caused Dr Rix to turn and gesticulate anxiously at her. She waved cheerfully at him. Derek had taught her how to steer into a skid, but she proceeded more circumspectly along to the vicarage.

Peter White was in his kitchen, and smiled warmly at Lois as she stamped snow off her shoes. 'Come on in, my dear,' he said. 'Just made a pot of tea. You must have a cup and warm up. How was your Christmas? Children happy?' It crossed his mind to ask whether they had gone to church on Christmas Day, but he knew the answer to that one, and abandoned it.

'Fine, thanks,' said Lois. 'And you?' Silly question, she thought. It was the vicar's busiest time of the year, she supposed. He looked so friendly and concerned that she broke her usual rule and sat down to sip scalding hot tea and allow him to chat. And anyway, something useful might come up.

He was in the middle of a long story about the children carol singing round the village, and her thoughts were wandering, when he got up suddenly and said, 'There's a policeman at the door, Lois. Better let him in, if you don't mind. I'll just tidy up,' he added. 'I'm afraid I haven't combed my hair yet!'

Not much difference when you do, thought Lois, but obediently went to the front door and opened it.

'Good morning,' said Hunter Cowgill, as if they'd never met before. 'Is the vicar at home, please?' His eyes were distant, and Lois caught on quickly.

'Yes,' she said. 'Who shall I say?'

Inspector Cowgill gave the tiniest of nods, and said, 'Police, madam. Detective Inspector Cowgill.'

'Wait here,' she said. 'I'll get him.' The Inspector looked faintly annoyed at being left on the doorstep, but it was only seconds before Peter White was there himself, ushering the Inspector into his cold sitting room.

Lois took her cup of cooling tea with her and made for the study, where she began dusting and tidying his papers. Better not use the cleaner yet, not until she'd had a chance to catch a word or two of their conversation.

'Sorry to trouble you, sir, but I wonder if you'd mind answering one or two further questions?'

'Of course,' said Peter White, but his voice trembled, and Lois frowned as she heard the door shut firmly. Why was he nervous? She walked quickly to the cupboard where he kept his old jacket and pulled it out. The stain was still there, and she sniffed. Creosote. Unmistakeably creosote. She put it back and returned to the study, switched on the cleaner and moved swiftly over the worn carpet. Nothing more to be heard now, so she might as well get on and keep her ears open for when the Inspector left.

He was there for a good half an hour and by the time he was on his way out the conversation was restricted to formalities. 'Thank you very much, sir,' said the Inspector.

'Not at all.' Peter White's voice was over-polite. 'Only too willing to help in this ghastly business,' he added. The door shut, and the vicar came quickly into the kitchen, where Lois was washing up last night's supper dishes. 'Strong coffee,' he muttered, and switched on the kettle.

'Let me make it,' said Lois. 'You're all of a shake.'

The vicar took a deep breath, and looked at her gratefully. 'Ah yes, how kind. Thank you, my dear,' he said, and slumped down into a chair by the table.

Lois made the coffee and found a packet of biscuits. 'Here,' she said, 'have a couple of these. Did you have any breakfast?' She had seen no evidence of it, no cereal dish with cornflakes stuck hard, no sticky marmalade knife.

'Um, no, actually, I wasn't hungry,' said Peter White, and pushed the biscuits to one side.

Lois took out a couple and put them on a plate. 'Here,' she said again, 'Mother's orders. Eat up.'

Peter White's face cleared for a moment, and he looked at Lois with a tentative smile. 'Goodness, Lois,' he said, 'I'm old enough to be your . . . er . . . brother. Still, I'm sure you're right. Thank you.' He began to nibble one of the biscuits and sip the hot coffee.

'Nosy parkers, these cops,' said Lois conversationally.

'Oh yes, but it is their job,' said Peter White quickly. 'Though I had told them all I knew already.'

'Fresh evidence come to light?' said Lois casually.

'I'm not sure,' said the vicar. 'The Inspector did go on asking questions about Gloria's personal life – whether she had confided in me in my professional capacity, had I heard anything from other parishioners, that sort of thing.'

'And have you?' said Lois, bluntly now.

Peter White looked at her in surprise. 'That kind of thing is told to me in strictest confidence, Lois,' he said reprovingly.

'Yeah, but have you?' said Lois again. To her surprise, instead of telling her to get on with her work, he laughed. 'Really, you're incorrigible!' he said. 'But I'm afraid I can't satisfy you any more than I did the Inspector. The only time I saw Gloria for more than a few minutes lately was that time she had been ill, and I made a pastoral visit. She was perfectly polite and nice, and I remember thinking what a comfortable home she had in her little cottage, but that was all. All very correct and blameless, I'm afraid!' But he didn't tell Lois about the dressing gown falling away from shapely legs, the glimpse of pleasantly full breasts. He did not mention that Gloria had insisted on mending his socks, or . . . No, enough was enough. Sins of omission, though, he warned himself.

'Ah well,' said Lois. 'Maybe you'll think of something. Oh, and by the way,' she added lightly, 'that old jacket of yours has a nasty stain on the sleeve. It smells like creosote. How did that happen?'

The vicar's reaction was swift. He jumped up and fetched the jacket at once, handing it to Lois. 'Quite right, my dear,' he said, 'would you drop it into the cleaners in Tresham for me? Many thanks.' He headed off towards his study. Lois looked at the offending jacket, sniffed again at the sleeve, and then quietly put it back in the cupboard.

Josie had hung the mouse tableau in her bedroom and though Derek had not been at all happy about it, he agreed that they should say nothing more to her. If they made a great thing of it, Josie was quite likely to go underground, meet Melvyn secretly and God knows what might happen. Lois had reminded Josie that she would have to start taking school work seriously now, and no more gallivanting with Melvyn's gang.

Josie had no intention of leaving it there. She had been astonished when Melvyn turned up with the present. How did he have the nerve? But he'd seemed so sure of himself, and now she knew he cared for her. That picture had been expensive and although he'd always got money, she knew he was on a fixed allowance. She looked at herself in her dressing table mirror. What does he see in me? she thought. She never believed her parents when they told her she was pretty and had a good figure and shouldn't worry about a few spots and pimples. They would go, they said, when she grew up. Well, if Melvyn Hallhouse fancied her, she was grown up enough. She took out a bottle of dark purple nail polish from her drawer and began to paint her nails. Her homework lay unopened on her bed, and she heard her mother calling from downstairs.

'Coming!' Josie yelled.

'Melvyn's here!' Lois added, her voice annoyed and sharp. 'I've told him you're not going out week nights.'

Sod it, thought Josie. She waved her hands about to dry the polish, and gingerly opened the door. The delicate mouse tableau caught her eye, and she smiled.

'Hi,' said Melvyn. 'Like your nails . . .'

Josie melted. 'Thanks,' she said. 'Has Mum . . . ?'

'Yep, and quite right, too,' said Melvyn, with a quick glance at Lois. 'Get your homework done first and then I could come back and have a cup of tea, maybe, Mrs Meade?'

Blimey, he never gives up! Lois nodded weakly, and opened the back door. 'Don't bother if it's raining,' she said. 'Usually takes madam here the whole evening to finish anyway. She'll see you tomorrow, I expect.'

'No problem,' answered Melvyn with his charming grin. 'I'll just call in and see. Got to fetch something from a mate on the estate. See you later, Josie.' He grinned again at Lois, and disappeared into the darkness.

Irritated, Lois shooed Josie back upstairs. Thinks he can charm the birds off the trees, she said angrily to herself, and went back to watching television. But when Derek asked her what the programme was about, she couldn't tell him.

Nineteen

Friday, and Lois was on her way to the Baers'. She could see Gloria's cottage at the end of the street and thought of the newly-creosoted trellis in the porch. So, they'd all brushed past it on their way in – Doctor Rix, Prof Barratt and Peter White. Not Derek, of course! It really didn't mean much, as far as the doctor and the vicar were concerned. There was every reason for them to be visiting Gloria, who had been ill. That left Professor Barratt and he'd done a bunk. She had heard no news of his whereabouts or his return, but the vicar had mentioned seeing the Detective Inspector talking to Rachel at the Barratts' front door. Lois wondered if Inspector Cowgill had revisited the Baers. It was unlikely that she would find out. She'd given the new 'arrangement' considerable thought and didn't have much confidence in the supposed help she'd get from Cowgill. Still, two could play at that game.

She turned into the Baers' yard and saw the blinds drawn down in the gallery. It was always closed for January and February and Evangeline was more often in the house, getting under Lois's feet and making conversation because she had no one else to talk to. Today Lois welcomed the thought. Perhaps she would glean something of interest.

She hardly ever saw Dallas. He was a mystery man, with his smart city suits and fashionable staccato speech. Lois had discovered a few details about Evangeline, from brief conversations here and there, and knew that she had married Dallas not long ago, when she was in her early thirties. She'd been a Somerset girl – still had a trace of the west country burr in her voice – and had once told Lois jokingly that she'd married beneath her. Dallas had been working for her father's company, and had carried off the boss's daughter, she'd said, laughing, but with a wistful smile at Lois, who had nodded non-committally as usual. Dallas went off early to business in Birmingham, and came back late, so Lois had little chance of getting to know him. She sometimes thought that Evangeline, too, seemed not to know him very well.

It was a shock, then, for Lois to find Evangeline and Dallas sitting at the kitchen table, clearly still having breakfast at nine o'clock on a Friday morning. What's more, they hardly glanced at her as she walked in, muttering 'Morning,' and then returning to what seemed to be a close study of the newspapers. This was so odd that Lois tiptoed through to the broom cupboard, collected her things, and decided to start on the dining room which had a hatch through from the kitchen. This was open, and as Lois began polishing the old rosewood table in which Evangeline took such pride, she heard the scrape of a chair as one of them got up.

'*I* don't care who hears,' said Evangeline in a strangely husky voice, but Dallas's hand appeared on the hatch cover and shut it with a bang. Then both voices started at once, raised and angry, but Lois could not make out the words. Now what? She shook her head sadly. This village is going to pieces. Old Malcolm on the run, the vicar scared out of his wits, Nurse Surfleet behaving like a priest sitting tight in the confessional, and now the cool and reasonable Baers at each other's throats.

She finished the dining room and went through to fetch the Hoover. Dallas Baer stood at the foot of the stairs, looking up. He ignored Lois and began to speak in a harsh, unkind voice.

'Don't threaten me,' he said, still looking up to the landing above.

'I shall do it, unless you tell me the truth!' said Evangeline's tearful voice.

'Don't be so bloody daft,' Dallas replied. 'And anyway, you won't. Women like you never do.'

Lois turned back, thinking a retreat to the kitchen was the best bet, but stopped when Evangeline suddenly screamed. Lois whipped round to see Dallas standing immobile as Evangeline tumbled like a rag doll from stair to stair, all the way from top to bottom, screaming as she fell.

*   *   *

112

'The doctor was there in minutes,' said Lois to Derek. She had come home early and by the time Derek appeared for what was usually a snack lunch, he found chops, potatoes and peas waiting for him. Lois had told him the story as they ate, and now explained that Evangeline had miraculously escaped serious injury. 'She should've at least broken an arm or a leg,' said Lois, shaking her head. Derek listened to Lois's description of Dr Rix's competent examination, his calm, reassuring manner with Dallas, who, said Lois with a frown, seemed perfectly calm himself. Lois took apple crumble from the oven and set it on the table. Giving Derek a generous helping, she continued, 'Dr Rix said there was no need for an ambulance, so they put her on the long sofa in the sitting room. She was crying a lot, but the doctor said it was mostly shock, and sent Dallas off to the chemist in Tresham. I said I'd wait until he came back and he wasn't long. She dozed off to sleep pretty quickly – something the doctor had given her, I think. But Derek . . .' Lois faltered, frowning.

'I could do with a cuppa,' said Derek blandly. Lois filled the kettle, and sat down again. 'Go on, then,' Derek encouraged her. 'What's bothering you?'

'It was Dallas,' said Lois slowly. 'The way he just stood there, watching her fall, without moving a muscle to catch her or stop her or anything . . .'

Derek shrugged. 'Took him by surprise, maybe. You said he taunted her, said she wouldn't do it. P'raps he really thought she wouldn't. Anyway,' he added, and his face was serious now, 'better be careful, my duck. Don't get mixed up with marriage problems. You can never see the whole picture, and shouldn't try. If this murder thing is going to get you into trouble, I want you out of it now. *Now*, Lois, d'you understand?'

Derek so seldom used a stern voice to her that Lois was taken aback. He was right, of course. Never come between man and wife. But she had no intention of doing so, and had asked no questions, made no comments. She'd just kept watch over Evangeline until Dallas returned, and then left. She tried to explain this to Derek, and he nodded.

'But just watch it,' he said. 'We got enough on our plate with the kids and that Melvyn, without getting in deep anywhere else. Better to forget the whole thing,' he added. 'Kettle's boiling.'

When Evangeline woke up, she could not for the moment remember what had happened, or why she was lying on the sofa in the middle of the afternoon. Then she saw Dallas in the chair opposite, his head slumped on his chest, snoring gently. As she moved to get up, she felt a sharp pain in her shoulder. She groaned loudly with the pain and woke up Dallas.

'Don't move, Angie,' he said. 'You've had a fall.' His use of the old nickname gave her a start.

'What?' she said. 'What d'you mean, a fall?'

'You tripped and fell downstairs,' said Dallas quickly. 'Dr Rix has been, and there's nothing broken. You've just got to rest for a couple of days. Bruises, and all that.'

Evangeline said nothing, but shifted her shoulder tentatively, trying to ease the pain. 'You can have some painkiller, Doctor said.' Dallas went into the kitchen and returned with a glass of water and tablets in his hand. 'Here,' he said, helping her to raise her head.

'Dallas—' Evangeline choked on the water and spluttered for a few seconds. 'Dallas,' she began again. 'What really happened? We were having a row, weren't we? I can't remember properly, but I'm sure we were having a row?'

'It was nothing,' said Dallas. 'You just got upset about something silly. That old jealousy again! And without cause, as usual. I expect that's why you tripped. Nothing to worry about. Just forget it and get some more sleep. I'll stay here. I've rung the office, and arranged a few days off, so I can look after you. Just rest, Angie pet. Take it easy.' He stroked her forehead gently until her eyelids drooped. 'That's it, take it easy. Old Dallas is here to take care of you.'

Twenty

Long Farnden parish council had always met in the village hall, surrounded by old sepia photographs of former chairmen and luminaries of the village who looked down on them benevolently. But tonight, the present chairman, Dr Rix, sat uneasily on his hard chair and tried to concentrate on the minutes of the previous meeting, banishing thoughts of Gloria and how she must have stood in abject terror in the kitchen behind him.

Janice Britton, the Special who had been so encouraging to Lois, was clerk to the parish council. She had not given much credence to the supposed collaboration with Keith Simpson and Lois on gathering information in the village, sensing Lois's animosity after being turned down in Tresham. Janice had contributed little, but she had tried to keep her ear to the ground. In fact, she had thought on her way to the village hall that tonight might possibly turn up a few clues. She had been clerk to the council for a number of years, and the members relied on her absolutely to come up with items for the agenda, papers to peruse and letters composed ready for Dr Rix to sign. He often said that without Janice he would not have been able to continue for so long, being such a busy man himself.

Tonight would be his last meeting. He had been expected to resign, and had put it off several times, but now he felt pressure on him from younger members. Three councillors had let it be known they were willing to stand as his successor: Evangeline Baer, Malcolm Barratt and Gillian Surfleet. Well, Evangeline was still recovering from her fall – a funny business, that – and Professor Barratt had not yet reappeared in the village. This left Gillian Surfleet and anyone else who might declare themselves willing. Andrew Rix had his doubts about Nurse Surfleet. Not that she was anything but excellent at her job, he just was not sure if she would be able to handle the strong-willed members, of whom Prof Malcolm was the most troublesome. There were times when arguments broke out, when old village confronted new village, and animosities rose to the surface. Then, the chairman was required to be diplomatic but authoritative. Subduing the natives, his father would have said. As for the other two, could they be elected *in absentia*? He could not see any objection, provided they were known to be still willing.

Andrew Rix turned to Janice. They had reached the relevant item on the agenda, and now he needed her guidance. 'Do we have names, my dear?' he said.

Janice nodded. 'We still have three, but only Nurse Surfleet is present. I tried to contact Mrs Baer, but her husband was reluctant to bother her with decisions to be made. Seems she is still quite poorly – shock, he said.' Dr Rix raised his eyebrows, but said nothing. 'And then there's Professor Barratt,' Janice continued. There was a pause, and members looked at each other.

'Ah yes,' said Dr Rix. 'Have we any news from that quarter?'

Janice shook her head. 'I tried a diplomatic approach to his wife, but she more or less shut the door in my face. I think she may have been taking a consoling nip of something,' she added with the faintest trace of a smile.

'So?' said Andrew Rix.

'So I was unable to check, and it seems that without the others being able to indicate their willingness to stand . . . are there any other proposals?' She paused, and looked around the room. No one spoke, and Janice continued. 'Then Miss Gillian Surfleet, who has confirmed that she is still willing . . .'

Janice looked at Nurse Surfleet, who beamed and said, 'Quite keen, actually.'

'Then Miss Surfleet is by default our new chairman . . . or perhaps I should say chairperson.' There was a spatter of applause, Gillian Surfleet smiled broadly and got importantly to her feet.

'Gentlemen, fellow councillors,' she began. 'I can hardly thank you for electing me, because really you didn't . . .'

She paused, and there were mutters of 'Would've done, anyway,' and 'You'll do, gel,' and 'Get on with it, then.'

'Well, thanks anyway,' she said briskly. 'But before we go any further, I have a very pleasant and important task to perform.' She began a clearly prepared speech of gratitude and praise to Dr Rix for his long and wise service in the chair which she was now about to occupy. Gillian had done her homework. She spoke of good deed after good deed, gave innumerable examples of the doctor's wise counsel and patience over difficult parochial issues, and finally groped beneath her chair and produced a smartly wrapped parcel. She advanced on Dr Rix, and handed to to him. 'With our deep gratitude and affection,' she said, and everyone clapped heartily, some sniffing a little with emotion.

It was Andrew Rix's turn to say a few words and they were short and to the point. He had loved every minute of his time as chairman, but hoped he knew when the time had come to step down, and he wished Gillian Surfleet every success. 'If she's half as good at keeping us in order as she is in administering an enema . . .' he said and the rest of his sentence was drowned in loud guffaws from the rest.

In this atmosphere of mutual admiration and goodwill, Janice began to suspect she would spot nothing suspicious this evening. It was only when they were packing up papers and putting their chairs back against the wall that she overheard something rather interesting. Dr Rix was still at the table, handing over files and papers to Gillian Surfleet, and she heard him cough in an embarrassed way and say quietly, 'A little word of warning, my dear.' Gillian Surfleet looked at him, surprised. Janice loitered behind them, pretending to search for something in her own document case. 'Lois is very curious,' he continued in a whisper that Janice could only just hear.

'What?' said Gillian Surfleet.

'Curious,' he repeated. 'More curious than usual. Noticed it at the Baers'. Just thought you ought to know.'

'Ah, well, thanks for telling me, then.' The usually confident Gillian Surfleet looked for a moment nonplussed. Then she gathered all her things together, and said loudly to the rest, 'Drinks on me tonight! See you all in the pub.'

'Hello, yes?' said Lois. She had heard the telephone ringing as she opened the front door. She and Derek had been to see a film – superbly horrible – and now she panted, out of breath.

'Lois? It's me, Janice Britton.'

Lois mouthed at Derek to put on the kettle, and sat down heavily. 'God, Janice, you gave me a fright. I thought it must be something to do with the kids. Josie was left in charge for the first time tonight while me and Derek went out, and I thought . . .'

Janice interrupted her. 'I shan't keep you,' she said. 'Just thought you should know what I happened to overhear at the parish council meeting tonight.' She relayed faithfully Dr Rix's words of warning.

There was a moment's silence from Lois, and then she said, 'Oh dear . . . Well, thanks for the tip. I shall have to watch it, shan't I? Still, funny he should be so bothered.'

'Yep, that's what I thought, too,' said Janice, and with a brief 'Cheers, then,' she rang off.

Lois decided not to tell Derek about the real reason for Janice's call, saying lightly that it was the Special Constable woman, just checking to see if anything new had come up. 'I told her I'd lost interest,' she said casually. She did not like lying to Derek, but she knew that he was now very worried in case she should become too involved. He has a point, Lois reminded herself. After all, there is a murderer out there somewhere and if she seemed to be probing too deeply, she could find herself on the slab next to Gloria. An involuntary shudder caught her. Yes, she'd definitely better watch it.

'Looks like Josie has gone to bed,' Derek said. 'Better go and check on Jamie.' He went upstairs two at a time, while Lois waited in the kitchen. She hadn't been keen on leaving Josie in charge, but Derek had said she was old enough now to baby-sit and, after all, he had his mobile with him and she could always call. Lois wandered into the sitting room waiting for Derek to come down, and switched on the light.

'Oh, my God!' she shrieked. There was a body on the sofa.

A long thin body, curled up and motionless. 'Derek!' yelled Lois, in such a terrified voice that he rushed down, followed by the boys, tousled and sleepy, and finally Josie, rubbing her eyes and looking anxious.

The body moved, then sat up and Lois saw that it was Melvyn. 'Oh, sorry if I scared you, Mrs Meade,' he said, instantly wide awake. 'Josie was a bit worried about being left alone with the boys, so I said I'd stay until you came back.'

'But what were you doing here in the first place?' said Derek, now furious and barely able to contain himself. 'Sneaking in behind our backs? You've been told to keep away during the week and if I had my way, it would be forever. Come on, out with it, what were you doing here?'

Before Melvyn could answer, Josie, white and trembling, burst in. 'Shut up, Dad!' she shouted, close to tears. 'Melvyn brought a book he said he'd lend me and I asked him in. The boys were playing up and I was scared, and . . . and . . .' She was crying now with loud, wrenching sobs.

'What book?' said Derek. He glared at Melvyn. 'I said, what book?' Melvyn took a paperback from the table and handed it to Derek.

'*Harry Potter*?' said Derek. 'This is a kids' book.' He opened it suspiciously. 'They're all reading it at school, grown-ups as well,' said Josie, sniffing her tears away. 'As you'd know if you ever read anything else but the racing results.'

Lois stepped in. 'That's quite enough, Josie,' she said. 'Go on back to bed, and you boys as well. There's been a mistake and it's time for sleep. Go on, all of you.' Sheepishly, they trailed back upstairs and after a few minutes muttering, there was silence.

Melvyn stood stiffly in the sitting room, mesmerised by Derek's hostile stare. 'Now then,' said Lois. 'I think we owe Melvyn an apology.'

'If you believe any of it, which I don't,' cut in Derek, angrily. 'I'm off to bed, Lois, and I suggest you do the same. Make sure he's well on his way out before you come up.' Without another look at Melvyn, he disappeared, leaving the two of them staring uncomfortably after him. Lois was the first to speak. 'Well, I believe you, Melvyn, because if I don't then Josie is a liar, too. I know all kids lie, especially to their parents, but she's only half a kid now and that goes for you, too. I just hope the grown-up bit is telling the truth. Better be off now.'

Melvyn nodded. 'It *was* the truth, Mrs Meade,' he said.

'OK,' said Lois. 'Then thanks for looking after them. Don't worry about Derek. His bark's worse than his bite,' she added, and ushered Melvyn out of the back door. As she locked up and put out the lights she wished things were more straightforward. After all, there was only that story of the factory assignation against him. Josie could have exaggerated it, or made it up. She wouldn't put it past her. Perhaps Melvyn was the pleasant, polite lad he seemed to be on the surface. She was sure things were not absolutely right at home for him, otherwise he wouldn't have turned up like that on Christmas Day. But it didn't mean he wasn't suitable for Josie. It was the age difference that worried Derek, she knew. Nothing would persuade him that Josie wasn't the complete innocent, or that Melvyn wasn't devious, streetwise and dangerous. Until tonight, he'd allowed Lois to convince him that it would blow over and Melvyn would find another girl who'd be easier to corrupt. But it looked as though that wasn't going to be the case.

He grunted as Lois got into bed. 'Get to sleep now, gel,' he said. 'Talk some more in the morning.' But Lois found it impossible to sleep and late into the night she was still juggling worries around in her head: fears about Josie, the message from Janice Britton, and Long Farnden in general. When the same worries came round for the third time she cuddled up against Derek's broad back and finally fell into a troubled sleep.

Twenty-One

Rachel Barratt sat up in bed. The little gilt bedside clock told her she'd overslept. It was nine o'clock and a grey light seeped in from behind the thick, drawn curtains. The girls! She rushed out of bed, clutching her dressing gown, and tried to ignore the pounding in her head. She'd really have to try and cut out the nightcap, but it helped her to sleep and was better than pills.

Downstairs it was quiet. There were traces of a hasty breakfast, with cereal bowls and toast crusts left on jammy plates. So they'd got themselves up and off to school again and she was a lousy mother and not fit to have such good kids. Rachel sat down heavily at the cluttered table and put her head in her hands. What was she going to do? That inspector kept coming back, though she'd told him all she knew. She'd heard nothing from Malcolm, not a word, and was beginning to wonder if she would ever see him again. The only way she could cope, she told herself, was by helping the days go by with an occasional glass or two. Nothing wrong with that, surely? She got up to put on the kettle, then abandoned the idea and went to the fridge. A nice glass of cold orange juice, that's what she needed. Her eye was caught by a tall bottle, still half-full of white wine. There you are, she told herself, I can still leave some in the bottle. Don't have to finish it up every time, like some old soak. Still . . . She glanced at the kitchen clock. It was nearly ten o'clock. Time for a mid-morning snifter, she thought, her father's old word coming involuntarily into her mind. She poured a full glass of wine, thought how nice it looked in the frosted glass, and sat down again at the table.

She stared at the crusts scattered across the abandoned

121

breakfast plates. They'd always left their crusts, ever since they were toddlers. Malcolm had tried all ways of persuading the children to finish them up: offers of extra jam, songs of crusty soldiers marching into barracks . . . The wine filled her mouth, cold and acidic. She swallowed and waited for the lift. Suddenly she was crying. It was the crusts and thoughts of little girls and happy families. Sodding Malcolm! She was angry now and stood up. All of this was his fault; her drinking and staying in bed and never washing or combing her hair from one day's end to the next.

'Bloody Malcolm!' she yelled and threw the glass into the sink, where it smashed into tiny shards.

'Did you call, dear?' said a voice. Rachel swung round to see a figure at the open door, a silhouette against the bright winter sun. He moved into the kitchen and she could see what she already knew. He'd come back. She stood up shakily and then her knees buckled and she descended with relief into an all-embracing blackness.

By the time the girls came back from school, walking in wearily from the bus, they found a tidy, clean kitchen. There were flowers in the hall and when they came into the high-ceilinged sitting room, they saw a leaping fire, either side of which sat their parents. Their mother was smartly dressed, her hair washed and brushed into the old, neat style, their father relaxed and smiling at them.

'Hi, girls!' he said.

'Say hello to your father,' said Rachel. But the girls were dumb. Malcolm stood up and went across to them, putting his arms around both.

'Come on,' he said, 'let's have some tea and talk. I've got some explaining to do, I know, and you're sure to have lots of questions. Mother and I have spent all day in serious discussion—'

'Here we go,' muttered one of the girls.

'. . . and resolved all our problems, haven't we, darling?' continued Malcolm with a persuasive look at his wife.

Rachel nodded, and with a reassuring, happy smile she said, 'Take your things off, girls, and I'll bring some tea in here. We can sit by the fire and relax.' She looked at them, and there was desperate pleading in her eyes.

'Got some homework,' said one girl.

'I'd rather watch the telly,' said the other.

They went, leaving Rachel looking at Malcolm, troubled that their careful plan had gone awry. Malcolm had indeed spent all day explaining his absence to Rachel, slowly convincing her that it was a teaching assignment in Newcastle to which he could have taken her, but was too angry to explain. He suggested their marriage had become stale, that they were too used to one another, and that perhaps this 'little break' might prove to have been a good thing. Such was the power he had over her, that by mid-afternoon he had convinced her. She had forgotten the panic and disbelief, the fear and loneliness. Her desperate retreat into the comfort of alcohol, which she had known all along would destroy everything she had left, had been put to one side. All her attempts at recrimination and blame had been answered and smoothed away.

Now she saw that Malcolm's manipulative charm had no effect on the girls. They've dismissed him, she realized. He betrayed them and they will not forgive him. They are strong and I am weak. She felt glad for them, but knew that she could only ever react the way she had done. I need him. I cannot live without him and so I have capitulated. She looked across at Malcolm, who had subsided once more into the big armchair.

He smiled at her. 'They'll come round,' he said, and stretched out his arms. 'Come and give us a kiss,' he said.

'Hello? Is that Inspector Cowgill? Ah yes, well, this is Malcolm Barratt here. I believe you have been trying to get hold of me?' Malcolm smiled at himself in the mirror by the telephone, and ran his fingers through his hair. 'Yes, been away on business. The wife? Ah. Just a spot of marital friction . . . A domestic I believe you call it?' Malcolm laughed lightly, and turned to wink at Rachel. 'Of course. Be glad to talk to you. About ten o'clock tomorrow? Fine. Look forward to seeing you.'

Malcolm put down the receiver and turned smiling to Rachel. 'There,' he said. 'All settled. We shall soon put all that nonsense behind us, and make a new beginning. Dear old Rachel . . . would you like us to go away for a weekend? Sort of a second honeymoon? There's this really super hotel in Eastbourne . . .'

Rachel nodded and smiled weakly. No matter that she had seen on his desk a special offer on his credit card for much-reduced weekend breaks at a choice of mid-price hotels around the country, one of them being in Eastbourne. No matter that she hated Eastbourne, with its echoes of wheelchairs and retirement. She'd go anywhere as long as he was there. She knew that now. 'That would be lovely, Malc,' she said. 'Just what I need. Oh, I *am* glad to see you back!' she added impulsively and ran into his waiting arms.

Though the Barratts had denied any possible connection Malcolm might have had with Gloria Hathaway, the ever-patient Inspector Cowgill needed to check. He stood for a few seconds looking up at the Barratts' house, and reflected – not for the first time – that houses with trouble brewing inside them had a certain closed-up look. This house had looked like that on his previous visits, but now it did not. The windows were open and the friction was blowing out in the cold January wind. A light was on in the attic room, which he knew was Malcolm's study. Mrs Barratt had given him permission to look around up there and, apart from a secret cache of body-building literature, he had found nothing. He walked quickly up the drive and knocked loudly. The door opened straight away – Rachel must have seen him – and he was ushered into the sitting room.

'I'll just call Malcolm,' she said, and asked if he would like a coffee.

'No thanks,' he said.

'Mustn't accept bribes?' said Malcolm, coming through the door with his charming smile.

The inspector's hackles rose. 'Not at all, Professor Barratt,' he said. 'Just don't drink coffee, that's all. But I'd love a cup of tea, if it's not too much trouble, Mrs Barratt,' he added with extreme politeness.

Most of the conversation between them covered old ground. Where had he been at the time of the crime? How well did he know Gloria Hathaway? That sort of thing. Then the inspector asked if he could have a detailed account of his movements while he'd been away, and Malcolm said he didn't see how that could be relevant?

'We never know what's relevant, sir,' said the inspector icily. 'But the more background information we have the more likely it is that we shall come up with an answer to this tragic business.'

Malcolm glanced at Rachel, who took the hint and left the room. 'It was a teaching assignment,' he said. 'Visiting professor, and all that. I'd suggested taking Rachel, sure that she would refuse and we had that almighty row, and I'm afraid I stormed out in a temper. Came to my senses, of course. Everything all right now.'

'And where was this . . . er . . . assignment?' said Inspector Cowgill.

'I see you get my drift,' said Malcolm confidingly. 'Well, yes, it was A.N. Other, as they say. Didn't work out, and we parted with no hard feelings. Just a brief fling, really. I'm not proud of it, of course, but no harm done. Edinburgh, the Grampian Hotel. They'll corroborate.'

Inspector Cowgill remembered Rachel, drunk and shattered, her pride gone, a broken woman. He recalled her pathetic attempt to cope on her own, propped up by alcohol, and felt a considerable dislike for this vain, confident man before him.

'Well, thank you sir,' he said. 'That will be all for now . . . except, oh yes, I wonder if you have a Barbour jacket?'

Malcolm was taken aback. 'Yes, as a matter of fact I do,' he said.

'Might I see it, sir?'

'Of course, I'll call Rachel.'

Inspector Cowgill made no comment, but the fact that it had a recent cleaner's ticket pinned to the lining, in the middle of the muckiest, wettest season of the year, when expensive cleaning would be an utter waste of time, seemed odd to the inspector, and he made one or two notes. 'Well, I'll be off now,' he said. 'Don't worry, Mrs Barratt, I'll see myself out,' and he was gone.

Malcolm was taut with anger. 'Why the bloody hell did you send it to the cleaners?' he said.

'It had that mark on the sleeve, you know . . . you said . . .' said Rachel, beginning to tremble.

'I didn't ask you to!'

'But I often send your clothes without . . .' faltered Rachel in a cracked voice.

Malcolm sighed. 'Oh well, I don't suppose it matters,' he said, deflating. 'Don't let's spoil it all now. We'll go down to the pub and have a curry.' He had made a big effort, he felt, but the coolness was there again and he didn't know what else to do for the moment.

The Farnden Arms stood at a crossroads in the village, where a narrow lane intersected the long main street about halfway down. The pub had been built three hundred and fifty years ago as a staging post on the main route to the west. It was large for a village pub, with a big yard with stabling at the back, but no horses, carts or carriages called there now for a rest on their long journey. The stables were converted into garages and, tacked on to the end, built in ugly pink brick, were the pub toilets. The new landlord – Don Cutt, late of the Standing Arms, Round Ringford – had put up new signs; a highwayman for the men's toilet, a simpering, crinolined lady for the ladies. This had caused some ribaldry in the pub and Malcolm Barratt had made a serious request for reinstatement of the old toilets. 'Those new things are right out of character,' he'd said to Don Cutt, who had made a silent vow to keep things exactly as he wanted them. Some of the older inhabitants of the village had been delighted with the new signs, and one old boy had told him a story of the legendary Ditchford Dick, a local highwayman who'd led a life of successful crime, but ended his days swinging from the gibbet on Fletching Hill.

'Morning, Professor,' said Don, with professional bonhomie. 'And Mrs Barratt. Nice to see you back, sir. What can I get you?'

'Pint of Old Hookie for me, and a gin and tonic for Rachel,' said Malcolm, perching on a bar stool and holding another out for Rachel.

'Um, no,' she said. 'I think I'll just have an apple juice today, thanks.'

Don Cutt smiled kindly at her, and said, 'Fine. Apple juice

coming up. The Old Hookie'll be a minute or so – just put on a new barrel.'

Malcolm took up the menu and glanced down it. 'How's the new caterer doing?' he said. Bronwen had grown tired and too old, she said, to cope with pub food any more, and they'd got in this Indian bloke, who filled the place with foreign smells that were nevertheless very appetising, and the new dishes were going well. They chose curries and went to sit down in the corner.

They were halfway through, at ease with each other again, when Dallas Baer walked in. 'Malcolm!' he said. 'Welcome back, old son!' Greetings were exchanged, and Dallas walked over to them carrying his half-pint.

'Join us?' said Malcolm, but Dallas shook his head. 'Got to get back to the wife. She's not been well, but you wouldn't have heard about that. A nasty fall. Well on the road to recovery now, though. Thanks all the same,' he added, and downed his beer in a couple of swallows. 'Where've you been, then, you old reprobate?' he said. 'Thought I caught sight of you one day when I was up in Edinburgh—'

Rachel turned swiftly to Malcolm. 'But I thought you said—'

'Must've been someone else,' said Malcolm smoothly. 'Sure you won't have the other half?'

Don Cutt had his hand ready on the pump, but Dallas shook his head. 'No,' he said. 'Have to get back. Evangeline is much better, but doesn't like being left alone for long.'

'Very understandable,' said Rachel acidly, and added, 'Give her my love. I'll be round to see her later with another book. She read the last one in three days, poor soul. Just as well the gallery's closed anyway at present, isn't it, so Evangeline can have a really good rest?' Her voice was not friendly. She'd heard rumours around the village. Did she fall or was she pushed? She had dismissed these as typical gossip, but after her own recent experiences she was tempted to lump all men into the same guilty heap. Men . . . who needs them? I do, she admitted, and fought a winning battle against the craving for a nice cool glass of white wine.

Twenty-Two

'Morning, Lois!' Malcolm's voice came as no surprise to Lois as she let herself into the Barratts' kitchen. A call from Janice Britton had given her the news of his return. Janice was wary of the new arrangement but had been told by Hunter Cowgill himself to co-operate with Lois. Janice had explained to Lois that she'd seen Malcolm in the shop, looking as full of himself as usual, with Rachel tagging along behind him with a meek expression on her foolish face. Janice had sounded annoyed, as if Rachel was letting down the whole of womankind, and Lois had momentarily agreed. Then afterwards, once she had thought about it, her sympathies moved to Rachel. After all, Rachel had the girls to bring up and no job of her own. It was easy for Janice to be judgemental when she was single with no children and a good career in front of her.

'Ah, you're back, Professor Barratt,' said Lois coldly. Malcolm had just come in from the garden, back in countryman mode, wearing his Barbour and a tweed hat which made him look like an actor playing the part.

'*Surely*,' he said in a mock stern tone, 'you know me well enough now, Lois, to call me Malcolm?'

She ignored this, and said blandly, 'Did you have a nice holiday?'

He nodded quickly, and said, 'I'd be glad if you could do my study first this morning? I want peace and quiet up there as soon as possible and no interruptions.'

'If that's all right with Rachel,' Lois said, and added, 'and the totally silent cleaner's not yet been invented. Perhaps *you* could do that, being a professor and all, Malcolm?'

Rachel was in the sitting room, plumping up cushions and

stacking newspapers. 'I don't expect you to tidy as well as clean,' she said. She had said this every week before Malcolm's disappearance, and then she couldn't have cared less whether the house was clean, tidy or burnt down to its foundations.

Lois recognised the old catchphrase as a return to normality, and smiled. 'Thanks,' she said. 'If only all my clients were as thoughtful as you, Rachel. I'm to start upstairs, then?'

'Please, if you don't mind,' said Rachel, apologetically.

Lois had all but finished in the attic study when she heard Malcolm's step on the stairs. She rapidly rewound the cleaner flex and made for the door, but suddenly there he was, barring her way.

'All done?' he said, but he was not smiling. Lois nodded, moving forward. He put out a hand and took her arm. A shiver of fear made her start back. 'Now, Lois,' he said, turning her back into the room. 'I have meant to say this to you before, but now it's even more important. A lot of my work deals with sensitive issues and anything you may see or hear in this room is strictly confidential. Do you understand? Papers, telephone calls, anything at all. Do I make myself clear?'

Stupid old fart! Suddenly Lois was angry. 'Excuse me, Professor Barratt,' she said sharply, pulling her arm away from his restraining hand. 'I'll thank you not to touch me again, ever, and if I hear any more so-called warnings from you like that, I shall be handing in my notice at once. It seems to me,' she said, warming to the task, 'that anybody who's been away from home for weeks without letting his wife know where he is – or been in touch with his daughters at Christmas – has no right to be talking about "sensitive issues". And now, if you don't mind, I'll get on with my work.'

To her surprise, Malcolm smiled. 'Wonderful!' he said. 'I love it when you're angry. Off you go, with your arms akimbo! Wonderful!' And he added to her departing back, 'Don't forget what I said, mind!'

Lois, furious, clattered down the stairs, all prepared to collect her coat and leave, but when she reached the hall she saw Rachel looking at her with a worried frown. 'All right, Lois?' she said, her chin quivering.

'I suppose so,' said Lois wearily.

'I'll make us a coffee,' said Rachel gratefully, and scuttled into the kitchen. Lois followed her and began to sweep the quarry-tiled floor. She hated it, with its liver-coloured tiles and dull surface that never came up to a good shine. As she simmered down, she reflected that after all it wouldn't be such a good idea to give up the Barratts. She'd learn nothing more about Malcolm's strange absence, nor about the reason he'd had that stain cleaned off his jacket. Maybe now would be a good time to get something out of Rachel.

'Oh, by the way,' she said. 'Where did you take the professor's jacket to be cleaned? Looks good as new. My Derek's got a nasty oily stain on his and he won't chuck nothing away . . .'

Rachel looked at her sharply. 'Johnsons in Tresham,' she replied. Then she added, as if to herself, 'Wretched jacket – what's so special about it?'

'Special?' said Lois, taking her empty mug to the sink and rinsing it out. 'What d'you mean?' she added casually. 'Is it Exhibit A, or something?'

It was meant to be a joke, a tactful reference to the mystery of the disappearing professor, but Rachel's reaction took her by surprise. 'What d'you mean!' Rachel stuttered. 'Has that Inspector been talking to you?'

Lois shook her head. 'No, it wasn't . . . I just meant . . .' She gathered her thoughts swiftly, and added, 'Why, Rachel? Was he interested in the jacket?' But Rachel had withdrawn, taken up a vase of flowers and gone rapidly out of the kitchen.

Halfway through the morning, Lois was dusting upstairs in the big bedroom overlooking the drive. She straightened the curtains and saw a police car draw up at the gate. Since nobody seemed to be answering the door, she went quickly downstairs and opened it. 'Morning, Inspector,' she said.

The Inspector's smile was warm. 'Good morning, Mrs Meade,' he said. 'Is the Professor at home?'

'I'll get him,' said Lois, but Malcolm had come up behind her.

'Thank you, Lois. I'll look after the inspector now.' Dismissed, Lois walked slowly back up the stairs, straining her ears to hear what was said.

She managed to catch the tail end of a sentence, just before the sitting room door was slammed shut by Malcolm. '. . . and so I wonder if you'd mind telling me about that evening once more,' said the Inspector.

'What made you think you'd be the only one to notice those jackets?' said Derek, pushing spaghetti around his plate. 'Stands to reason. If an amateur like you can spot a thing like that, it's a sure thing a professional will notice it, too. They're highly trained, y'know. PC Plod is a thing of the past. 'But,' he added, looking at Lois crestfallen face, 'he might not have come up with the connection. Not noticed the creosote on that trellis.'

'Bet he has,' said Lois miserably. Still, the whole jacket business might not be all that important. She'd only to find a reason why Malcolm Barratt visited Gloria, and she'd already come up with his oft-declared intention of 'getting to know the locals' by taking on the delivery of the village newsletter. And the doctor and the vicar had every reason to be there.

She brooded on this for a while, until Derek said, 'Penny for 'em,' as his fork chased the last piece of pasta across the table.

'Worth more than a penny,' said Lois, thinking quickly. 'It's the boys. They'll soon both need new shoes.' She got up and kissed the top of Derek's head, his springy hair tickling her nose. 'You'd better get back to work,' she said. 'Else we'll never be able to afford them, the price trainers are these days. They'll want the latest, of course.'

'Of course,' said Derek. 'And as long as I can connect a couple of wires, they shall have the latest.'

The shoe shop was crowded, as always on a Saturday. Most of the customers had helped themselves to a single shoe that took their fancy, and stood about trying to catch the eye of one of the very few assistants. After a long wait, the boys finally had their shoes, and Lois said they could go off for half an hour, but to meet her again by the entrance to John Lewis without fail. Josie had tagged along in the hope of new shoes herself, but Lois had very little money left.

'Next month, Josie,' she said. 'Then it'll be your turn.'

They walked up the shopping centre boulevard, and Lois thought funds would stretch to an ice-cream while they waited for the boys. The ice-cream parlour was brilliantly lit. Too bright, thought Lois, to be welcoming. It's like standing under a spotlight in a torture chamber. She squinted against the whiteness, wondering if they should go somewhere else, when Josie's voice drew to her attention the tall figure of Melvyn Hallhouse standing in front of them, smiling broadly.

'Hi, Mrs Meade. Hi, Josie. Ice-cream all round? Er . . . like, it'd be an apology for getting it wrong the other night?'

Josie accepted quickly, before Lois could refuse, and they perched on uncomfortably high stools eating silently. Someone's got to say something, thought Lois, and wiped her mouth with the paper napkin.

'Josie's Dad came round, more or less,' she said. 'Better not come to the house for a week or two, but after that I reckon it'd be all right . . . just at weekends.'

Josie beamed at her. 'Fine!' she said.

But Melvyn shook his head. 'Might not be around for much longer,' he said portentously.

A warm sense of relief flooded Lois, but Josie gasped. 'Why? Where're you going?'

'We might be movin' away, up north,' said Melvyn. 'Dad's being moved in his job and Mum says where he goes we all go. They've sussed out a house to rent already. None of the rest of us want to go, but Dad says he has to be where the work is. Sensible, I suppose.'

Lois agreed quickly, adding that it always took a while to move house, so he'd be sure to be in Tresham for a few weeks yet.

Josie failed to cheer up, and threw her half-eaten ice-cream into the bin. 'I'm going to look for the boys,' she said. 'See you around, Melv.'

'Oh dear,' said Lois, getting off the stool. 'She's upset, Melvyn, that's all. I'd better be off after her.' Something made her look back as she walked away from the parlour. Melvyn was watching her, grinning as if he'd just won the lottery. Well, thank God *he* doesn't look exactly broken-hearted, Lois thought, and hurried on her way.

Twenty-Three

Monday morning in Byron Way was chaos, with the boys rushing in different directions looking for homework books, library books, violins, recorders, football boots, coats, scarves, gloves. Josie had shut herself in the bathroom for some unexplained purpose and wouldn't come out. Lois's mother stood at the door, saying that if she, at her age, could get herself ready and out of the house, and walk up that steep hill in time to collect everybody, surely the least they could do was be ready.

'Quite right, Mum,' said Derek. 'Get a move on, you boys. Your mother has to go to work, and so do I, and poor Gran is getting cold waiting on the doorstep, and –' he added without pausing for breath but his voice rising several decibels – 'Josie Meade! Come down here at once. I don't care if you're still in your pyjamas! Serve you right if I made you go to school in them.'

'Derek, that's enough,' said Lois, and went quickly upstairs. 'Is something wrong, Josie?' she said through the bathroom door.

'Nope,' said a tearful voice.

'Let me in, dear,' said Lois. 'Better tell me what's up.' She sat with Josie on the edge of the bath and put her arm round the narrow shoulders. 'Now then . . .'

'It's today Melvyn's movin',' Josie finally croaked. 'Shan't see him no more.'

'*Any* more,' said Lois automatically. 'The move's happened very quickly, hasn't it?'

'Well, his Dad's found a place to rent, and it's empty, so he said no point in waiting. Melv doesn't want to go . . .'

'Oh dear,' said Lois, hovering between a wish to comfort her only daughter and pleasure that at least one of their problems would now be solved. She finally got Josie dressed and, despite being rather limp, Josie was now at least dry-eyed. Gran had waited, sensing that her granddaughter might need support. Derek told her sharply to get a move on. Lois made a face at him and encouraged Josie out into the porch.

'There'll be other fish to fry,' she said cheerfully, knowing as she said it that at Josie's age there is no such thing as tomorrow, let alone next week or month or year.

Derek was overjoyed when Lois told him. 'Good riddance,' he said. 'Perhaps Josie'll concentrate on her school work now.'

And perhaps she won't, thought Lois. There will be others, but none of them will be good enough for Derek's little girl. Still, we should get a bit of respite now Melvyn's gone. She pulled on her coat and went out to start her car. The doctor's house today. As she drove along past leafless trees and bare fields, noisy seagulls driven inland by storms flew up in a curving flock. I could do with a bit of sunshine, a warm beach and blue sea, said Lois to herself. She had been watching a travel programme the previous evening and wished they had enough money for a winter holiday. It'd make spring come all the quicker. 'Instead of which,' she said aloud to the small dragon talisman swinging over her windscreen, 'I am on my way to clean another woman's house because she's too lazy to do it herself.' Her thoughts circled on and as she thought about Mary Rix and her empty days, she wondered again what had happened about the baby they should have had, the one they made a nursery for and kept as a shrine. Time to find out, Lois. You never know what might emerge.

'Morning!' she called as she stepped into the big kitchen, wiping her feet carefully on the mat.

'Ah, there you are, Lois,' said Mrs Rix, as though Lois was already half an hour late. Lois checked with the handsome wall clock, and saw that she was dead on time.

'Punctual to a fault, that's me,' said Lois, hanging up her coat. 'You could set your watch by me, Mrs Rix.'

'Yes, well, I'm sure you're right,' said Mary Rix. 'This morning I'd like you to help me make up the beds in the spare room and then give the whole of upstairs an extra good going over. We have friends coming to stay from Sweden and you know how houseproud *they* are.'

Lois didn't, but nodded and went to the linen cupboard for sheets and pillowcases. Mary Rix was at her heels and as they passed the firmly shut nursery door, Lois said, 'Shall I go round in there with a duster? Freshen it up a bit?'

Mary Rix's reply was cold. 'No thank you,' she said. 'No one but myself is allowed in that room.'

'Not even the doctor?' said Lois. 'After all, I suppose the baby was his, too?' Oh Lord, that's gone too far.

Mrs Rix had pulled up short and was glaring at Lois. 'I don't know what you mean,' she said and followed it up with the closest she dared to a reprimand. 'I don't think it has anything to do with you.'

'But Mrs Rix,' said Lois. 'I don't mean any harm,' she continued quietly. For all her reputation, Lois knew when to be gentle. 'I've worked for you long enough to be trusted, surely? It seems silly if I'm up here with the cleaner and dusters and things not to go in and clean round. I'll be very careful and you can tell me what's what.'

There was a long pause, and then Mary Rix's face crumpled and reddened. 'Tell you what's what?' she said. 'I don't know what *is* what, Lois, and that's the truth,' she blurted out. 'There's no baby and never will be. I don't know why I . . .' Then she was in real tears and Lois opened the nursery door slowly, taking Mary Rix by the hand.

'Show me,' she said. 'It'll not do any harm.'

It was dark in the room and Lois drew back the curtains, noticing prints of yellow sailing boats on a blue and white sea. A weak wintry sun penetrated the room and Lois led Mary Rix to a chair by the small white wicker cradle. 'There,' she said. 'I'll just dust round carefully and you can tell me about it. If you want to, that is.'

Lois felt a pang of deep sympathy for Mary Rix as she lifted up fluffy dogs and plastic ducks, dusted underneath, and then moved on to an unused dolls' house, the door standing open and all the furniture and tiny inhabitants standing inside, waiting.

'You don't want to hear my sorry story,' began the doctor's wife.

'I do,' said Lois simply.

Mary Rix hesitated, and then said, 'It's common enough, but still cruel, for all that. I'd tried so many times for a baby and always lost them in the first few weeks. Then it looked hopeful. I got to five months and could feel her kicking. It was a girl, they told me, when –' she scrubbed her eyes with a handkerchief and pulled herself together – 'when I began to lose blood, and finally miscarried. No baby, nothing to show for those weeks of waiting and hoping. No little person to occupy the nursery we'd finally dared to set up. No little girl for Andrew to spoil and cuddle. Only emptiness inside me and between us in this big old house.' She paused and put her hand over her eyes.

The silence became embarrassing, and Lois said, 'Didn't you try again?'

Mary shook her head, sadly. 'I was really too old and Andrew wasn't keen. He said the disappointment was too hard for me to bear, but I think he meant himself as well. Then we didn't talk about it again. I shut the door on the nursery and didn't go in for weeks. After that, I started creeping in here when Andrew was out, just to think about that little one who almost made it. I mean, nowadays they can do wonders with premature babies, can't they?'

Lois quietly opened the window a notch. 'Shall we let in some fresh air,' she said. 'It's a bit stuffy in here. Blow the cobwebs away, an' that.'

Mary Rix sat for a long time as Lois busied herself about the room. Without realising it, Lois was humming and an ordinary sort of calm spread around the room. It was as if time had started again in that room and everyday life had been allowed in.

Mary Rix sighed deeply and stood up. 'Lois,' she said, her voice shaky at first, then stronger. 'Next week, I want you to help me turn out this room.'

'Oh, but—'

'No, I mean it. It's time. We'll sort out stuff to take to the local hospital's premature baby unit. I could do with a sewing room, now I've taken up patchwork. We had a demonstration at Open Minds and we're all at it now! Yes, that's it, that's what we'll do.' She smiled at Lois. 'You're a good girl,' she said. 'I shan't forget your kindness. Now I'll go and put on the kettle and you can carry on as usual.' She put her hand briefly on Lois's shoulder, and then was gone, her step firm on the stairs.

Lois finished cleaning the sad little room and moved on to the landing. She shut the door, but then changed her mind. 'Let's see if you mean it,' she said softly, and opened it again, leaving a small draught that made the yellow sailing boats dance upon the blue and white summer sea.

'Hello? Oh, it's you.' Lois, back home as the telephone began to ring, looked round to see if anyone was listening. 'What? . . . Hunter Cowgill again? . . . Well, I suppose so, but I haven't got much . . . Where, then? Round the back of the bike sheds? No, no, it was a joke . . . Yes, I'm at the nurse's on Wednesdays . . . Difficult? Well, I'll have to think of something. Shall I come to the cottage back door? And will he wear a red carnation so's I shall recognise—' Before she had finished her sentence, Keith Simpson had replaced the receiver.

'Who was that?' said Josie, coming through the door with a miserable expression. 'Not Melv?'

Lois shook her head. 'No, not Melv. Just someone for me. And for goodness sake cheer up, child. You look like something the cat's brought in.'

'Funny you should say that,' said Josie, delving into her school bag. 'Melv sent me a goodbye present . . . one of the kids down his road brought it in. Ouch!' she added as she pulled out a spitting kitten, its claws extended and a wild look in its blue eyes.

'Oh God!' said Lois. 'That's all we need – and a ginger tom, too! I don't know what your father will say.'

'He likes cats,' said Josie confidently. 'I'm going to call him Mel, to remind me of my own true love.'

Twenty-Four

Both Barratts were out when Lois arrived the next day, so she used her own key to enter the quiet, tidy house. Her feelings were mixed. She could always get on faster in a house where nobody was at home, but now she felt it was an opportunity lost, no chance of a conversation that might give her a useful lead.

At least I can have a snoop, she thought, as she climbed the stairs to the bedrooms. She paused outside the bathroom, where she usually began, but thought perhaps today she'd start right at the top, in Malcolm's attic study, and work her way down. Won't matter, with nobody at home, she said to herself.

The door to the study was open and, feeling suddenly nervous, Lois peeped round the door. 'Yoo hoo!' she called. There was no answer, so she went over to empty the waste-paper basket. She recalled Malcolm's nasty habit of catching her bending whenever he got the chance, and from force of habit whipped round quickly as if to catch him at it.

There was nothing of interest in the bin, but as she dusted his desk she saw an address book open at the 'P' page. Idly glancing down the names, her eye was caught by a single Christian name – 'Pamela'. No surname, no address, just an enigmatic telephone number. Lois recognised the code. Was it Malcolm's unlucky day? Auntie Ginnie, her mother's sister, lived in Edinburgh and kept in touch, and Lois knew the code off by heart. Well now, it might be interesting to dial this number and pretend a bit. Better do it from home, thought Lois, oddly scrupulous about wasting the Barratts' money.

The uneasy feeling that someone might be in the house followed her from room to room. It seemed sad to Lois that she would probably feel the same in all her houses, now that the murder had spread poison round the whole village. It wouldn't be any different until the murderer had been discovered and all the circulating suspicions could die down and the village get back to normal.

She found nothing more of interest in the Barratts' house. In fact, she stopped looking. Can't do it, she thought. Not while they're out. It's not right. Some rules, it seemed to Lois, must be established if she was going on with this. She did not have the legal right to search private property and anyway felt dishonest. Information picked up by chance was fair game . . . but not this snooping around. She wouldn't ring that Pamela woman after all, whoever she was. She left promptly and called in at the village shop for a loaf of bread before going back to Tresham. The bread was wonderful here and though the kids preferred Tesco's sliced white, Derek and she ate the village shop wholemeal loaf as if it was cake. Mmmm . . . a slice of toast with butter and honey. Lois dreamed of sitting by the fire, indulging herself.

'Morning, Lois!' It was Gillian Surfleet, bustling into the shop with a big smile for everyone. 'Finished at the Barratts?'

Lois nodded. 'I'll see you tomorrow,' she said, and found herself wondering why Gillian was so smiley, so anxious to please this morning. There it was again. Suspicion is an evil thing, creeping everywhere, and she hated herself for her own thoughts about a woman she would have trusted with her life. 'Bye, then,' she said, and drove home through the empty lanes. Confused and unable to sort out her own part in all this, she thought of her meeting the next day. Perhaps that would make things clearer. As she drove into the quiet estate and saw her own house, the warm centre of her life, she was tempted to forget all about Gloria Hathaway, not turn up tomorrow, and cancel the arrangement. But then she remembered how much she knew already and what new avenues might open up. Was it her duty to continue? She couldn't decide, and then thought of Cowgill's casual warning. She might be in danger herself. The murderer might strike a second time.

Wednesday dawned with a clear, pale blue winter sky. The sun sparkled on the early morning frost in the gardens of Tresham's

Churchill Estate, and Derek leaned out of the bedroom window to breathe in the clean air. A line from a school poem of Josie's ran through his head: 'And chimney cowls like little owls, turn in the morning air.' Lovely, that was. He'd seen one of those turning cowls somewhere on his travels. Farnden, it was. Yes, it was in Lois's cleaning village. Now which house? He'd done work in several of them. Ah yes, that was it, Miss Hathaway's. The chocolate-box cottage belonging to poor old Gloria. Well, she wasn't poor and she wasn't old, but she was certainly dead, mused Derek with a sigh.

'You at the nurse's this morning, Lois?' Derek thought he should show some interest, though he was determined to keep any discussion of Farnden to a minimum.

'Yes, as usual on a Wednesday.' Lois was sharp, still in a gloomy mood from yesterday's confused deliberations. 'I shall be a bit late back. Got some shopping to do.' She hadn't told him about the meeting in Gloria's cottage. There were quite a few things she hadn't told Derek about her investigations. She knew he was getting fed up with it all and had lately changed the subject every time she opened it. Now she didn't try. Well, that was all right. Naturally a bloke didn't want his brains bothered after a hard day's work. All he asked for was a good tea, feet up and the television on. If the kids needed help with their homework, he was always willing, but even that was getting difficult for him now they were older. Education was a very different thing from when he was a lad.

'I'll get me own dinner, then,' he said. 'Working in Tresham today, so I could go to the pub and have a sandwich.'

'You needn't make it sound like a penance,' said Lois. 'No doubt a pint or two will go down well with the sandwich.'

'Blimey! What's eating you this morning? Better go back to bed and get out my side. Anyway, I'm off. See you at teatime.'

He left without kissing her goodbye and this added to the dismal beginning to Lois's day. She'd be better out of it. Leave it to the police and those who know how to go about it all. Floundering about, she thought. That's me, and I could be doing more harm than good.

Her mother bore off the kids, with Josie lagging behind, not wanting to be seen in the company of her grandmother. Lois had noticed Josie was quiet this morning. She's got the hump too, she thought, same as me. Poor kid. Lois remembered the pangs of first love only too well. She emptied the kitten's tray into the back garden and made a face. Ugh! She thought she'd done with all that. Josie would have to take responsibility. It should cheer her up to be looking after something connected with Melvyn.

Gillian Surfleet's welcome was as vigorous as always and her face as sunny as Lois's was dark. 'Lovely morning, Lois! Winter mornings like this really lift the spirits, don't you think. All my old ladies will be just a bit brighter. Sunshine should not be underrated as a cure for depression, I reckon . . .' She looked closer at Lois. 'Speaking of which,' she added, 'you don't look so cheerful yourself. What's up? Anything I can help with?'

Lois shook her head. 'It'll pass,' she said. 'Just a few things getting on top of me. They'll sort themselves out. Thanks anyway,' she added, and was ashamed at another pang of suspicion. Is she hoping to pump me for what I know? Lois dismissed the thought and got on with her work. She found herself hoping that she wouldn't find out anything suspicious today. I'll just have the morning off from being supersleuth, she decided. Maybe I'll give up altogether. Nurse Surfleet conveniently went off on her rounds after coffee and Lois finished her cleaning a few minutes early.

Hunter Cowgill was waiting for her in Gloria's back garden and allowed himself a small smile. His wife had given him hell this morning for breaking a bottle of milk, and the sight of Lois, fresh and slim in her working overall, pleased him. 'This way,' he said briskly, and led her into the damp kitchen. 'Let's go upstairs,' he said, and Lois couldn't resist.

'Is that an offer?' she said, and was delighted to see the Inspector blush.

'I'll ignore that,' he said. He led the way into Gloria's bedroom, and grimaced. 'This whole cottage needs opening up and cleaning properly,' he said. 'Let's hope it won't be too long before we can turn it over to the executors to put it on the market.'

'Might be difficult to sell,' said Lois. 'What with the previous owner being murdered, and that.'

'But not in the cottage,' said Cowgill. 'It wasn't on the premises. Anyway, let's get down to business.'

After a few seconds hesitation, Lois made a decision. It was neither a good nor a bad decision, as it turned out. Perhaps a bit of both. 'There is something,' she said. 'Might not be news to you, but I've noticed some funny stains on one or two jackets in houses where I go. All in the same place, on the sleeves,' she said. 'And I think I know where the marks come from.'

Cowgill looked disappointed. 'Creosote,' he said. 'Off Gloria's front porch. We were on to that one ages ago.' He sighed, and then added, 'Still, it was clever of you to spot it too, Lois. Just for the record,' he added, 'tell me which jackets you're talking about.'

Lois answered flatly. 'The vicar's, the doctor's, and Prof Barratt's. And all had good reasons for standing in Gloria's porch.'

Cowgill nodded. 'Yes, we've checked on those,' he said. 'Professor Barratt is the weak one, but he does –' and they chorused together – 'deliver the village newsletter.'

'Goes to every house,' added Lois sadly. 'Ah well, not much help, I'm afraid.'

'Oh, never say that,' Cowgill consoled.

He sounds quite human, Lois thought.

'You never know where enquiries might lead. One thing connects up with another and before you know it the trail is hot,' continued Cowgill.

A jealous wife and a dangerous fall downstairs might make it hotter. Or a shrine to a long-lost baby? Something was stirring again. I can't help it, Lois realized. Nosiness or duty, I can't help it. Whichever, Lois cheered up. She told him about Evangeline's fall and Dallas's odd reaction. 'Might not mean anything,' she said, but he looked interested and made a note in his book.

'Keep your eyes open there,' he said. 'Anything else?' She

thought of the Rixes and their sadness, but decided to keep that to herself for the moment.

She shook her head and said, 'Well, now it's your turn. What were you going to tell me?'

'*Ask* you, I said.' Cowgill was back to being professional again. 'It was something I wanted to show you and see if it rang any bells.' He did have something to tell her, but that could wait.

'Well, come on then. Show me.'

Hunter Cowgill walked over to the small cabinet by Gloria's elaborate bed. He opened a drawer and fumbled at the back. 'They missed this when they searched the place,' he said, 'and I found it afterwards, tucked underneath.' He handed her a small photograph, dog-eared at the corners. It was no bigger than a credit card, but the picture was clear; a close-up of a new baby, wrapped in an intricately woven shawl in its cradle. It was touching and tender, as all new babies are, and Lois felt her heart contract.

'Oh God,' she said, and then looked up at Cowgill, who was watching her closely. 'Was it hers?' she said.

It was not that impossible, Lois reasoned as she drove home. After all, Gloria Hathaway was known to go off on long holidays, for several months, so Nurse Surfleet had said, which was easily enough time to have a baby. But would this private, self-reliant and selfish woman have chosen to have a baby out of wedlock? Gillian Surfleet had talked a lot about Gloria lately, building up a picture in Lois's mind. She was a pain, that was for sure. Gillian had had no hesitation in describing a difficult neighbour. But a secret baby? No, not the Miss Gloria Hathaway known by the village of Long Farnden.

It could have been a god-child, Lois considered. Certainly not very precious to Gloria, if she had shoved it to the back of a drawer. She turned into Byron Avenue, resolving to get back to her neglected notebook after a quick snack. She slowed down and saw a car parked outside her house. It was a familiar car, and Lois frowned. He must have found a quicker way back to town. It was Inspector Cowgill's car and she could see his tall, commanding figure at her front door.

'Ah, there you are, Mrs Meade,' he said with no sign of familiarity. 'You're later than usual. I wonder if I might come in and have a word?'

Twenty-Five

The inspector followed Lois into her sitting room and, though invited to sit down, remained standing.

Fair enough, thought Lois, if that's the way we play it. 'How can I help you, Inspector,' she said in a neutral voice.

'It's not so much what *you* can do, Mrs Meade. It's your husband we'd like to have a chat with, but I see he's still at work.'

In spite of herself, she registered surprise. 'Derek? Did you say Derek?' What on earth was the man talking about? 'What d'you mean? Of course he's at work. Where else would he be?' I'm rambling, she thought. Steady, Lois. 'He'll be home this evening, as usual,' she said. 'What do you want him for? He doesn't know anything about Farnden.' What had she got Derek into? Oh God, he was going to be furious.

Hunter Cowgill looked at Lois's worried face and wished he did not have to go through with this. 'No, I'm sure you can find what we want, unless, that is, he's wearing it. His jacket, Mrs Meade,' said the Inspector. 'I wonder if I could have a look at his waxed cotton jacket?'

'He took it *away!*' Derek's face was thunderous. 'What the bloody hell's going on, Lois?'

'Derek, please . . . the boys . . .' Lois put her arm around Jamie to protect him from his father's unusual rage.

Derek took a deep breath and sat down heavily on a kitchen chair. 'Go on upstairs and get on with your homework,' he said, and as soon as the frightened Jamie was out of earshot, he turned to Lois. 'So, this is where your daft notions have got us!' he said. 'Suspect, am I? About to be taken to the station for questioning? Detained for twenty-four hours while I help those buggers with their enquiries?'

Lois said nothing for several minutes, feeling resentment rising. After all, the jacket was nothing to do with her dealings with Cowgill. And there was something else. She faced Derek, and said, 'He wasn't unpleasant, so you needn't get so hot and bothered. It was Inspector Cowgill. He looked at that oily stain on the sleeve—'

'Yes!' butted in Derek, 'oil! . . . not creosote!'

'I *told* him that, of course I did Anyway, it smelt like creosote to me!' Lois shouted back at him, and added, 'And what are you so worried about . . . if you've got nothing to hide?'

Derek glared at her. She had never seen him so angry. '*What* did you say?' His face was dark-red now, his eyes narrowed.

'I said,' Lois replied, her voice icy, 'why are you so worried if you've got nothing to hide? And I said that because Cowgill produced something else. His reason for asking. He said you'd come to their notice because Nurse Surfleet told them you'd done work for Gloria Hathaway. Been there several days, coming and going.' Derek looked as if she'd struck him. Then Lois's strength suddenly gave out and tears began to roll down her cheeks. 'You never said, Derek. Why didn't you say?' She looked at him pleadingly, and stretched out a hand towards him.

He didn't take it. He glared at her and stood up violently, shoving the chair back so hard that it toppled backwards on to the floor with a crash. 'I'm going for a pint,' he said in a tight voice. 'I need it. Be back later.'

'Derek! *Please* . . . don't go!'

But he'd gone and Lois was left alone in her small kitchen, listening to the sounds of the boys quarrelling overhead and Josie's music turned up full blast.

Twenty-Six

The Reverend Peter White had had a bad night. He'd dreamed of women, one after another, and the dreams had not been innocent. A failure, that's what I am, he told himself as he sat at the kitchen table with his head in his hands. Too scared to have a proper relationship, and too scared to do my job properly. He forced himself to face the fact that his advice was never sought, nobody ever came to him when they were in trouble, and no one wanted to confide in him. He actively discouraged it, he admitted. If even the smallest approach was made, he changed the subject and got out fast. What a failure! He should probably resign.

He stood up, hearing a car pulling up in his driveway. It was Lois. Of course, it was a Lois day. He made an effort to pull himself together and managed a fairly cheery 'Good morning,' as she came into the kitchen. To his surprise she did not answer. 'Lois?' he said, peering anxiously at her.

'Oh, yes, morning, Vicar,' she said absently, and went to the cupboard to get her things.

'Is something wrong, my dear?' he said. Here it was again, that shrinking feeling, not really wanting to know. But facing up to the truth had cleared his head and maybe here was another chance. 'Anything wrong, my dear?' he repeated, but Lois shook her head.

'Just a bit tired,' she said. 'I'll be fine.'

'You don't look fine,' said Peter White and ordered her to sit down while he made a cup of coffee. His unusually firm tone took her by surprise, so she sat down, brush and dustpan in hand. He took them from her gently, and set a steaming mug in front of her. 'Chocolate biscuit?' he said and without waiting for an answer, put two on a small plate in front of her. It was his turn to play mother, he thought wryly.

He sat down again, sipped his own coffee and waited. He usually made sure he did not wait long enough, but this morning was different. Here was Lois, his friend, obviously miserable. He waited.

After a few gulps Lois spoke. 'It's the murder, isn't it?' she said. 'It's getting to everybody. Even me and I don't even live in Farnden.'

'Everybody?' said Peter White. It was certainly getting to him.

'All the houses I go to,' Lois said, head bent. She kept her eyes fixed on her hands, unwilling to look him in the eye, in case he should get out of her the real reason for her misery. Derek had come home late last night, drunk and morose. He'd clambered heavily into bed without speaking, turned his back on her and gone instantly to sleep. Or pretended to. And then this morning, he'd been up early and away in his van before breakfast, shouting out to the kids that he had a long day ahead and would see them at teatime.

'All the people, the Rixes, the Barratts and Baers, even Nurse Surfleet.' Lois shivered involuntarily when she thought of Gillian's duplicity. 'They've all changed. All edgy and suspicious. Nobody trusts anybody any more. The whole village is under a cloud, if you ask me,' she said. 'It's enough to make me give up.'

Peter White frowned. 'Gracious, Lois,' he said. 'You mustn't do that. What would we do without you? We must just soldier on and hope it all comes to an end very soon.' Not brilliant, he said to himself. Soldier on? Lois was in considerable distress and this was all he could think of to comfort her.

Vicar could be right, thought Lois. Cowgill probably knows a lot more than he's told me. And anyway, it's too late now. I've done the damage and Derek is in trouble with the police and he hates me. No, giving up would be no help now. She stood up and rinsed the mugs under the tap, turning them up on the rack to drain. 'I expect you're right,' she said. 'It'll be finished soon, and then we'll all forget it and get on with our lives.'

As she took up her cleaning things, she felt a sudden lift of spirits. It was all a storm in a teacup. Derek would be cleared by the police, get back his jacket with the oily stain, and be her loving husband again. 'Thanks, anyway,' she said to Peter White, who remained sitting disconsolately at the table. 'All part of your job, helping, I expect,' she said. She managed a laugh and was surprised at the relieved smile flooding Peter White's face.

'It's not an easy job, Lois,' he said, looking up at her. 'Some of us are naturals – seem born to be Christ's servants.' Lois winced. She hoped he wasn't going to start preaching to her. Still, better listen in case anything interesting turned up. 'Did you always want to be a parson?' she asked casually. From past experience she knew that he hated personal conversations and was quite likely to stalk off to the privacy of his study. She would have to tread very carefully.

However, this morning, Peter White was in a different mood, and he shook his head. 'Gracious no,' he said. 'My dad was in the army, and I always assumed I'd join up too, when I was old enough. Cadets at school, and all that kind of thing. Camp in the summer, drilling in the school hall. I loved it and he was so proud.'

'So what happened?' Lois leaned against the sink. She felt tired from worry and the lack of sleep and was glad of this moment's rest, a chance to listen.

'He left us,' Peter White said baldly. 'Walked out when I was thirteen. Turned out he'd had loads of girlfriends and finally ran off with his sergeant's wife. Got the boot from the army, of course, and that was the last we saw of him. I was an only child and Mum relied on me to be the man of the house. She kept on saying that. I was so disgusted with him, so knew I'd never follow him into the army, if that's the kind of man they turned out.'

'But the Church?' said Lois. 'Why that?'

She saw his face shut down suddenly and he became a different person. 'Why not, Lois?' he said in a cold voice, standing up and opening the door for her to go through. She

149

felt an unexpected shiver of anxiety as she passed close by him. 'It would be too hard to explain,' he said, as she went upstairs.

What was so hard to explain? That shiver made her realize she would have to be on her guard with them all. Hunter Cowgill was not joking. She heard the study door close, and was left to speculate as she changed the sheets, trying not to notice anything untoward.

An only child with a deserted mother, she pondered. Father spreading it about and buggering off. No wonder the bloke had problems! Rotten parents do a lot of damage, one way and another. God, he was mixed up! Just the sort to . . . Her thoughts were interrupted by a terrible noise and as blue smoke rose up from the vacuum, she switched it off quickly. All I need this morning, she cursed. She forgot about Peter White's troubles and was reminded inexorably of her own. Derek wasn't being much of a parent at the moment. If anything happened between her and Derek to damage their kids, she would kill him.

Twenty-Seven

Friday, Lois's day at the Baers, and she had been sorely tempted to stay at home. There had been no opportunity to challenge Derek the previous evening. He'd come home late again and gone up to bed early, soon after Josie, saying he was dead tired. This morning, he had grunted at her when he could not avoid speaking, and the poor boys were creeping around looking scared.

Lois's anger had evaporated and with it her courage to face whatever Derek had to tell her. Now, all she wished for was to discover that everything had been a bad dream. Her mother, when she arrived, looked at her hard and asked what was wrong, but was sensible enough not to pursue it. The last thing Lois wanted was to go to Farnden and hear Evangeline Baer rabbiting on about her fall, and how kind Dallas had been to her afterwards. And then, of course, the murder. It was still the favourite topic of conversation in Farnden. The gallery was still closed and Evangeline would be under her feet all round the house. Dallas might even be there, too. He had taken time off after Evangeline's fall. Still, he was probably back at work by now and she could get rid of Evangeline by cleaning around her feet. It might cheer her up to bruise a few ankles.

Lois opened her front door and was making her way to the car when she saw the inspector, tall and smartly dressed, approaching.

'Morning, Mrs Meade,' he said formally. 'Have I missed your husband again?' He saw the expression on Lois's face and came quickly to the point. 'We're keeping the jacket just for the moment, but perhaps you'd ask him to call in at the station for a couple of minutes. This evening,' he added firmly.

'About six-thirty would be fine.' He turned on his heel and left Lois standing quite still on her path.

What now? Should she try to get hold of Derek at work and warn him? But what would be the use of that. And anyway, she wasn't sure she wanted to get involved with this problem, right now. Let him sort it out. She might just as well carry on, use Evangeline Baer as a distraction, and earn her money. Lois drove off, grating her gears and moving forward in a series of painful jerks.

'Most unlike you to be late, Lois!' Evangeline Baer tried her best to make it sound humorous. But really, she could not allow this to go on. She limped away from the kitchen, but not quickly enough.

'Perhaps you'd rather I didn't come any more,' Lois said in a harsh voice. She had had enough and at that moment would have been quite happy not to set foot in Farnden ever again.

'Hell!' said Evangeline under her breath. Then louder, 'Of course I don't want you to leave. And it doesn't matter anyway. The gallery is closed, but when it opens up again, you know I rely on you to be here at nine o'clock sharp to take over the house. Can't manage without you,' she added with a forced laugh.

Yes, well, I'm fed up with being indispensable, thought Lois. Her confidence had taken a nasty knock in the last twenty-four hours, and she shook her head. 'You'd manage,' she said. 'Is Mr Baer at home? Shall I start in his room?' Dallas kept what he called his den for getting away from Evangeline, though he claimed he brought work home and needed a quiet room on his own. He was not there this morning.

'Dallas has gone to London on business,' volunteered Evangeline, following on Lois's heels, as anticipated. She seemed about to say more, but a loud sigh made her hesitate.

Lois followed up the sigh with a request for more bags for the cleaner, 'I did ask you last week.' Then switched on the cleaner and zoomed so close to Evangeline's feet that she retreated rapidly, saying she had some letters to write and would Lois make her own coffee, as the letters would take a long time.

'Serious business,' she said, smiling hopefully from the doorway.

Stupid old bat, I don't know what she's talking about, thought Lois, and bashed the cleaner against a table leg without caring.

It would all have become quite clear to Lois if she had been able to look over Evangeline's shoulder. The words almost leapt off the page with joy. *Dear Susie,* wrote Evangeline to her sister. *You're not going to believe what I'm about to tell you, so hold on to your seat. I'm pregnant! Yes,* pregnant! *It's a bit embarrassing for a woman of my age, but I really am over the moon. Dallas is too. We can hardly believe it. I was a bit worried about safety at my age, and all of that. But Dallas says if the PM's missus can do it, so can I, and he's gone off this morning to make all kinds of special arrangements to be sure I'll be OK.*

The letter covered three pages and took most of the morning to write. When Lois brought the coffee, Evangeline covered the writing with her hand, but realized too late that Lois was irritated by this. How unfortunate! Evangeline had planned to tell Lois the wonderful news over a companionable mid-morning break, but somehow it had gone wrong. Lois was banging about in a bad temper and Evangeline had no wish to spoil her own elation by listening to tales of woe from her cleaner. No, it would have to wait until next week. Meanwhile, she must start on another letter to her old school friend in Sydney. Goodness, wouldn't *she* be surprised!

By six o'clock in the evening, Lois was shaking with nervous anticipation of Derek's return from work. She had to tell him what Inspector Cowgill had said and feared his reaction. She wished now she had rung him on his mobile and got it over with earlier.

'Mum, what's up with you and Dad?' It was Josie, dressed in funereal black, draped round the newel post at the foot of the stairs. 'You've hardly spoken for days, and me and the boys are upset. We think we ought to know.'

Lois snapped. 'Oh, I see,' she said icily. 'You think you ought to know, do you, Miss.' Josie nodded, frowning at her mother's tone. 'Well, perhaps your father and I ought to know why you've been going round like a bloody wet week of Sundays ever since that bugger left town!'

Her mother's swearing was so excessive that Josie began to feel a twinge of fear. Was there something seriously wrong? Her imagination flitted through images of kids at school whose parents had split up, kids from broken homes, lost, miserable, dopey kids. 'I only asked, Mum,' she said in a quavering voice.

Lois glared at her, and then collapsed into a chair. 'Come here, Josie,' she said, shaking her head in self-disgust. 'Come here, baby.' Josie went to her mother and Lois put her arms around her daughter's slender waist. 'Sorry, love,' she said. 'Things aren't too good at the moment, but it'll soon be sorted out. Don't worry and I'll tell the boys everything's fine. We all have difficult days, don't we?'

At this point, Derek came in, bag in hand, and over his shoulder was slung the waxed cotton jacket. 'Hi, everybody,' he said. 'Hi, Lois, Josie. What're you two up to?'

Lois got up and held Josie's hand for support. 'Derek, the inspector was here again.'

'I know,' said Derek. 'I called in at the cop shop on my way home. Time to get my jacket back, I thought. I saw him and we had a chat. All sorted out. So what's for tea?' he added, but he would not meet Lois's eye.

Twenty-Eight

The weekend that followed was, on the face of it, no different from any other. Saturday afternoons were always taken up with football. Derek and the boys supported Tresham United and travelled around the local area decked out in cheerful red and white, joining their fellow supporters with an enthusiasm that was clearly not dependent on their team's prowess, since Tresham United was bottom of the league. 'Fair weather or foul, you got to be loyal,' preached Derek, regularly. Lois could rely on a peaceful afternoon at home or, occasionally, a shopping expedition with Josie. More often than not, though, Josie was off with her friends. It had probably been Melvyn when he'd been around, but now she was back with the gang of girls who'd been together since primary school.

On Sundays, none of them went to church. It was rare for anyone on the Churchill Estate to go to a church of any kind, though a big family at the end of Byron Way set off regular as clockwork, dressed in their best, to attend the Baptist Chapel in the town. If you happened to be passing during a service, Douglas had told Derek, you could hear them singing at the tops of their voices. 'Talk about a row!' he'd said, but there'd been a wistful edge to his voice. There was joy in those voices and he wouldn't have minded being a part of it. Derek had said no son of his was going to join the happy clappies, and that was that.

Lois had occasional thoughts of her own childhood, when she'd gone to the local Sunday school under protest. Had any of it rubbed off on her permanently? She doubted it. Often enough she'd heard Rev White bemoaning the tiny congregation in Long Farnden. She had once or twice asked him why people didn't go to church any more, but he'd never given her a satisfactory answer.

Now, this Sunday, because this weekend *was* different and Lois was feeling restless, she took Josie into town to look at the sales. Most of the shops were open, and they bought several bargains. Then, after a good Sunday dinner, Derek went to sleep in his chair by the fire, and the boys went off to the playing fields. Josie went up to her room and Lois sat opposite Derek, trying to read the newspaper.

I wish it *was* the same as every other weekend, thought Lois, watching Derek out of the corner of her eye. I wish Gloria Hathaway had never existed. Derek was snoring with his mouth open and looked as if he hadn't a care in the world. But he had told her nothing about his talk with the police and had refused to discuss anything to do with Farnden, saying they'd all heard quite enough of that place, thank you very much. Douglas and Jamie had raised a small cheer and Lois had felt squashed and humiliated, as if it was she who had something to explain, to apologise for. Last night, when Derek came back from the pub, he had climbed into bed and turned away from her. When she had tried to talk to him, desperate to know about the job he'd done for Gloria and why he had kept it secret from her, he had breathed deeply, feigning sleep. Today, she just couldn't pluck up the courage to confront him and ruin another evening.

Now it was Monday morning, and Derek was out of the house early, saying that he wouldn't be home at midday as he was working over at Fletcham and it was too far to come back. 'See you at tea-time,' he called out, and was gone.

'Everybody ready?' Lois's mother appeared at the door. She was determined to say nothing more to Lois, knowing from experience that her daughter would tell her if anything was wrong in her own good time. No good asking questions. That made her clam up even more.

Good old Mum, thought Lois. She knows there's something up. I couldn't tell her, though. I wouldn't know where to begin.

Lois drove thoughtfully to Farnden and found the Rixes both

at home, the doctor in his surgery as usual, and Mary waiting in the kitchen.

'Morning, Lois,' she said. 'Ready for the big turn-out?' She smiled at Lois, who thought she'd never seen Mrs Rix looking so cheerful. But what was she talking about? Turn-out? It was hardly spring-cleaning weather yet, surely?

'I've collected up lots of boxes and bought a roll of black bin-liners, so we shall have somewhere to put all the clobber.' Mary Rix laughed, delighted with herself for being able to speak like this about the contents of that sad room.

Of course! Lois remembered. They were going to turn out the baby's room, pack up all the little garments, the toys and books and pictures, give it a good clean, and set it up as Mary's sewing room. Good! That was something positive to think about and Lois gradually fell in tune with Mary's mood. The pair worked away with a will, Lois helping Mary over the occasional tearful moment, and by coffee time the boxes and bags were stacked in the hall ready to be taken away.

'Now, you let *me* take them to the charity shop in Tresham,' said Lois firmly. She remembered only too well her mother's distress when they took her father's clothes to Oxfam after he had died. She'd watched helplessly as her mother hugged an old jacket, tears dropping on to the worn tweed. No, it would be far better for her to take away the last vestiges of Mary's dream. She could say goodbye to it here and make a new start.

'Time for a break,' said Mary Rix, setting off downstairs. 'Coffee or tea, Lois?'

Alone in the now almost empty room, Lois looked around. There was only that chest of drawers in the corner. A nice little piece, it would be useful for Mary's cottons and pins and things. She pulled open the top drawer and found a baby record book. Oh dear, she thought, and put it straight into a black sack. It opened as it hit the bottom, and something fell from between the pages. It looked like a piece of blank paper, and Lois was about to empty the next drawer, when on impulse she reached down to pull it out. It wasn't blank both sides. It was a photograph, and peering closely she could see a tiny, new-born baby, wrapped in a shawl, fast asleep. But it couldn't be! Mary said she'd miscarried! Lois heard footsteps coming up the stairs and swiftly slipped the photograph into her overall pocket. She was shaken and couldn't concentrate on what Mary was saying. Luckily, Mary was so preoccupied with her plans for the room that she didn't notice Lois's monosyllabic replies to her endless excited comments.

The morning was quickly over and Mary Rix helped load boxes and bags into Lois's spacious car boot. 'One good thing about this old banger,' said Lois. 'Plenty of room, if not much speed.' She had recovered her equilibrium and, making sure everything was safely packed, she turned to say goodbye. The doctor stood in the doorway, looking at the two women. His face was stony, and Lois thought she had never seen anyone look so sad. 'Well,' she said, 'see you next week, then.'

To her surprise, Mary leaned forward and kissed her cheek. 'Thank you, Lois,' she said. 'You've probably saved my life. Take care, now.' Lois started her car and drove slowly down the drive. She looked into her driving mirror, and saw Mary waving cheerfully. But the doctor had disappeared, and the doorway was empty.

The photograph lay on Lois's kitchen table and now she had Douglas's magnifying glass to look more closely. It was very much like any other baby of that age, she thought, and very like the one Cowgill had shown her in Gloria's cottage. What was it doing here? Now she could swear it was the same shawl and the same dark little head. She needed to check, and realized she had no idea how to contact the inspector. That was one small thing he had overlooked, she thought sourly. Best thing would be to ring Keith Simpson for help. She quickly dialled the number and he told her to wait one moment. His voice was friendly, but cool. After a few seconds, Cowgill came on the line.

'Yes?' he said. She explained quickly, and he said three words before putting down the telephone. 'Jock's Café. Three.'

Luckily, Lois knew where the café was. It was behind Woolworths and some of the girls used to go there for a snack at lunchtime. Not a good place for me, she thought. She could see through the window that the café was empty of customers, except for Hunter Cowgill's unmistakeably upright figure sitting at a table in the corner. But the waitress was still the same, hair greying now, and much stouter. Lois caught Cowgill's eye through the glass and beckoned, then walked on very slowly, causing a log jam on the pavement.

He caught her up, touched his hat and said, 'Good morning, Mrs Meade. How are the boys today?' What the hell is he talking about, thought Lois. He had stopped walking, and was smiling at her as if they had just met unexpectedly in the street. 'Are you on the way home?' he continued, and added, 'My car's just round the corner. I'd be happy to give you a lift.'

'This is bloody daft,' said Lois, as she sat in the front of Cowgill's car and they cruised slowly off towards the Churchill Estate. He didn't answer her, but felt in his pocket and pulled out the small square photograph. She frowned and matched it up against the one in her bag. It was the same, without any doubt, though taken from a slightly different angle. Even the shadow of a hand was the same.

'Right?' he said.

She nodded. 'But there's nothing bad about the Rixes,' she added defensively. 'I'd stake my life on it.'

'I hope that won't be necessary,' said the Inspector, and gave her a brief smile. A crack in the concrete, thought Lois. 'This is too dangerous,' she said, 'being seen in your car.'

He nodded. 'Send me a message through Simpson, if you want to meet,' he said. 'Then go to Alibone Woods near Farnden at the time I say. People walk their dogs, but not at this time of the year.'

Lois knew the woods, though she'd never stopped there. 'Bit cloak and dagger, isn't it?' she said.

'Nothing fictional about this murder, Lois,' he said, stopping at the entrance to the Churchill Estate. Nobody about, she noticed with relief, and made her way home. It was only while she was filling the kettle that she realized he'd called her 'Lois' and she hadn't minded.

The day had been so full that Lois had been able to put the necessary confrontation with Derek to the back of her mind. When she reached home, her mother was there in the kitchen, smiling at her and unwrapping a chocolate sponge she had made for the family.

'I know Derek likes chocolate best,' she said, as she had planned, to give Lois an opening if she needed one.

'We all know Derek likes chocolate!' agreed Lois, and then, with a miserable shrug, 'I'm beginning to wonder if I know anything else about him, though.' Her mother said nothing. 'He's a close one, you know, Mum,' Lois continued. 'Doesn't tell me everything . . .'

'Like what?' said her mother simply.

'Like he did a job in Long Farnden that he didn't tell me anything about. Not a squeak. And he always lets me know where he is, in case there's an emergency with the kids or anything.'

'What kind of a job?' said her mother, frowning.

'You may well ask,' said Lois, and then, as if deciding she'd said quite enough, went off into the garden, where she began taking in washing that was still as wet as when she had put it out. 'Waste of time pegging it out,' she said on returning. 'Put it in the drier for me, Mum.'

So, end of conversation about Derek, thought her mother. Still, it's a start. She stayed for half an hour, drank a cup of tea and attacked the cake. There was not much left when the boys had had their fill and Lois put the rest in a tin, saying they must leave some for their father, since it was made specially for him. After her mother had gone, and only Josie was left in the kitchen, an uncomfortable silence fell.

'What was that about, Mum?' Josie trod carefully, well aware that she was on thin ice.

'What was what about?'

'You know, that stuff about Dad and not telling you about a job in Farnden?'

'Nothing to do with you,' said Lois briskly. 'Now go on upstairs and get going on your homework.'

'No, well, it's just that Dad said something to me about it at the time,' said Josie.

'What?'

'I remember him saying something about that old spinster in Farnden and how she was a pain in the arse.'

'Sounds about right,' said Lois bitterly.

160

'Well, I expect he just forgot to mention it,' said Josie hopefully.

Lois looked at her and felt so angry with Derek that it was a good thing he didn't choose to come in at that moment. All this anxiety had spread to the kids and it was his stupid fault. 'Expect you're right,' she said to Josie. 'We're all so busy dashing here and there, there's never time for a proper talk. Go on, love, get your books. Dad'll help you if you get stuck.'

The confrontation had to wait until the boys and Josie had finally gone to bed and were sure to be asleep. Derek was dozing in front of the television and Lois folded away the newspaper as she steeled herself to begin.

'Derek! Wake up!'

'Not asleep,' he mumbled. 'Just thinking . . .'

'Well, think with your eyes open then,' she said sharply.

He opened them and looked at her. 'What now, Lois?' he said wearily.

'We have to talk.'

'Do we? What about?'

'You know very well. About Gloria Hathaway, and that mysterious job you did for her and didn't tell me about.'

'Oh God, it was ages ago . . .'

'I want to know. Now.'

Derek sat up straight in his chair. 'Are you sure you want to know?' he said, and added, 'some things are better not spoken of.'

Lois was really frightened now, but having come this far she had to pursue it to the end, however disastrous. 'Yep,' she said, 'I want to know.'

It was a pathetic little tale. Derek had been looking for Nurse Surfleet to make a date for rewiring her cottage, and, unable to find her, he'd called in at Gloria's, asking if she'd give her neighbour a message. 'She said she might have some work for me and would I go in and have a quick look.'

'Huh!' said Lois.

Gloria had given him a cup of coffee and offered to dry his coat by her fire. 'It was a dreadful day, tipping it down,' he said. They'd got talking, gone upstairs to look at a dodgy plug in her bedroom, and one thing had led to another.

'You didn't . . .' Lois could hardly speak.

'Yes, I did. And after that I went back a couple of times to complete the job.'

'Huh!' said Lois.

Derek frowned, and rubbed his hand across his eyes. 'She was good at it, Lois,' he said in a low voice. 'Though you'd never have thought it. And it was that time when you'd gone off it, didn't want to know . . . after Jamie was born . . . God knows I've regretted it since and hoped you'd never need to know, so's not to be hurt. She was a real tart, y'know. Got all the tricks.'

Lois shook her head unbelievingly. Not her Derek, no, it couldn't be true. 'And you did it more than once, you said?' Somehow, that made it very much worse. The pounding in her ears was horrible and the room was hazy. 'I'll kill you,' she said in a pinched voice, and took up the poker.

'Don't be so bloody daft,' said Derek, getting up quickly and advancing on her.

'I'll kill you like *somebody* killed her,' said Lois, shouting now.

'*What*?' said Derek, and then, grabbing Lois's wrists he began to laugh. 'Have you forgotten I was here, in this bloody room that night she was done in? For God's sake, Lois, sit down.' He took the poker from her, made her sit on the sofa, and then sat beside her. 'Now you listen to me, young woman,' he said. 'That Gloria Hathaway had been around. She knew exactly what she was doing and I was just one on her list. She chatted me up, knew how I was feeling. It was three times at the most, and then I got out. I was ashamed of myself, yes, and I'm very sorry now that I've hurt you. But that wasn't the only thing. She was trouble, real trouble. If you want to solve your murder mystery, Lois, I can tell you more than a thing or two about Gloria Hathaway. Now, are you going to listen, or would you rather hit me over the head with a poker?'

Lois subsided into a muttering heap and Derek got up to open a medicinal bottle of brandy. 'Here, drink this,' he said, and poured another one for himself. The minutes ticked by and it was so quiet they could hear Douglas snoring.

Then Lois downed the last of the brandy and turned to look

162

Derek straight in the face. 'You sod,' she said. 'You stupid, silly sod.' He said nothing, waiting for her to go on. 'I never thought you . . . of all people . . . not you, Derek. But there it is.' She took a deep breath, glared at him and said, 'Right, since you know so bloody much about Gloria Hathaway, you can answer a few questions . . .'

Twenty-Nine

Tuesday at the Barratts' was a dull and unproductive morning for Lois, who could have done with some enlivening
new scrap of information to take her mind off last night.
Although she and Derek had come to a kind of truce, and he'd
certainly given her some very interesting stuff about Gloria
Hathaway, she still felt sick at such betrayal. She felt like
talking to someone, but the Barratts were cemented together
in an embarrassing reconciliation and had no time for gossip
with their cleaner. She had a solitary lunch and sat staring at
her notebook most of the afternoon. After a while, she began
to write notes on what Derek had told her and slowly her spirits
began to rise. By the time her mother came in with Jamie and
Douglas trailing behind, she had gained enough confidence to
answer her tactful questions as best she could.

With the boys safely in front of the television and Josie not
yet home, she gave a more or less complete account.

'So that's it,' said her mother. 'No wonder you look so low.
But it won't do, Lois.'

'What d'you mean, "it won't do"?' said Lois angrily.
'Haven't I got a perfect right to feel low?'

Her mother nodded. 'But it's not the end of the world, you
know.' And then she smiled broadly. 'I like him a bit better
for it, to tell you the truth. He's always been so perfect . . .
your Dad and I used to call him Mr Smug in the early days.'

'Wonderful!' said Lois. 'First my husband confesses to
having it off several times with some scraggy old spinster
and now my mother says she approves!'

'I didn't say that, Lois. I just don't judge, that's all. So he's
had one small fling . . . it's quite likely you'll do the same one
day. When you get to my age—'

164

'Oh, spare me that,' said Lois rudely. 'So what do you suggest I do? Congratulate him on his success with lonely old women?' She knew she was being unfair. Gloria had not been old and in her way not unattractive. But Lois was a woman scorned, and they are never fair.

'Think about it, Lois,' answered her mother. 'What really matters? He's still the same old Derek; a good husband and father. What's important is that he still loves you – which he does, of course – and you both have a lovely family, home and jobs. Some people would give their eye teeth—'

'I know, I know,' said Lois. 'Well, I expect you must be getting back now,' she said unkindly, and ushered her mother to the door.

Later, though, she pondered over what her mother had said and knew it was sensible advice. She was still angry, though, and knew that Derek had to suffer some more for his transgression.

Then, when she was still feeling adrift, without the firm footing at home that had given her confidence, there was another confrontation for Lois the next day. She was not looking forward to it. She had to discover why Gillian Surfleet had known about Derek visiting Gloria and had said nothing. Common sense told her that there was no reason why Nurse Surfleet should have mentioned it to her, but still . . . She probably assumed Lois knew about it. To an incurious neighbour, an electrician turning up at Gloria's cottage on more than one occasion, meant nothing more than that he was doing an electrician's job in a house riddled with electrical problems.

Well, he was on the job, that's for sure, thought Lois, reluctant to listen to common sense, and I reckon Gillian knew all about it. There's a lot she knows, according to Derek.

The nurse's cottage was warm and Lois took off her coat in the small kitchen. 'Hot in here,' she said abruptly. Nurse Surfleet was in her chairman of the parish council role this morning, seated at the table surrounded by council papers, working on village business.

Of course she knew, Lois assured herself. She knows

everything that goes on in Farnden. 'I'd like you to tell me something,' Lois continued, dispensing with polite frills.

'I'm rather busy, Lois,' said Gillian, brusquely. 'Can't it wait?'

'No,' said Lois flatly.

'Well . . . all right.' Gillian looked apprehensive. 'We could have a coffee break now, if you like, though it's earlier than usual.' Lois quickly made coffee and set it down. 'Now then,' said Gillian in a brisk voice. 'Sit down and tell me what's up.'

'Would you say you were my friend?' Lois looked at her, unsmiling.

Gillian looked surprised. 'Of course I am, you know that,' she said.

'If you thought there was something I ought to know, would you tell me? Even if it was likely to hurt?'

There was a long silence, during which Gillian studied her hands, bit the end of her pencil and shuffled her papers. Finally, she spoke quietly. 'I know what you're talking about, Lois,' she said. 'It's Derek, isn't it. Yes, I knew about it, but it was such a little thing—'

Lois gasped. 'A *little* thing!' she shouted. 'My God, if you were a married woman you'd know that your husband knocking off another woman is a *big* thing!'

Gillian's eyes widened and she put her hand in front of her mouth. Perhaps she had not expected such vehemence. Lois had shaken her, but she was quick to regain her composure, stood up and walked round to where Lois was sitting. She put a hand on her shoulder, and Lois had great difficulty in not brushing it away.

'It'll fade,' she assured Lois. 'As time goes by it will fall into place. Don't be too hard on him. Gloria Hathaway could be very persuasive . . .' Her voice was sad now, and she squeezed Lois's shoulder in a way that was not wholly pleasant. Lois was silent, thinking hard. 'Am I forgiven, then?' Gillian walked back to her seat, and began turning over papers. 'Or have I got the sack?' she added, looking up at Lois with a smile.

Lois sighed. 'Nope,' she said. 'I need the money.'

They hardly spoke again before Lois left, but as she went

out of the door to her car, Gillian Surfleet called her back. 'Look,' she said. Her voice was odd, and Lois felt a shiver of apprehension. 'I want to show you something.' She went to her desk and pulled out a newspaper clipping. It was old and yellowing with a photograph and some text. 'That was Gloria, when she was still at school. Champion that year at swimming,' she said. The picture showed a slight, slim girl in a black swimsuit posed against the sun. Her smile was wide and her hair long and glinting. 'She was lovely once, you know,' said Gillian. 'And she knew it. Don't be too hard on Derek, my dear.'

Lois fled. 'Something stinks,' she muttered to herself, and drove off much too fast. She felt like rushing home and having a hot shower, but until she calmed down and slowed down to a reasonable speed along the country lanes, she could not acknowledge what she had known for a long time. 'Oh no, what a mess,' she said at last. She felt sad and sick at heart for Gillian Surfleet, in spite of everything. It was true, then, what Derek had said about her. There was love – lust, even – in the way she had stroked that creased bit of newspaper.

Lois had much to think about and when she went upstairs for a pee she didn't question that Josie's bedroom door was not standing open as usual. It was firmly shut and though it registered with Lois, she thought no more about it. Derek would be home at any minute for his lunch and she put on some water for boil-in-the-bag cod steaks. Quick and easy and not all that bad for you, she thought. Anyway, I don't feel like slaving over a hot stove for my lord and master just at the moment.

She stood waiting for the water to boil and thought again about Josie. Maybe she had come back for something and shut her door behind her? She had a key of her own now. Lois dropped the plastic bag in the water and went back upstairs to check. She pushed open the door and peered into a darkened room. 'Josie?' The curtains were drawn, and Lois could make out a hump on the bed that was Josie, curled up under the duvet, either fast asleep or pretending to be so.

'Are you OK?' she said gently. Josie had been very quiet lately, but Lois could not remember exactly when it had started.

167

After Melvyn left, she supposed. She felt guilty that her own troubles had taken up all her thoughts. She should have asked Josie, tried to find out what was wrong.

'Josie? Aren't you feeling well?'

A muffled voice said, 'Go away,' but Lois sat down on the edge of the bed. 'Please, Mum,' said the voice. 'I've got a sore throat, so they sent me home. It's really bad and I just want to sleep.' Lois frowned. A sore throat didn't sound bad enough to be sent home for. Still, perhaps it was 'flu. There was a lot of it about. 'Shall I get you a hot drink, love?' she offered.

'Just leave me alone.' Josie was shaking, but Lois couldn't tell if it was crying or the start of a temperature. She stood up and walked to the door. 'Try to sleep, then,' she said. 'I'll come up again a bit later. See how you are.'

Derek was worried. 'She's not been right for quite a while,' he said. 'You don't think . . . ?'

Lois's reply was sharp. 'Think she's pregnant? Or on something? Well, it could be either. But then again, it could be 'flu. Let's give her the benefit of the doubt, shall we? Not everyone has a guilty secret.' She might as well have slapped his face.

'Fair enough,' he said, and without touching his ice-cream, he put on his coat and left. He didn't say goodbye and he certainly did not blow her a kiss. Her heart rose again when the door opened and he poked his head back round the door, but all he said was, 'Better get the doc if she's no better by teatime.' And then he was gone again.

Well done, Lois. You really handled that well. She cleared away the dishes and washed up. Maybe a little quiet thinking would be good for her. She took out her notebook and began to write. *Doctor, vicar and professor . . . and businessman?* Thank God she didn't have to add electrician, since Derek had been safe in the bosom of his family that night. But now the nurse. Any one of them could have strangled the very lovely Gloria Hathaway. None of them had a watertight alibi. The doctor had said he had driven to the other side of the county to see a friend who was not at home, the vicar was on his own in the vicarage, but had no witnesses to prove it, and the professor said he'd been waylaid on his way to the pub by a motorist asking the way to Tresham. Lois reckoned this had delayed him by just enough time for him to have nipped up to the village hall, done the deed, and been in the pub by the time Don Cutt remembered seeing him. Then there was Dallas Baer. Lois had not forgotten that row about jealousy and suspicion, and Evangeline's disastrous fall, while he had stood by and watched. He'd been at home on his own that night. Now, of course, they were all lovey dovey, but she wouldn't trust him round the corner, smarmy bugger.

And Gillian Surfleet? She was strong. Her arm muscles were well developed from heaving old ladies about. If she'd been in love with Gloria herself – and been spurned – she might have been unhinged enough to take revenge. Lois did her best to imagine the strength of feeling Gillian might have had for her unfriendly neighbour. Maybe Gloria hadn't always been quite so unfriendly? Where had that faded newspaper cutting come from? Had Gillian known Gloria as a girl? Perhaps they had been at school together. Started as a schoolgirl crush, perhaps. They must have been about the same age. Gillian was perhaps a few years older, but they could still have coincided for a year or two. Ah, there were still so many unanswered questions.

Had Gillian been at the Open Minds meeting that night? Lois knew she was a member, and if she'd been there it would certainly knock her off the suspect list. Keith Simpson would know. Perhaps she should give him a ring anyway. She should keep him sweet, if only to make use of him. What could she tell him as a reason for ringing? She didn't want to set him onto Gillian until she had found out much more about her. Well, she would think of something.

In the end it was easy. 'Hello, Lois,' he said. 'Nice to hear from you. Need some help?'

'I'm not sure I've got that Open Minds meeting quite straight,' she said. 'Who was there and who wasn't. Nurse Surfleet, for instance?'

'Rachel Barratt was, definitely,' he said, after a small pause. 'And Mary Rix. But not Nurse Surfleet. She was on duty, apparently. I remember that distinctly, because she was annoyed that the old woman she went to see in Ringford was fast asleep in her chair and wouldn't let her in. Could see her through the window, Gillian said, but couldn't wake her up. What a job, eh, Lois? Still, I suppose it's like ours in a way, dealing with people in trouble. Anyway, is that a help?' Keith had his instructions, and was following them to the letter.

Lois thanked him and took up her pen again, adding Nurse Surfleet to the short list of suspects. Doctor, nurse, businessman, vicar and professor. Tinker, tailor, soldier, sailor, rich man, poor man, beggarman, thief . . . murderer. This Long Farnden group were important people in the village and all with a lot to lose. If Derek was right, Gloria Hathaway had been trouble, a dangerous person to know. Once in her clutches, he'd said, it'd be hell to break away.

'You managed it,' she'd said acidly.

'I could see the way the wind was blowing,' he had replied bluntly. 'Easy for me. I didn't care tuppence about her. It was just—'

'I can just imagine what it was,' said Lois, and she had shut him up then. It was the last thing she wanted to talk about, but now she needed to know more, and Derek could tell her. She glanced at the clock. Time to check on Josie. She closed her notebook with a snap.

Thirty

Peter White drove through Tresham and out on the Ringford road. He was sure Lois had said this was the way. He had never before had any reason to visit the Churchill Estate, but now he could not wait until tomorrow, when it was his Lois day. He had to talk to her now, before he drove himself mad in his quiet, chilly vicarage. He was not sure how much she knew about Long Farnden, but suspected her perambulations round the village had given her considerable insight into what was going on. It had come to him suddenly – as he was shaving – that Lois could be very vulnerable, in danger, even. She might know too much. He'd known what was going on long before Gloria Hathaway had been murdered and was well aware that he should try to put a stop to it. But how could he, implicated as he was himself? He knew that the old-time Farnden inhabitants looked on with contempt at the newcomers, and that included him.

The ringleader had been Malcolm Barratt, of course. It had all been cooked up in the pub one night when they'd had too many pints. They all drank pints, of course. They were country people now, and country people drank pints of warm, flat beer and played darts and dominoes. They'd ousted old Fred from his time-honoured position as captain of the dominoes, and organized tournaments with pubs from other villages, where similar teams of newcomers had taken over the best seats by the fire and put computer-generated notices on the noticeboard exhorting everyone to join this and that, take part in quizzes which the old guard despised, could never answer the questions and saw no reason why they should. Yes, Malcolm Barratt and Dallas Baer had been the ringleaders, bounding into the village like overgrown Tiggers, without biding their time or waiting to take their natural places in the hierarchy of village life.

Peter White slowed down and wound down his window. 'Excuse me,' he called to a middle-aged woman walking on the opposite side of the road. 'Can you direct me to the Churchill Estate?'

Lois's mother looked at the parson in his rusty old car and wondered what he wanted with the Churchill. 'You're practically in it,' she said. 'Turn right over there and that's it. What road did you want?'

'Byron Way . . . a Mrs Meade.'

'Ah,' said Lois's mother, her face bland. She did not believe in giving anything away for free. 'Second on the left, then turn right. You can't miss it.'

As Peter White drove off, she wondered what on earth the parson wanted with Lois. Then she remembered. Lois cleaned for a Reverend in Long Farnden. Probably him. Weedy-looking specimen, she considered. She wondered if his visit had anything to do with her daughter's marital problems, but dismissed that thought at once.

Lois poured steaming water on to a lemony cold cure and took the mug carefully upstairs. 'Josie? Are you awake? I've brought you a drink, love. It'll do you good.' She pushed open the door and walked in.

Josie was on fire. Her face was scarlet and every limb trembled to Lois's touch. Her hair was wet with perspiration and her nightdress clung to her body as if she'd just emerged from a bath. Her eyes were half-open and she mumbled something which Lois could not catch.

'Oh my God!' Lois rushed to the bathroom for the thermometer, but could not get Josie to put it in her mouth. Well, for God's sake, she didn't need a thermometer to tell her Josie had a very high fever! She rushed downstairs, and was about to lift the telephone receiver when the doorbell rang. She pulled open the door, saw Peter White standing there, and without querying this unusual visitor, dragged him into the house.

'Quick,' she said, 'help me wrap her up and then you can drive us to the hospital.'

His mouth dropped open. 'But, Lois . . .'

'But nothing,' she said. 'Don't argue. Just do what I tell you and I'll explain later.'

They bundled Josie into a warm blanket and manhandled her downstairs and out into Peter White's car. The trembling was worse, and her eyes seemed to have rolled up into her head.

'Quicker, for God's sake,' said Lois.

'Shouldn't we have waited for an ambulance?' he said tentatively.

'You could wait for ever,' Lois said. 'She could be dead by the time they arrived.' This abrupt statement galvanised Peter White. He put his foot down as hard as it would go and shot lights that were turning to red. They swung round corners, narrowly missed cyclists and frightened an old dog ambling along the curb. 'Hold tight,' Peter White said, as the hospital finally came into sight.

Another set of lights were turning red and Lois had a quick look from left to right. 'Nothing coming,' she said, and they shot over the crossing into the hospital entrance.

By now, Josie was limp in Lois's arms, and it took all Peter White's best efforts to help them into reception. A nurse looked expertly at Josie and to Lois's huge relief, took over.

Peter White stood quietly, his face anxious, but he had Lois's hand in a firm grasp. He was still there three hours later, when Josie's face, now as white as the sheets covering her, was at rest on the pillows.

'Is she . . . ?' Lois's voice trembled uncontrollably.

'She'll be fine, Mrs Meade,' said the sister. 'It'll take a while. A very nasty infection. But you got her here in time and with rest and antibiotics she'll be fine. She's young and that's a big advantage in itself!'

Pneumonia, the young Indian doctor had said. He had been so gentle and kind, and when Lois had finally collapsed and couldn't stop crying, he'd whispered to Peter White that he should stay and look after her.

'Are you Mr Meade?' the doctor had asked and the vicar had shaken his head vigorously.

'No, no, just a friend.' He had felt ridiculously pleased to be mistaken for Lois's husband. And Josie's father. He had a sudden vision of what he had missed. 'I'll just go and get us a cup of tea, Lois,' he said. 'If you'll be OK by yourself for a minute or two?' He felt strong and responsible for something that really mattered. When he returned with mugs of tea, he saw a man standing by the bed, close to Josie.

'Thanks a lot, Vicar,' said Lois, standing up. 'This is my husband, Derek. They got hold of him and he came straight over.' She was whispering and he noticed her hand now clutching Derek's.

'Oh, right,' Peter White said. 'You'll be all right now, then. Not need me any more?' They shook their heads kindly at him.

'Thanks a lot,' whispered Lois. 'I don't know what I'd've done if you hadn't . . . well, you know . . .'

'Oh no,' said Peter White. 'It was just lucky . . . Well, I'll be off now. Let me know if . . . well, you've got Derek now, and I'm sure . . .'

He backed away from the still figure asleep in the bed, her parents watching over her. As he walked away down the long corridor and out to his car, loneliness, his old enemy, gripped his heart. Self-pity, he told himself. That's all it is. You could do something about it. Not too late to find a wife and make a real home. He sighed, and drove out of the hospital car park. It was not until he was driving into Farnden that he remembered the urgent warning he'd set out to deliver to Lois, and wondered if she would be at work tomorrow. Very unlikely, he thought, and planned to call her in the morning if she didn't turn up.

As Peter White had expected, Lois did not come to work. He had every reason to speak to her and ask after Josie, so soon after breakfast he made the call. She answered at once, as if she had been standing by the telephone.

'Oh hello,' she said. 'I thought it might be the hospital. They sent me home to get some sleep, but I can't. I just can't help worrying about her and—'

'Lois, listen to me,' said Peter White, a new authority in his voice. 'It doesn't matter a bit if you can't sleep. Just relax – watch the telly – any old rubbish will do. You can catch up on

174

sleep later. And now, if you don't mind, I'm coming over to see you. It'll help to talk to someone, and anyway, I do have something important to tell you. Is that OK, my dear? I shan't stay long.'

To his relief, she agreed listlessly, saying that she had to go back to the hospital shortly, but would wait for him to come over. 'I've got this feeling that if I'm not there, she'll wake up and really need me. You know . . .'

Both she and Derek had come home in the early hours, and neither wanted to go to bed. They had sat without speaking for a while and then Derek had asked what exactly had happened. She told him about the vicar and Derek wondered why the doctor had never turned up. Then, Lois had broken down again and confessed that she hadn't ever sent for him.

'I wanted to wait and see if she got better after a sleep. You know how kids do.'

Derek had accepted this, but Lois knew that the truth was something different. She'd been so full of her new discoveries about Nurse Surfleet and Gloria that she'd all but forgotten her sick daughter upstairs. And then that call to Keith. She'd laughed in triumph as she got what she wanted from him. Laughed! And Josie upstairs getting sicker and sicker! Lois had flushed with shame and Derek had put his hand on her forehead.

'Now, Lois, we don't want you coming down with the bug. Off to bed now,' he had urged. 'I'll be up in a minute.'

Now here was Peter White, worried and pale, sitting in her best armchair, asking about treatment and visiting times and breaking into her endless thoughts of self-blame and condemnation.

'Sorry, what did you say?' He was looking at her closely, as if wanting an answer to some question he had asked.

'Don't worry, Lois,' he said. 'It's just that I thought I should warn you to be careful. In Farnden, you know. With the other people you clean for. Epecially the Barratts,' he added, ploughing on, though he was not sure that Lois was listening.

175

'Barratts? Why . . . what do you mean?' Lois's eyes had focused on him now, and he had her attention.

'Well, to do with the murder, really,' he said. 'There was something not very nice going on in the village. I knew about it, of course. But I considered it none of my business.' May God forgive me, he thought. 'I felt sorry for their wives, of course, but you know what they say: Never come between man and wife.' He tried a small smile, but met no reciprocal one from Lois.

'What exactly are you saying, Reverend White?' said Lois. She was sitting up straight now.

'It was mostly Malcolm Barratt and Dallas Baer,' he said. 'They were at the root of it. Some book they'd read about couples in America – yes, that was it, *Couples*, that was the book. Swapping, you know. And poor little Gloria . . . At least, that's how it started. But now, what with Gloria's untimely death, they're very anxious to hush it all up.'

'And me? Why is it dangerous for me?' said Lois, completely alert.

'Because you have the opportunity to . . . well, not to put too fine a point on it, snoop, my dear. Not that you would, of course,' he added hastily. 'But I believe you should be careful. Very careful. Somebody killed Gloria Hathaway and in my view it was not unconnected with what I've just told you. And that somebody may be capable of further violence.' Had he gone too far? He didn't think so. 'There's no need for you to worry any more about it. You have quite enough to think about now. Just be careful, that's all.' He stood up, and patted her shoulder.

She nodded. 'Well, thanks,' she said. 'Thanks a lot.'

In the long vigil by Josie's bed, Lois had plenty of time to think. As she watched her daughter's face slowly change from parchment to something more resembling a living creature, she began to relax at last. She had sifted all the information that Peter White had told her a thousand times through her brain. He could have been trying to put the blame on Prof Barratt to cover himself. She knew that things were beginning to fall into place. But first things first, she said to herself.

Then Josie opened her eyes, frowned, and said in a frightened voice, 'Mum? What's happened? I feel sick . . .'

Long Farnden suddenly seemed a very long way away.

Thirty-One

Two weeks had elapsed since Josie's illness and she was beginning to regain her strength, pottering around at home. It had been a worrying time for Lois. Hard on the heels of the shock of Derek's dalliance with Gloria, the anxiety and feeling of guilt about Josie had reduced Lois to something of an automaton. She organized her household and family into a rigid routine, and even her mother was given orders each day for what was required.

'It's the only way I can be sure everyone is taken care of,' she said when Derek suggested she might relax and give them all a break. She returned to work, but went through her cleaning tasks efficiently and without, if possible, conversation with her employers. If it was unavoidable, she kept her replies to noncommittal banalities.

She did not want to think of anything but home and family. Remembering the vicar's warning, she convinced herself that nothing she could do would bring Gloria's murderer any quicker to justice. The police would succeed. It was time to forget the whole business and concentrate on what was most important. She suspected she had made an idiot of herself, and it was time to make amends.

It was a fine Monday morning and she was just back from the doctor's house, where Mary Rix had been blithely singing along with her sewing machine in the new, light and airy little room. Dr Rix, too, had been cheerful and self-assured. Lois comforted herself that at least she had done *some* good in the last few months. Who cared now about that tiny baby in a faded photograph? Gloria was gone. Lois could only do harm by pursuing Mary Rix's connection with the baby and bringing new shadows into the doctor's house when his wife had swept them all away with such courage.

'Josie! How nice . . .' She looked at the kitchen table, all set ready for lunch for three, and the tempting smell of pizza coming from the oven. 'You shouldn't have done this,' Lois admonished.

Josie smiled. 'Better than mooning around doing nothing. I'm fed up with the telly, Mum. And the doctor said I could start being more active.' Lois saw that Josie's cheeks were pink and her eyes bright, and realized that she had finally more or less recovered.

'Well, thanks, love,' she said. 'Something in the oven smells great!' She took off her coat, and washed her hands. 'Maybe we could go shopping this afternoon? Get you some new things for going back to school?'

To her surprise, Josie shook her head. 'No, I think I'd better stay around here,' she said. 'Might get a visitor, if I'm lucky.' Though Lois asked her twice who the visitor would be, Josie refused to answer.

She laughed. 'You'll see,' she said. 'And anyway, he might not be able to make it.'

Then Lois knew. It was Melvyn, the only 'he' that was guaranteed to bring that blush to Josie's face.

'I see,' she said with a sigh. They had thought he was safely out the way. Well, maybe Melvyn wouldn't make it. And maybe he would.

It was around half past two when the doorbell went and Josie rushed to answer it. Lois heard Melvyn's voice and a silence that could only have been a warm embrace. She stayed in the sitting room, praying for guidance on how to handle this, until the pair came into the room. Josie's smile was wide and Melvyn looked somehow older, although he hadn't been away for long.

'Hello, Mrs Meade. Nice to see you again.' He came forward and gave her a peck on the cheek and brushed her with an adult scent of aftershave and soap.

Such charm, such self-assurance in one so young. Lois felt uneasy, certain that whatever it was about Melvyn that now made her feel vaguely threatened, was not imagination, nor to do with being an over-protective mother. He was too smooth, too confident that he could win her over. She remembered now how easily he had gained her sympathy, against Derek's strongly expressed disapproval. No longer sure of her own judgement after recent events, Lois was coolly pleasant to Melvyn, but made it plain to him that Josie was still convalescent and he should not stay too long and tire her. Josie protested that she was fine, but Lois made a point of saying she was only fourteen, and would have to do what her mother told her for a few more years. She said it lightly, made a little joke of it, but Josie could not mistake the authority in her voice.

Melvyn just smiled his warm smile and after a while suggested that as it was such a lovely day, perhaps Lois would allow Josie to come for a short stroll. The fresh air would do her good, he urged. Lois could not reasonably argue with this, but made them promise to be back in half an hour at the latest. Josie took Melvyn's hand as they went down the path and Lois fought back an irrational desire to pull Josie back.

'So the bugger came, did he,' said Derek. They were preparing for bed after an evening in front of the television. Things were not good between them. Derek said little and many of Lois's remarks were still barbed, in spite of knowing that this was getting them nowhere.

How long does it take? she wondered. She could see all the arguments for taking a reasonable line, for putting Derek's unfaithfulness behind her, for making a new start. All good common sense, but wounded pride, she supposed it was, kept breaking the surface and out would come a taunt, or a sharp remark, that set them back again. But why should she do all the work? Derek was the transgressor! Let *him* mend the fences, and make her feel secure again. But he didn't. He came and went, did all he could to help Josie's recovery, was his usual fatherly self with the boys, and teased Lois's mother in the same old way. With Lois, he was guarded. It was almost as if he was frightened of her. He was polite, of course. He didn't rise to her taunts, and most of the time she realized he was keeping out of her way.

'Yes, Melvyn came,' said Lois. 'They went for a walk and he got her back home at the time I said. He was charming, friendly and affectionate. Josie was over the moon.'

'Huh,' said Derek.

Lois was silent for a few seconds. 'Derek,' she said.

'Yes?'

'Why don't you like him? He doesn't seem to put a foot wrong.'

'Have you forgotten?' he said. 'That time in the factory?'

'No, but Josie could have been exaggerating . . .' It was no good. She knew Derek was right and it was a relief to admit it. 'No, she wasn't, was she,' she continued. 'There's something about him . . . I didn't feel comfortable about him and Josie today. I should've listened to you before.'

It was a small advance, but Derek saw his chance. 'Probably nothing in it,' he said magnanimously. 'But I think we should make sure she doesn't get involved with him again. With luck, he'll get interested in some new girl where he now lives. Anyway, Lois,' he added, hopping into bed and looking at her hopefully. 'Fancy a cuddle? Kiss and make-up, gel?'

He held his breath, and to his enormous relief Lois managed a smile. 'Cheeky bugger,' she said, and slipped in beside him.

Next morning, Derek whistled as he went off to work, and Lois's mother noticed. 'Thank goodness for that,' she muttered. 'Come on, boy,' she said cheerfully, helping Jamie into his jacket. 'The Professor's this morning, isn't it?' she said to Lois. 'Well, Josie's coming home with me and then we're going up the shopping centre. OK?'

'Fine,' said Lois, grinning at her mother.

On her way to Farnden, for the first time since Josie's illness, Lois realized she was thinking about the murder again. She tried to banish the thought, but it returned. Many times since that awful day when Josie had been taken ill, she had remembered Peter White's kindness and support. She had also noticed the concern in the vicar's expression when Derek had joined her in the hospital and there was no longer any need for him to stay. Afterwards, when he'd frequently asked how Josie was progressing, she had looked at his serious face and told herself that such a man was not capable of committing murder.

She stopped at the village shop for bread and as she emerged Rachel Barratt drew up in her car. She wound down the window and called out to Lois that she was going to see a friend for the day, but Lois could carry on as usual. 'Malcolm's there,' she added. 'Perhaps you'd make him a coffee? He's working on something urgent, so you'll probably not get into his study!' She laughed gaily, and drove off, leaving Lois muttering that she wouldn't care if she never went into his study again.

The house seemed quiet to Lois, as if no one was there, but if Malcolm was high up in his study, she wouldn't hear anything anyway. She began cleaning up the kitchen, thinking resentfully that Rachel usually cleared the breakfast things before gadding off on a jaunt. She put on the radio softly, as she always did if left alone in a house. Suddenly, she wasn't alone, and there was Malcolm at the door.

'Shut that thing off!' he said, with no preliminaries. 'I want a word with you,' he added, and advanced into the room.

Lois backed towards the sink, her heart thudding. For God's sake! It was probably only about coffee . . . She said quickly, 'I'm busy. It can wait until I bring your coffee.' She tried to edge round towards the door.

'You can do what you're bloody well told!' he shouted at her. 'What did I say, Lois Meade? Keep out of my private business! And what do I find? You've been ringing a friend of mine, pretending to be a wrong number! My God, I'll . . .'

He advanced further and grabbed her arms. She had time to see that his eyes were bloodshot and his breath stank . . . but, then her head began to swim.

'Lois?' Malcolm's voice was far away, coming to her through a thick fog. It was such an effort to hear him that she gave up. But she had been frightened . . . wasn't that it? Something had terrified her and the feeling was coming back. Threatened . . .

someone was threatening her, coming closer. She could smell his breath. She could still smell it, very close, and suddenly she was conscious, and very frightened indeed.

Malcolm's face was close to hers and she pushed him away violently. 'Leave me alone!' she tried to shout, but it came out as a squeak.

'Now, Lois,' he said, his voice controlled now and full of oily concern. 'You fainted, my dear. Probably been doing too much, with your daughter's illness and all of that. Just relax for a few minutes, then I'll make you a cup of tea. Hot and sweet?' He smiled at her and backed away as she sat up, shaking with the effort.

'I don't want tea,' she said. 'I'm going home and I shall not be back here . . . ever again.' Holding on to the edge of the table, she managed to stand up. The kitchen was revolving again and she grabbed the draining board with both hands. But the realisation that she now had her back to Malcolm gave her strength enough to turn around. She took a tentative step, then another, and to her huge relief the whirling vertigo settled down and she was able to reach the door. 'I don't know what happened,' she said, 'but I expect it'll come back to me. I just know I have to go. No, don't come near me!' she added quickly, as he moved to hold the door open for her. 'I'll give Rachel a ring.'

She got the car going with difficulty. It was as if she was driving alone for the first time. She had to remind herself of each step. Turn the key . . . foot on clutch . . . into gear . . . When the car moved away slowly from the Barratts' house, she noticed a car behind her. In her driving mirror she saw Keith Simpson at the wheel and she raised her left hand in salute. Once outside Farnden and approaching Alibone Woods, she suddenly began to feel dizzy again and decided to stop. She wanted to think, anyway, in peace and quiet. It was her best hope of recalling what had happened. Keith slowed up, opened his window and yelled, 'OK Lois?' She felt dizzy, but the last thing she wanted was anxious attention from Keith Simpson, so she nodded and waved him on, pulling into the layby. He accelerated fast and disappeared.

Alibone Woods in spring shimmered with bluebells and

crowds came from town to see them, but now it was winter, quiet and deserted. This was where Hunter Cowgill had suggested they should meet, but she'd had no occasion to call him. She got out of the car and walked up a wide track under the tall beech trees which extended across the landscape as far as she could see. The brilliant sun had gone and heavy clouds hung over the woods. The chilly solitude surrounding Lois cleared her head. She had been frightened, terrified, and it was something Malcolm Barratt did or said. He'd appeared suddenly, making her start with surprise. The radio had been on, she remembered. That's right . . . he'd told her to turn it off and then he started shouting at her. Why? She took a narrow path deeper into the woods and a rabbit scuttled across her path. Normally, she thought, I should be scared stiff of a running rabbit. Nothing would have persuaded me into a lonely wood on my own, but now, she thought, there were far worse things to be scared by.

A mossy tree stump, the remains of an ancient oak, served as a damp seat. She felt shaky again and hoped she'd be able to find the car again. She'd left her mobile there, so she couldn't phone Derek to come and rescue her. Telephone . . . It was something to do with a phone call . . . Pamela! He'd said that name, shouted it at the top of his voice. Suddenly, she remembered it all. The accusation, his spitting rage as he advanced on her in the kitchen. She'd fainted then. Did he touch her? She felt her throat tentatively, but it was not in the least sore. No bruises anywhere, so he didn't touch her. But if she hadn't fainted, she was sure he would have attacked her. He'd been out of control, with flecks of white at the corners of his mouth.

Pamela . . . It was the name in the address book on his desk, and she had been going to ring her up and pretend to be a wrong number. She'd decided against it because she couldn't see anything to be gained from it. After all, the woman would hardly be likely to say anything of interest to a perfect stranger. Someone had phoned Pamela, though. It must have been Rachel. Perhaps she'd noticed the name just as Lois had done, and had suspicions. After all, she had every reason. Malcolm was an old letch and had just returned from some mysterious absence. Rachel was only human.

Lois stood up, brushing the back of her damp coat. People'll think I've wet myself, she thought, and began to laugh. It was such a relief to know she would not be going back to the Barratts. There would be no problem about getting another job, she knew. Mary Rix was always asking if she had any free time to clean for other people in the village. 'Good riddance, Professor Barratt!' she yelled to the silent wood. Lois set off back down the narrow path, looking down at her feet as she picked her way through puddles and heaps of fallen twigs. Suddenly there was a shadow in front of her and she looked up in terror.

'Morning Lois,' said Inspector Cowgill. 'I hope I didn't startle you.' But Lois was swaying and he had to reach out quickly to support her. 'Here, steady!' he said and put an arm around her, furious with himself for being so insensitive. Simpson had telephoned him from his car and he'd come straight out to the woods, sure that something was up. Clearly Lois had had a shock of some kind.

She straightened up and shook off his arm, then leaned against a tree trunk, breathing hard. 'Sorry,' she said. 'I'm OK now. It was just that . . .' She frowned and looked at him fiercely. 'What the hell are you doing here, anyway? I didn't . . .' she said.

'Keith Simpson,' he said, and waited. 'Sure you're all right?' he said after a few seconds.

'Yep,' she said. 'And the reason I'm here is that I wanted to be on my own.'

'Fine,' said Hunter Cowgill, turning round. He was getting used to Lois now.

She followed him slowly, but before they reached the wide track, she stopped again. 'Listen,' she said, and he turned and faced her, eyebrows raised. 'There was something. Malcolm Barratt. He had a go at me. At least, if I hadn't passed out, I think he was going to. Something about one of his women. Anyway, I got out quick, and shan't be going back. Told him so. Now, I just need to settle down for a minute and then go home. So you can go. I don't want you doing anything about it.'

185

She could see now that he'd backed along the track into the wood so that his car would not be seen from the road. He thought of everything.

Now he said, 'Fair enough, Lois. We'll keep an eye on him. But I'd be glad if you'd think again about leaving the Barratts. Can't influence you, of course. Just give it some more thought.' She said nothing and he walked away from her. She followed slowly and as he got into his car he turned back and raised his hand. 'Take care,' he called, and drove off.

Lois's car started without trouble this time and she felt calm enough to call in at the supermarket in Tresham for supplies. It was lunch time when she arrived back in Byron Way, her spirits restored. For the moment she saw no reason to question her mother's presence, sitting there in her kitchen in the middle of the day . . . until she saw her face.

'Mum? What's up?' Her mother looked at least ten years older and seemed on the verge of tears.

'It's Josie,' she said. 'She ran away from me.'

'What d'you mean?' said Lois. 'She's not a little kid. She wouldn't run away?' She still felt soothed by Hunter Cowgill's reassuring remarks, and wondered fleetingly if her mother was wandering a bit. After all, she was getting on.

'It was that lad,' said her mother and suddenly Lois's composure evaporated. 'Melvyn. He turned up in the centre. Came out of nowhere. And before I knew it, Josie was taking his hand and saying she was just going off to have a coffee with him and would meet me outside John Lewis in half an hour.' She stopped, and her eyes filled.

'And?' said Lois urgently. Her heart was pounding and she could hardly breathe. 'For God's sake, Mum, what happened! Where is she?'

'She didn't turn up. I waited an hour, then went to the information office and they made an announcement . . . you know, like they do for lost kids. But Josie didn't turn up and her mobile was switched off. In the end, they told me to go home and see if she'd gone back alone. After all, they said, she is fourteen.'

'She wasn't at your house, then,' said Lois. 'So you phoned the police, for Christ's sake?'

Her mother nodded. 'They told me not to worry, she'd be sure to turn up. Probably gone home, they said. Let us know if she doesn't turn up by bedtime, they said. I expect they thought I was just a silly old woman.' Her mother was crying now, and Lois slumped down into a chair.

'So now what?' she said. Her immediate instinct was to telephone Derek. But he was working twenty miles away, the other side of Fletching. A big job, he'd said, and he was anxious to finish it today. With all the recent troubles, he'd got behind with his schedule, and was planning to work solidly until he caught up. He wouldn't thank her for ringing now, when Josie might turn up at any moment.

'What time did you get to the centre, then?' she said handing her mother a tissue.

'Ten-ish. We went straight there after dropping the boys off at school. Lois . . .' she added. 'I waited and waited. Where can she have gone?'

Lois shook her head. Her imagination had begun to work and, although she tried to subdue rising panic, she knew she'd have to ring Derek. He had to be told, angry or not, and might have something useful to suggest. After a conversation that began acrimoniously, then became accusatory when Derek said Lois shouldn't have allowed Josie to go in the first place, and finally settled down to practicalities, he suggested they wait at home for a while, then ring round Josie's friends. He'd be back as soon as he could.

Feeling a little reassured, Lois gave her mother a cup of strong coffee and went upstairs to look for clues in Josie's room. From her mother's account, it seemed to Lois pretty clear that Melvyn had arranged this meeting. That meant they probably fixed it up on that walk. Josie was sure to have known where he was staying in Tresham. Lois turned over school books, lurid teenage magazines full of stuff about how to get your man and piles of tapes littering Josie's work table. Nothing. If she could only find Josie's address book . . .

Think, Lois, she told herself. Put all your famous powers of detection to work. Telephone pad. If Josie had made a call to Melvyn, there was just a chance. She rushed downstairs and saw an unfamiliar Tresham number scribbled on the pad. She dialled, holding her breath, but the ringing tone seemed to go on for ever. Finally it was answered.

'Who's that?' said a gruff voice.

'You won't know me,' she said.

Before she could continue, the voice said, 'Well, I don' wanna talk to ya, then,' and the call was cut off.

She dialled again. 'Who's that!' said the same voice, more irritated now.

'I'm a friend of Melvyn's,' said Lois quickly. 'Can I speak to him?'

There was a silence, and then, 'E's not 'ere. Gone. Get it? And don' ring agen.' Once more the receiver was banged down.

But he had been there. And Josie had spoken to him and arranged to meet, and now they had disappeared together. Panic rose again in Lois, but this time she could not subdue it. She lifted the receiver once more and dialled Police Constable Keith Simpson.

Thirty-Two

'Are we nearly there?' said Josie. She was tired. They had been travelling for two hours and although Melvyn had stopped twice, buying her cans of drink and sandwiches, she felt weary and dispirited.

'Yep, only five more miles on the motorway, then about twenty minutes up the lane to my uncle's farm.'

'What will he say?' said Josie.

'He's nearly blind now,' said Melvyn. 'He won't think nothing of it. He's Dad's brother and we often go and stay with him. Help him on the farm in summer. He's a bachelor and his house is a tip. But he's nice. He'll make us welcome.'

Josie didn't fancy staying in a tip, but she looked across at Melvyn's profile and felt proud that he had chosen her. He could have had any of the girls in his year, all seventeen and streetwise. She came from a sheltered home by comparison. The thought of home gave her a nasty jolt. She blinked hard and looked out of the window. It was growing dark and she couldn't see much.

'I've got to phone my Mum and Dad,' she said.

'When we get there,' Melvyn replied. 'You can tell them you've come away for a break. Some north country air in your lungs. Do you a power of good.' He reached for her hand and brought it up to his mouth, kissing the tips of her fingers. 'You'll be fine with me, Josie,' he said.

'Where did you get this car?' Josie said. It was a small, newish Renault and had mopped up the miles with ease.

'Borrowed it from a friend,' said Melvyn casually. 'He said I could have it for a few days. He owes me.'

'What for?' asked Josie, but it was an idle question. She did not really want to know. The wonderful, exciting feeling of being with Melvyn, alone in a car, miles from home, was wearing thin. Would they be worrying? She could imagine Dad having a go at Mum and probably Gran as well. She would phone as soon as they arrived.

The track up to the farm was bumpy and the small car, so brilliant on the motorway, now jerked Josie about until her chest hurt. Potholes threw them from side to side and she was nearly in tears when they finally stopped. It was pitch dark, with only a dim light showing the stone wall of an old house. Melvyn got out and walked round to her side of the car.

'Out you come,' he said kindly. He took her hand. 'Come and meet Uncle Ned, then we'll get the bags out.'

The farm kitchen was dimly lit, warm and very smelly. Two squirming spaniels greeted them with delight, but Josie pushed them away with growing panic. What had she done? Where on earth were they? The old man shuffling towards them, his eyes looking all over the place, everywhere but at her, terrified her.

'Melvyn!' she said. 'I want to go home!'

'Don't be silly!' he hissed at her. 'You'll annoy him. Just say hello and then we'll find a room to sleep.'

Suddenly Josie was very frightened. 'I want to phone home,' she said.

The old man cackled. 'Got no phone, me duck,' he said. 'Tomorrow, you can go down to the box on the corner. If it's working, that is . . .'

He cackled again, and Josie began to shake. 'I don't feel well,' she said.

'Oh, for God's sake,' said Melvyn. 'Come on, I'll take you to the phone box, if that's what you want.' He turned and led her out of the door, back into the yard, and then, tripping and half-running, they made their way down the dark lane.

Keith Simpson had been a tower of strength, suggesting that he would report Josie still missing, then get on down to the station to get things moving. 'She's probably gone to the pictures with him and will give you a ring. They'll have a quick burger and then home, I shouldn't wonder,' he said. 'She'll turn up, Lois. You said he wasn't a bad lad. Try not to worry.' She hadn't told him about the factory incident, and wondered if she should. There was still this nagging doubt about the truth of Josie's account, and she was reluctant to blacken the lad's name unless it was really necessary. She'd tell Keith later.

Now it was tea time and still no Josie. Derek had gone off into Tresham to the house where the Hallhouses used to live, to see if he could get their new address or telephone number and he hadn't come back yet. Lois had lost count of how many cups of coffee she'd made and when Derek came through the kitchen door she realized her hands were shaking uncontrollably.

'Well?'

'I got the number,' he said, making straight for the telephone.

Lois subsided on a kitchen chair and clenched her fists to stop the shaking. She heard the ringing tone stop and the sound of a voice. Derek asked if Melvyn was there, and she heard a woman's voice saying that he was staying in Tresham with a friend for a few days.

'Do you know where he's staying?' said Derek.

'Not sure of the address,' said the woman. 'But I've got a phone number.'

Derek wrote it down and then asked that the minute Melvyn got in touch to tell him to phone the Meades.

'Is there something wrong?' said the woman.

'I hope to God not,' said Derek. 'He's got my daughter with him . . . she's only fourteen and if he does her any harm, I'll have his guts for garters.' He banged down the receiver and checked the number with Lois. It matched the one on the pad, and he dialled again.

'Hello! What'ya want? . . . no, for Christ's sake, bloody Melvyn's not 'ere. 'E was, and 'e's gone.' The phone line went dead, just as it had with Lois and she realised they had got nowhere.

Derek sat down at the table and put his head in his hands. 'It's getting dark,' he said.

'The police have got all the details,' said Lois. 'They'll find her.'

'Wanna bet?' said Derek. 'Fourteen-year-old kid from the Churchill Estate gone missing? Must be an everyday event for them.'

'Shut up, Derek!' Lois burst out. 'We've got to trust them.' She thought of Keith Simpson, moving into action straight away, full of reassurance. He would have told Cowgill by now and Lois was glad of that.

Silence fell between them. Her mother had got Douglas and Jamie and had said she would keep them for the night. They had been excited about staying with Gran in the middle of a school week and had gone off cheerfully. Now there was nothing to say. The silence lengthened and when the telephone rang, both of them jumped up and rushed to answer it.

'Hello! Is that you, Josie?' Lois had got there first and Derek was holding her fast, his ear as close to the receiver as it would go.

'Mum?' The voice was faint, but it was unmistakeably Josie. 'Mum, I'm all right.'

'Where are you, Josie? Tell me where you are and we'll come and get you.' Derek nodded violently, clinging on to Lois in his anxiety to hear Josie's voice.

'No, I'm all right. Melvyn's looking after me . . .' Lois could hear his voice, but not the words.

'Josie, listen to me,' she said. 'It's not legal for him to take you away. He'll be in big trouble if you don't tell us where you are this minute.'

'I don't know where I am,' said Josie, and Lois could hear tears in her voice.

Oh God, what could they do? 'Don't ring off,' she said. 'Whatever you do, don't ring off!'

'I'm a bit frightened, Mum . . .' Melvyn's voice in the background again, but once more Lois couldn't make out what he was saying.

'Put Melvyn on the phone,' she said, and then wished she hadn't. She wanted to hold on to Josie, if only through the telephone line. It was her only hope.

''Lo, Mrs Meade. Don't worry. I'm looking after her. Give her a few days of good Yorkshire air and she'll be right as rain in no time.' His voice sounded firm and controlled, although not threatening.

'Where are you?' she said. 'My Uncle Ned's farm,' he said, with no apparent effort at concealment. 'Near Skipton. Lovely country here. You can come up too, if you want.'

'He's not right in the head,' muttered Derek. 'Give us the phone. What's the address?' he said.

'Stone House Farm, Easedale,' said Melvyn. 'But she'll be OK. I'll look after her,' he repeated.

'You'd better,' Derek said.

They had another talk with Josie, tried to reassure her and without saying what they were going to do next, finally and reluctantly put down the telephone. Derek marched into the hall and got his coat.

'Come on,' he said. 'Bring the map and we'll be up there in two hours. Hurry up, gel,' he added. 'Sooner we get there the better. And don't bother ringing your police pal. We can settle this without them.'

Josie awoke to the sound of doves cooing loudly outside the window and for several moments had no idea where she was. She rubbed her eyes and sat up. The bed was iron-framed and somebody had some time ago painted it white and gold. The gold was chipped here and there, revealing black metal beneath, and the boss of roses in the centre of the headboard showed traces of a virulent salmon pink, also peeling. The mattress she sat on was lumpy and now as she looked around her she saw that everything in the tiny room was old, scratched and unsteady. But it was clean. Mum would notice that straight away.

Last night came back slowly to her as she shook the sleep out of her head. Melvyn had found sheets and blankets and together they had made up this narrow bed. He'd made sure she had everything she wanted (except her mother and that was what she wanted most) and had disappeared, saying he would see her in the morning, when they would go for a lovely long ramble over the moor. The last thing she remembered was thinking that she'd never get to sleep in this strange and lonely place.

She slipped out of bed and went over to the window. The sun was up, and everything glistened with hoar frost. It was like fairyland. The nearest thing to it Josie had seen was the Christmas display in the shopping centre. But this magic transformation stretched as far as her eye could see. The farmyard below was swept clean and, like an illustration in a children's book, a horse's head peered out over the top of a stable door. As she looked out, the horse whinnied and plumes of steam came from his flared nostrils into the frosty air. Beyond, she could see a grassy meadow and tall, bare trees. The grass sparkled, and every bare branch bore a miraculous coating of shining, glittering frost. She struggled with the window catch, and managed to open it, gasping at the inrush of sharp, cold air. When she got used to the icy clearness of it, she took deep breaths and found herself smiling.

'Hi! Did you sleep OK?' It was Melvyn, dressed already in jeans and a thick jersey, below in the yard. He was grinning at her, and Josie pulled her nightdress tightly around her.

She nodded. 'It's great!' she said, gesturing widely with one arm. 'Never seen anythin' like this!'

'Get dressed, then,' called Melvyn. 'Breakfast's ready. Uncle Ned's gone into town to get chicken feed. We can go for a walk later . . . get some of this air into you.'

He made her sound like a flat tyre, she thought, but she splashed freezing cold water from a jug on a wash stand over her face and hands and got dressed quickly. She looked around the room, wondering what to do with the dirty water in the flowery china basin. A strange-looking bucket stood under the washstand. It had a lid with a hole in the centre, and, hoping it was the right thing, she carefully tipped the water into the sloping sides of the lid. It disappeared with a gurgle and she reminded herself to empty it later. By now she desperately wanted the lavatory and ventured out into the narrow dark corridor outside her bedroom. One or two doors opened into bedrooms with similar beds, but bare of everything except lumpy mattresses. None of them was a lavatory. Blimey! What did the rest of them do?

'Josie?' It was Melvyn at the foot of the stairs. 'Come on, I've boiled you an egg.' She rushed downstairs and with her legs crossed asked him urgently where she should go.

'Down the yard,' he said with a grin.

'What?' shrieked Josie, unsure of whether Melvyn was joking or not.

'Down there.' He pointed to a small, slate-roofed hovel at the far end of the yard. 'Used to be a two-holer,' he said. 'But it's a proper one now.'

Not waiting to ask him what a two-holer was, Josie ran down the yard, nearly came a cropper on the slippery cobbles, and bolted herself in the hovel with relief. It was clean, and hanging on a nail was a farming magazine, which Josie realized was in lieu of a toilet roll. The shiny paper did not do a very good job, but she had a tissue in her pocket, and that helped. She emerged again into the sunlit yard and began to walk back towards Melvyn, who stood waiting for her at the kitchen door.

How did he get to be so grown-up? she thought. Not once had he wavered, or seemed unsure, during their journey north. And after that call to Mum and Dad, he'd put his arm around her and taken her back to the house. She'd seen that Uncle Ned was a wizened, but friendly old man and soon Melvyn had suggested they go to bed. She had felt a moment's panic, but then he'd led her to the little room with a single bed and she knew that she wasn't expected to share his. She knew her parents would be here sooner or later, but had been quite glad they hadn't turned up in the middle of the night. Probably on the way right now.

The smell of toast wafted across the yard towards her and she felt hungry. She ate a boiled egg and three pieces of toast and butter – butter like she'd never tasted before – and felt good. Mum and Dad knew where she was, Melvyn was not pushing her to do anything she didn't want to do, and outside that door was an amazing world of space and light, and just the sounds of birdsong and the cackling of hens from the yard.

'Come on, then, gel,' said Melvyn. He handed her a pair of old wellington boots. 'These look about right for you,' he said and helped her pull them on over a pair of thick socks that smelt of dog. One of the spaniels was jumping about in excitement, barking sharply.

'Shall we take the dogs?' Josie said. 'Where're the leads?'

'Leads?' said Melvyn. 'They don't need no leads.' He led the way across the yard and out into the field through a heavy gate. The spaniels ran on ahead, their paws leaving a trail on the frosty grass. Suddenly Josie was laughing, not at anything in particular, but just in delight at the beauty of it all. She skipped along beside Melvyn, trying to keep up with his long strides.

He looked at her and smiled. 'That's right, Jose,' he said, and reached for her hand.

It had been a difficult task persuading Derek not to set off for Yorkshire straight away.

'How are we going to find this farm, right in the middle of nowhere, in the dark?' Lois had argued.

'I'll find it,' Derek had replied grimly. They had quarrelled violently, then, with Lois bringing up all the old anger. She said irrationally that if she hadn't been so shocked about him and Gloria, with her mind distracted away from where it should have been, on the family, she wouldn't have . . .

'Wouldn't have what?' Derek had shouted at her. 'Let Josie go off with your mother? Gone back to work in Farnden? If you hadn't been so taken up with playing detective, more likely . . . Don't be ridiculous, Lois,' he had added more calmly. 'It's just one of them things. Would've happened sooner or later whatever we'd done. That Melvyn is a weirdo, and he's not having my Josie any longer than is absolutely necessary. Get your coat!' he'd ordered.

Lois had refused, saying they'd do more harm than good arriving in the small hours. 'Won't stop anything happening. It'll have happened by the time we get there, if it's going to happen at all,' she said. 'We'll leave first thing in the morning and arrive at a sensible hour. If we can put this thing right without going mad, or getting the police storming in, it'll do the least damage to Josie. Surely even you can see that, Derek? After all, the lad's not an escaped loony, or anything . . .'

She had persuaded him in the end and they'd gone to bed, where neither of them had slept at all. As dawn broke, Lois went downstairs and made strong tea. They forced down a plate of cereal and, aware of curious eyes at several neighbouring windows, set off in Lois's car, through a silent estate, and on round the bypass to the motorway.

'His mother sounded quite nice,' said Derek, as they drove uninterrupted up the misty motorway. They had both calmed down and were talking together in a way they hadn't for quite a while.

'You know all them boys are fostered, except Melvyn, and he's adopted?' said Lois. 'Nosy-parker postman told me. The parents couldn't have kids of their own. She's a very good mother, according to him. Kids are always well turned-out, and more polite than most. Not that that means much,' she added, with a lurching stomach. 'Lots of criminals are very gentle, polite people.'

'Speaking from experience?' said Derek.

Lois did not reply and there was silence for a few miles. She had not told Derek about yesterday's scene at the Barratts. It had seemed unimportant compared with Josie's disappearance. She was reluctant for another reason; she knew Derek was fed up with the Farnden murder mystery, and would for two pins forbid Lois to go there any more. He knew as well as she did that she could get work anywhere. Of course, he couldn't actually forbid her. She had more than once told him to get stuffed and done what she knew he disapproved of. But they were little things. This was a big one. Maybe she shouldn't leave the Barratts' after all. Perhaps she should go along with Malcolm's deception that the whole row had never happened, that she had just fainted from tiredness and overwork? Ah well, time enough to worry about that one.

'Sun's coming out,' said Derek beside her. 'Got any coffee left in that flask?'

'How much further?' she asked, handing Derek a beaker of coffee.

'About another hour,' he said. 'Should we stop for something to eat?'

Lois shook her head. 'Keep going,' she said.

The car wouldn't do much more than sixty-five and the motorway stretched endlessly away into the distance. The mist had cleared and the sun shone into Lois's eyes. She closed them and leaned her head back against the seat.

'You can have a nap,' said Derek.

'Some hope,' said Lois, but three minutes later she was asleep.

High up on the hill above Uncle Ned's farm, Melvyn and Josie stood looking across the valley. 'It's fantastic!' said Josie. 'Why don't we all come and live up here, instead of that muck-hole Churchill Estate?'

Melvyn shook his head. 'This is for holidays,' he said. 'Towns are for school and work. I'm getting a job soon. Earn some money, then I'll get a place of me own. Will you come and live with me, Josie? We could get married later . . .'

Josie looked at him. 'I'm only fourteen,' she said, a tremor in her voice.

'Yes, I know. Not straight away. Later, I said.' He kissed her cold face and hugged her tight. 'I'm going to have me own home and kids, one day. I'll be a real father.' He let go of her, and looked away. 'You know my dad's not my real father,' he said.

Josie shook her head, but didn't say anything. He seemed to be talking more to himself than to her. 'I know who my real one is, though,' he continued. 'And me real mum. Though I don't often see them.'

He fell silent and neither spoke for a minute or two. The road lay beneath them, a whitish scar across the silvery green landscape. Josie could see a line of heavy lorries crawling along like her brothers' toys. Behind them, she made out a familiar shape.

'Hey!' she said, grabbing Melvyn's arm. 'Hey, that's our car, isn't it?'

Melvyn lifted the binoculars he'd taken from his uncle's cupboard and studied the motorway. 'Yep,' he said flatly. 'That's your Mum and Dad. Come to get you. We'd better be getting back.' His expression was empty. He took Josie's hand, and they set off across the frozen fields, back towards the farm, where retribution awaited them.

Thirty-Three

'I felt sorry for him,' said Lois quietly. They were driving back down the motorway, Josie apparently fast asleep in the back of the car. It had been unexpectedly easy. The runaways had been waiting for them in the farmyard as they climbed unsteadily out of the car. Josie had not rushed into her mother's arms, nor had Derek punched Melvyn in the face, as he had threatened several times on the journey. Josie had smiled and remained close to Melvyn, holding his hand tightly.

It was Melvyn, polite as ever, who had spoken first. 'Morning Mrs Meade,' he'd said, and nodded to Derek. 'I expect you'd like something to eat and drink.' The normality of his suggestion had rendered the Meades speechless for a few seconds. Then Lois had stepped forward. It took all her strength to suppress a furious outburst. She had done a lot of thinking on the journey and decided that angry confrontation would get them nowhere.

She took a deep breath and said in a reasonable voice, 'We need to talk, Melvyn,' she had said. 'And you, Josie –' she'd added, giving her daughter's red cheek a brief kiss – 'can get your things together.'

'But—' Josie had stuttered.

'But nothing!' Derek had found his tongue and in spite of Lois kicking his shin warningly, he'd laid into the pair of them. He had no thoughts of sweet reasonableness. All his pent up anxiety spilled out in an accusing tirade.

Melvyn had said nothing. He allowed Derek to come to a spluttering halt, then said, 'I didn't mean no harm. Honest, Mr Meade. I just wanted Josie to get properly better.'

Derek had taken a breath, but before he could speak, Lois had interrupted. 'Let him finish,' she'd said. 'Go on, Melvyn.'

It seemed Melvyn had planned it all carefully, with Josie's

collusion. He had wanted to ask their permission, he said, but Josie said they would never allow it.

Derek had grunted, 'Too bloody right we wouldn't have!' but then waited for Melvyn to continue. He was soon through with describing their journey, Josie's being upset, and the telephone call home.

'She's fine this morning,' he'd said pleadingly. 'Don't you see, Mrs Meade? She looks great already . . .'

'Where's this Uncle Ned?' Derek had demanded. He clearly didn't believe he existed.

'Gone to town. Be back this afternoon,' answered Melvyn.

'Huh!' Derek had said. 'We shan't meet him, then. Come on, Lois, get back in the car. This is the end of it, young man,' he'd added to Melvyn. 'Just stay clear of Josie or by God I'll make you wish you had.'

Josie had reappeared, carrying her bag, but sobbing now. They'd driven away down the pot-holed lane, and Lois had a fierce pain in her stomach as her muscles clenched with tension and their success in finding Josie felt strangely nothing like a happy ending. Josie had watched Melvyn until they turned the corner into the main road and he was out of sight. Then she'd slumped in her seat and closed her eyes. She hadn't spoken since.

'Sorry for him?' Derek said in disbelief and Lois put her finger to her lips.

She nodded. 'It was his face,' she whispered.

'And what about what he's done to our Josie?' Derek was having difficulty keeping his voice down and Josie stirred in the back seat.

'He never done nothing,' she said in a small voice. 'So there. Never touched me. Well, not like . . . you know. Had my own bedroom. It was nice. Clean, Mum, in case you were wondering.' There was a pause and Lois and Derek looked at each other, but said nothing. 'We went for a walk. It was magic. And the dogs didn't even have to have no leads . . . I wish I could've stayed there for ever!' Then she was crying as if her heart would break. Derek drove on in silence, and Lois, for once, could think of nothing to say.

*　　*　　*

The police accepted that they wished to take no action and Keith Simpson repeated how pleased he was that it had all turned out reasonably well. 'She's probably had enough of a fright not to try anything like that again,' he said to Lois.

She agreed, but as she put down the telephone, she muttered, 'I'm not so sure.'

Nurse Surfleet had called later, anxious and a little annoyed. 'When you didn't show up,' she said, 'I naturally thought something was wrong. You always let me know, otherwise . . .' Gillian Surfleet had indeed been anxious, but for herself rather than Lois. There was an unpleasant atmosphere in the village, very like the ominous presage of a storm. Lois had not told her the truth, but invented a really bad headache.

'Even I get ill sometimes,' she'd said shortly.

The remains of the day were spent sorting out Josie's clothes, retrieving the boys from her mother and attempting to fix her mind back on the routine of house and family.

'School tomorrow for you, young lady,' Derek said to Josie. 'If you can go gadding round the country, you can damn well survive a day at school.' He was still angry, but Lois could see he was thawing. Josie kept out of his way until bedtime, but ventured a quick goodnight kiss on her father's cheek. 'Night,' he said gruffly. 'Tomorrow's another day.'

As Lois parked outside the vicarage on the Thursday, she reflected that although she had had one of the worst times of her life, here she was, back at work, greeting the Reverend White, just as if nothing had happened. Her hands trembled a little as she dusted and polished, and while she had the vacuum cleaner going, Peter White suddenly appeared, yelling at her that he was going to the shop. She jumped like a shot rabbit and switched off the machine.

'Sorry, Vicar. Startled me.'

Peter White looked at her pale face, at the black smudges under her eyes and said, 'Anything wrong, Lois? You know you can talk to me.' Even as he said it, he doubted very much that she would confide in him.

To his surprise, she slumped down in his desk chair. 'I

wouldn't mind a quick chat, if you've got time,' she said. The shabby familiarity of Peter White, his air of being defeated before he began, suddenly made it easy for her. Her earlier suspicions of him faded. He was just what he seemed to be, an ordinary bloke, not very good at his job, but with his heart in the right place. She told him the story of Josie and Melvyn without a pause. She did not include Derek's defection, or her nasty experience with Professor Barratt, but stuck to the terror she had felt when Josie, aged fourteen and very vulnerable, had gone missing. She told him about the long journey north, and the relief in finding Josie, but tempered with fears of what the pair might have been up to. 'According to Josie –' she said, now almost talking to herself, unaware that Peter White had moved across his study and was perched on a window seat staring at her intently – 'and I believe her though Derek doesn't, nothing wrong happened between them. He's a strange lad, that Melvyn. Not like the other kids at school. Old for his years.'

As she came to the end, there was a small silence, and then Peter White said, 'Lois dear, there is something you should know.' He was very serious and she turned to look at him enquiringly. She had expected soothing words, assurances that would set her mind at rest. But what he said next was far from soothing. 'I have come across the Hallhouse family in the past. There was gossip there a while ago. It might be as well to keep Josie away from Melvyn.'

'What kind of gossip?' said Lois sharply.

'It was the father . . . well . . . he's very strict . . . belongs to some bigoted religious sect.'

Oh, so that's it, thought Lois, and relaxed a little. Vicar has it in for them because they're not Church of England. But it wasn't that, she soon learned.

'The wife is a very good woman, apparently,' he continued. 'Does all kinds of charity work in the town and the boys love her dearly. But there was gossip about the father. Seems he was a bit more strict than we're used to these days and the young ones were very afraid of him, so the story went. It was just local gossip, but I did hear some rather unpleasant rumours about violence and aggressive behaviour.'

'Well, what's that got to do with Melvyn?' Lois asked and found herself thinking defensively that whatever else, he seemed one of the most gentle lads she had met. None of the crude belligerence of the other kids on the estate. He handled Josie as if she was a china doll.

'Probably nothing,' Peter White said slowly. 'I just thought I'd mention it. You know what they say about violence breeding violence.'

'Oh right, yes, thanks, Vicar,' she said. 'Derek has threatened Melvyn with God knows what if he comes near Josie again. Looks like Josie'll need watching, too. Mind you,' she added, 'Derek gave them such a blasting I don't think they'll try anything on again.'

Peter White's expression did not change. 'I wouldn't be too sure about that,' he said quietly. 'Don't forget Melvyn is a young man in many ways. Not a child any more. Not like Josie. Now, Lois,' he added with unusual confidence, 'it is time for coffee for both of us. And you are going to sit down with me in the kitchen, whether you like it or not!'

Ten minutes before Lois was due to leave the vicarage, there was a knock at the door. She heard the vicar open it and then the unmistakably brisk tones of Nurse Surfleet. 'Just delivering these parish council papers,' she said. 'I'd like you to have a good look at them before the meeting, if poss.' Lois eavesdropped idly. She wasn't really interested, still brooding about Josie. Then she heard her name. 'Is Lois still with you?' Gillian Surfleet said, and then the vicar came to the foot of the stairs and called.

'Just a little word, Lois,' said the nurse, when the vicar had shown them both into the sitting room and shut the door. 'I just thought I should warn you.'

Oh God, thought Lois, not another sodding warning!

Gillian Surfleet was continuing, 'It seems Professor Barratt has been saying to one or two people – I heard him myself in the shop – in a jokey way that we should all beware of Lois Meade, the snooping house cleaner. "Lock up your papers!" I heard him say to Dr Rix. The doctor was buying stamps and looked very surprised.'

Lois was stunned. How bloody dare he? She resisted the

impulse to rush out and tackle the Professor. Instead, she asked, 'What did Dr Rix say?'

'Snubbed him good and proper,' Gillian Surfleet said. 'Told him you had an exemplary record and had been a good friend to his family for some time.'

'And what did he have to say to that?'

'Unsquashable, that one. Just laughed, said one of his stupid Latin things, and added that the doctor couldn't say he hadn't been warned. Then he left the shop, still laughing!'

Gillian patted Lois on the arm, told her not to worry, but just be a bit cautious, then she was gone, saying she had to rush off to Fletching on an errand of mercy. Lois's first reaction was to go at once and sort out that disgusting Malcolm Barratt. What did he think he was playing at? When she calmed down, she began to think more rationally. There must be some reason for his actions. Was he scared she would make public his threatening behaviour? Was he frightened of something else, something she might have discovered about him if she had indeed been shuffling through his papers? Better do nothing, she decided finally. Give him enough rope and he could quite possibly hang himself.

The rest of the week and the weekend at home with Derek and the kids passed in an unnatural calm. When they spoke to each other, it was about trivial household matters. And at the Baers' on Friday, neither Dallas nor Evangeline had talked much to Lois, beyond the usual greetings, instructions and polite enquiries about her family. Lois had noticed that there were no papers on Dallas's desk. This was unusual. There were always piles of papers and an expensive onyx desk set. That was still there, but the trays of papers had gone. So, the distinguished professor had been talking to Dallas, too. Well, what did it matter? If Dallas Baer had anything to hide, he was sly enough to make sure he left nothing around by accident. He hadn't put a foot wrong since that episode of the fall, and he and Evangeline were both behaving like cats who'd got the cream. Lois had noticed the sudden appearance of baby books and waited for the news to be broken to her. She remembered the morning Evangeline had spent writing letters. That was probably when they'd found out. Well, she was not keen to rejoice with the Baers just at the moment. They could guard their wonderful secret for as long as they liked.

Lois decided to keep Malcolm Barratt's outburst to herself for the moment. If Dr Rix was in a good mood, she might mention it to him on Monday. Thank him for sticking up for her. She had grown fond of the doctor and his wife since they'd opened up the baby's room, and she trusted him to tell her the truth.

Derek had begun to tidy up the winter garden, pulling up yellowing stalks of sprouts and raking up leaves that had escaped his autumn sweeping. Spring won't be long, he'd promised her. She had told him about Peter White's warning and he'd looked alarmed. He never wanted to hear Melvyn's name mentioned again, he said sternly to Josie, and she'd flounced off upstairs, slamming her bedroom door behind her. The subject was closed, Derek had decided firmly, and it was time he got back to earning a living for them all.

Lois could not forget, however. She thought more than once of contacting Hunter Cowgill. Keith Simpson was helpful, but he didn't give her that comforting feeling of authority in charge. Josie's troubles were nothing to do with Gloria Hathaway, of course, so she would probably just get a polite brush-off from the Inspector. It would have to be Keith, then, she decided. He might remember something about the Hallhouses, something to reassure her. Lois could not get out of her mind that last sight of Melvyn, his face taut with misery as he watched their car bumping down the rutted track, his hand raised in a hopeless salute to a disappearing Josie.

Thirty-Four

D r Rix was in his surgery when Lois arrived on Monday as usual. She noticed that Mary Rix was still cheerful, full of promises to show Lois how the patchwork was going and plans for attending an exhibition of embroidery and needlework at Ringford Hall in the spring. The house was warm and friendly.

It was half way through the morning when Lois heard the doctor emerge, shouting to Mary that it was all clear and could he please have a cup of strong coffee. He joined his wife and Lois at the kitchen table and the three sat companionably drinking and talking about village events.

'The dreaded J. was waiting for me again this morning, first in the queue,' the doctor said, and his wife grimaced sympathetically. Lois had no idea who he meant, but smiled anyway. 'There every week, Lois,' he continued. 'One imagined ailment after another. Poor soul is a bit lacking, you know. What a family!' He went on to describe them, being careful not to name names, full of compassion and a sincere wish to do more than he was able.

Lois was fascinated. She looked at Dr Rix with admiration. This was a real doctor, who knew all the village people and listened to their most intimate confidings as well as just their ailments. She thought of the medical practice in Tresham, where you were lucky to see your own doctor and where each patient was given the allotted few minutes' attention, with no time for the chatting that often led to the real cause of illness.

It was with absolute confidence that Lois said, as Dr Rix finished his coffee and stood up to go, 'Could you spare me a few seconds, doctor? I just wanted to ask you something.'

He paused and looked at his wife. She nodded imperceptibly and he said that Lois should fire away, he had no secrets from Mary. For some reason, this took away all Lois's resolve and she stuttered something about rumours of Professor Barratt going round the village saying bad things about her. 'Still,' she added, 'I believe you stood up for me, doctor, and I just wanted to thank you.'

To her surprise, Dr Rix said shortly, 'I don't know what you're talking about, Lois. It doesn't do to listen to gossip. Now, Mary, if you'll excuse me, I must get on.' And he walked out of the kitchen before Lois could say anything more.

Left with Mary Rix sitting in silence at the table, Lois felt small and foolish. 'Right,' she said. 'Better get on myself,' and made to get up from her chair.

Mary stretched out her hand and patted Lois's arm. 'Don't worry about it,' she said. 'We all know you're completely reliable. Good gracious!' she continued, 'there's nobody less likely to snoop than you, Lois!'

So they did know. Then why had the doctor behaved so strangely? Oh, sod them all, thought Lois, and went back to work. Halfway through the morning, Dr Rix had a caller. It was Nurse Surfleet and as she was ushered into the doctor's surgery, she heard her say, 'Well, Andrew, I think the time has come now, don't you? Something will have to be done . . .' The study door shut behind them and Lois felt that nasty twinge of fear again. She lingered as long as she could, washing out dusters and tidying the broom cupboard, until Mary Rix reminded her of the time. The two were still closeted together as she left. Gillian Surfleet must have walked to the doctor's. Wouldn't she usually have had her car?

For goodness sake! Lois mentally rapped herself sharply across the knuckles. Wasn't it the most likely and normal thing for the community nurse to be in confidential consultation with the local GP? And why shouldn't she walk? It was only a matter of yards from her house to the surgery. Ridiculous to suppose that they were talking about her. On the other hand, it was Gillian who had warned her against accusations of snooping. But then Dr Rix had denied any knowledge of it. What were they up to? It was beginning to look very much as if they were in league together. But what for? And how was it all connected with Gloria Hathaway?

Lois thought hard about it on her way home and began to see connections. It would soon be time to contact Hunter Cowgill. She had just started on the ironing, and was immersed in a radio play, when the telephone rang.

'Hello, Lois,' said Keith Simpson. 'How's things now? All sorted out with young Josie?' Lois was grateful for his call and said that Josie had gone back to school and Derek had forbidden any more contact with Melvyn Hallhouse.

'By the way,' she said, 'I wanted to ask you something.'

Keith had heard none of the gossip about the Hallhouses and suggested she should forget about it. 'There aren't many of us who haven't given the kids a quick smack in the heat of the moment!'

'Yes, but this might have been a bit different . . .'

Keith Simpson sighed. 'I'm sure we'd have heard if there'd been anything serious, Lois,' he said. Then he announced the real reason for his call. The Inspector would like to meet.

'When?' said Lois, not sure that she was really ready.

'Now . . . well, as soon as you can get to Alibone Woods,' said Keith.

'But I've just started the ironing.' There was no answer to that, as she knew there wouldn't be, and she put away the ironing board, took her coat, and left the house. It was raining and she stepped straight into a puddle by her car. Her mood was not good by the time she reached the woods.

Hunter Cowgill's car was out of sight along the track, as before, and Lois walked on past it. He was waiting for her, leaning against a tree. 'Ah, Lois,' he said. 'Understand you've been having a spot of family trouble.'

'Yes,' said Lois, 'but that's not why you want to see me. I haven't got much time before the kids come back from school, so can we get on with it?'

His face changed, hardened, and he said, 'What do you know about the Rixes?'

Lois raised her eyebrows. 'Quite a lot,' she said. 'I've been there a long time. What d'you want to know?' Her mind was racing. She would have had no problem telling Cowgill everything she knew about the Rixes; Dr Rix's long record of dedication to his patients, his kindness to her, Mary's courage in dealing with the little nursery. Nothing to hide, not with the Rixes. That is, until this morning. First the doctor's strange reaction to her thanks for defending her against Professor Barratt, and then the conference with Nurse Surfleet. Try as she might, she could not get rid of a suspicion that something was out of kilter, something to do with her . . . the snooping cleaner.

'Well, have you ever heard anything said in their house about Gloria Hathaway? More than just the proper reaction to her murder? Were there any quarrels in your presence, between doctor and wife? Ever heard any gossip about the doctor's private life . . . you know?'

'Dr Rix? You mean having it off with somebody?' Lois was shocked. The very idea was so unthinkable that she laughed. 'He's like a nice old bear, only cleverer,' she said. 'Quite cuddly, in his way, but never sexy!' But as she said it, she knew that this was ridiculous. The doctor was not all that old, late fifties, and every bit as sexy as any other bloke who'd been good-looking and ambitious in his time. She'd never seen any hugs or kisses with Mary, but they were not that sort. Not in front of the servants, especially snooping ones. What on earth had they got hold of now? His next remark was another shock.

'We are investigating the possibility that Gloria Hathaway may have been closer to Dr Rix than just a doctor-patient relationship,' said Cowgill, in a very official voice. 'One or two leads have pointed us in this direction. We shall be asking for his help, of course, but I thought you might be able to come up with something to consolidate our suspicions.'

'Shop the doctor!' said Lois. 'Why should I do that when I've never seen or heard anything out of the way? I know for a fact that Gloria Hathaway was a disgusting old cow, but not with the doctor. He'd never have had anything to do with her . . . couldn't get her out of his surgery fast enough. No, you're barking up the wrong tree there, Inspector.'

Cowgill said, 'Disgusting old cow? Do you want to tell me more about that?'

So Lois gave him an edited version. It was a relief to tell someone outside the family, someone who scarcely knew Derek.

He just nodded and put his hand on her shoulder. 'Bloody men,' he said sympathetically. He asked no more questions about that and returned to questions about the doctor.

'We just need to find out a bit more,' and he gave her that half smile. 'There are, of course, other people who have come to our notice as suspects. They're not confined to your clients only! We have had information about the doctor from a village source . . . no one you know,' he added, his voice warming. 'And I'm afraid it is important enough for me to get you out here in the middle of a damp wood in winter when you could have been ironing and preparing tea for your family.'

'Have *you* got a family?' Lois asked suddenly.

His face closed up. 'Yes and no,' he said. 'But you won't want to know about that. Anyway, Lois, if you could just tell me anything . . . your routine at the doctor's, who lets in the patients, how much Mary Rix is involved in the practice, that kind of thing?'

He looked quite human now, even a bit sad, so Lois told him about Gloria being a regular at the surgery, about Mary Rix being cross that she took up so much of the doctor's time. She said it was nothing untoward. Everyone knew that Gloria was a creaking door, always some small ailment, but never anything really serious.

'It was serious in the end,' said Hunter Cowgill, and Lois waited for him to continue, but he changed the subject. 'Anyway, thanks, Lois. And if you think of anything else, just get in touch. Simpson thinks a lot of you, you know. Said you'd had a really rough time with your daughter. I do appreciate your coming.'

Lois shrugged and started back along the track. She half tripped over a concealed tree root and at once Hunter Cowgill was at her side, his hand under her arm. 'Careful,' he said smoothly. 'We don't want you coming to any harm.'

The ironing was finished by the time Josie came trudging through the door, shoulders drooping as if carrying the cares of the world.

'Hello, love,' Lois said. 'Busy day at school?'

'It was all crap,' said Josie. 'I'm tired. Don't want any tea.' She dumped her bag on the floor and went through to the hall and up the stairs without answering Lois's questions. Lois forgot all about the Rixes and Detective Inspector Cowgill and rushed upstairs after her.

'Don't you feel well?' she repeated anxiously. 'Let's have a look at you.'

With relief, she saw that Josie's eyes were clear, her cheeks a healthy pink from the cold rain and that apart from an expression of utter misery, she looked fine.

'I suppose it's Melvyn,' she said. Might as well come straight to the point. 'You think you're missing him?'

Josie gave her a contemptuous look. 'I *am* missing him,' she said and sat down on her bed, cuddling the ginger kitten and turning her back on her mother.

'Got a telling-off today,' she said after a few minutes' sulky silence.

'What for?' said Lois.

'Not doing my homework,' said Josie, with no sign of remorse. 'Why can't I leave school and get a job?'

'Because you are too young, as you very well know!' said Lois, losing patience.

'Melvyn said I could go and stay at his house, with his Mum and Dad, in the Easter holidays,' Josie said tentatively, as if knowing the answer to that one.

'Don't be ridiculous,' said Lois. 'You know your father would never hear of it. Don't even suggest it to him.'

'But *you* could, Mum. He listens to you.'

'I agree with him!' said Lois.

'Oh, go away,' said Josie.

Lois took a deep breath. 'Josie Meade,' she said. 'Look at me, please! I am not going away. You are my daughter and you're still a child. Your dad and me are responsible for you and until you're old enough to support yourself, you'll do what you're told. And be cheerful about it.' Josie was sitting up straight now, alarmed at her mother's sharp tone. 'And as for Melvyn,' Lois continued angrily. 'You can just forget he exists. There'll be plenty of boyfriends for you, you stupid girl. Nice lads, with proper ideas of how to go on. If you carry on with this nonsense, you'll end up with a social worker and quite likely put into care, being out of our control. So, if that's what you want, OK, carry on. Please yourself. But in the meantime, Dad and me will give the orders, and you'll do as we say.'

She steeled herself against weakening as she saw tears slide down Josie's face. 'Now get yourself cleaned up and come down and give me a hand with the tea,' she added briskly. 'Oh, and there's something else,' she said. 'Did you ever go to Melvyn's house when they lived in Tresham?'

Josie nodded. 'Once or twice,' she said.

'And meet his Mum and Dad?' Josie nodded again. 'They were nice,' she said. 'At least, his Mum was.'

'What about his Dad?' said Lois.

Josie hesitated. 'Bit funny,' she said.

'What d'you mean?'

'Well, sort of quiet and serious. Not friendly and nice like our Dad is most of the time. They were all a bit scared of him, I reckon,' she added.

'Right,' said Lois. 'Now, downstairs in five minutes, young lady, and no more of this nonsense.' She patted Josie's back forgivingly. But inside she felt uncomfortably apprehensive. I wish none of this had ever happened, she thought. Gloria and Derek, the doctor and Mary, horrible Malcolm Barratt, Josie and Melvyn. What was coming next? She went slowly downstairs to welcome her mother and Douglas and to give Jamie a bit of a hug.

Thirty-Five

Lois parked outside the Barratts' house instead of driving in. She was unsure of her reception this morning, her last words flung at Malcolm Barratt having been on the lines of good riddance to bad rubbish. She had intended never to go to the Barratts again, but Hunter Cowgill's gentle hint had convinced her that she should carry on, see it through to whatever nasty end was in store. She was sure now that Gloria's murder had been the result of circumstances involving more than one of Farnden's respectable residents. Not that the actual killing was necessarily done by more than one person – and she still was not sure who did it – but she was quite sure that the Rev Peter White, Professor Barratt, and possibly Dallas Baer were all entwined in something very nasty. The doctor and Nurse Surfleet were also involved, she was sure of that. Gillian Surfleet had certainly been fond of – possibly in love with – Gloria Hathaway. That could well have meant jealousy, revenge, collusion . . . And Dr Rix, well, she could not bring herself to think ill of him, and put it to the back of her mind. No, the other four were definitely guarding a slowly emerging secret, and all of them were rattled.

It had to be sex. One single woman living alone and, as Lois knew, one who was more than willing. So far, so clear. Lois was beginning to have more than glimmerings of what exactly had been going on.

Her thoughts were roughly interrupted by the Barratts' front door being jerked open as she walked up the path to the house.

'Lois! I thought you said you weren't coming back!' It was Malcolm, still in his pyjamas, feet bare and hair wild. 'Thank God,' he continued. 'I had no idea what to say to Rachel if

214

you didn't turn up . . . come on in, woman, quickly.' He took her hand and pulled her into the house, releasing her at once when he saw her face. 'Sorry! Sorry! No offence . . . Now listen, quickly, before Rachel comes down.' He followed her into the kitchen and shut the door.

'I know now it wasn't you. It was Rachel, sifting through my papers. Tidying them, she said. Saw that name and number and tried it out. Big scene! But it's all sorted out and if you could forget our little contretemps the other day, I'd be eternally grateful . . . *please*, Lois?'

'Oh, for God's sake,' said Lois, turning her back on him. She began collecting her cleaning things, and added, 'I shan't say nothing. But if you ever try anything on again—'

He put up his hand, as if to ward off a blow. 'Never! Trust me, Lois. Friends again?' His smile was sickly and anxious. Sounds of footsteps down the stairs sent him charging out of the kitchen, and Lois heard voices, not raised, but some commonplace interchange. Then Rachel came into the kitchen.

'Morning, Lois. Are you feeling better?' Lois did not know what to say to this, but presumed that Malcolm had made illness an excuse for the lack of cleaning done last week.

She nodded. 'Fine, thanks,' she said.

The morning passed slowly. With Rachel back in full control, the house was clean before Lois began. But why should she worry? Rachel had asked her to go over the inside of the bedroom windows, so she began on the big bedroom which overlooked the main street. As she worked, her eye was caught by a couple of figures standing on the doorstep of Dr Rix's house. One was Keith Simpson, she was sure. He had a peculiarly upright stance that matched his official language and his undoubtedly righteous nature. The other, she now saw, was Detective Inspector Cowgill. Lois's heart sank. The door opened, and she saw the two men disappear inside. If only she could hear what was being said. And yet . . . she was glad that she could not. Of all the people involved in what she now thought of as a conspiracy to murder, Dr Rix was the one who concerned her most. She was sure that whatever his involvement, it was not a cruel or violent one. A man who on

215

almost every occasion had been kind and considerate to Lois, with an excellent reputation in the village, could only have been caught up against his will, surely?

As she moved on to the next room, again with windows facing the road, Lois was so astonished at what happened next that she dropped her duster out of the open window on to the flowerbed beneath. The doctor had appeared at the door, with Keith and the Inspector on either side, and they were clearly *escorting* Andrew Rix from his house to the police car waiting outside.

Lois rushed downstairs and out to the gate. What am I doing? she thought, as she watched the police car drive off slowly and then disappear up the Tresham road, villagers outside the shop staring as it passed, She had a mad impulse to stop the car, demand an explanation. How stupid, she thought, as she retrieved her duster from the flowerbed. Poor Mary Rix. Lois walked back into the house, holding out her duster in explanation, and met Rachel coming into the hall with a vase of fresh flowers.

'Everything all right, Lois?' she said brightly. She laughed when Lois told her about dropping the duster and said they might as well have coffee now, while Lois was downstairs.

As Rachel set out mugs and biscuits, Malcolm's footsteps came thudding down from the attic to the kitchen, his face showing an expression of pure panic.

'Got to go out!' he said.

'But your coffee . . . ?' Rachel turned in surprise.

'Later,' he said. 'Shan't be long . . . just thought of some . . . er . . . parish matter . . . urgent . . . catch Nurse Surfleet before she goes off on her . . .'

He was gone before Rachel could reply, and she shrugged. 'I don't know, Lois,' she said. 'Men . . . I'll never understand them.'

But Lois was beginning to understand only too well. She had remembered that the attic study windows also overlooked the road.

Malcolm returned very soon from his flying visit looking haunted.

216

'Not at home,' he said briefly, as he passed Rachel in the hall, and retreated to his study, banging the door behind him. Lois heard the telephone ping once as the study extension was lifted, but the faint murmur of Malcolm's conversation was too far away for her to hear his words. She noticed that Rachel was singing in the sitting room, rearranging cushions and ornaments from where Lois had just put them, apparently oblivious of her husband's drama.

The morning finally ended and Lois breathed a sigh of relief as she went towards her car. Then her heart lurched; there was someone sitting in it, in the passenger seat. She promised herself that once this whole business was sorted out, she would never set foot in Farnden again. Then she saw that it was Mary Rix and she knew that there might, after all, be something she could do, if only listen.

The deserted wood was chilly, but Lois still had the rugs in the car that she had taken on the long journey to retrieve Josie. Wrapped in these, she and Mary Rix sat on the broad tree stump, and Mary talked while Lois listened.

'They've taken Andrew for questioning, they said,' she began. 'I don't know what that means, but they said they'd bring him back. Everything's going round and round in my head and I can't tell anyone else,' she continued, close to tears.

'Go on, I'll help if I can,' said Lois quietly.

Mary looked at her gratefully and continued, 'I don't really know how many were involved in the village. It was so awful, Lois. Like something in one of those films. At first I couldn't believe it. Not Gloria Hathaway, surely, I thought. But she was wicked, you know. That's the only word for it. Prim and proper on the outside, certainly. She could play the innocent spinster better than anyone I knew. Of course, when we first came to Farnden she was quite young. Never seemed to have any real job, yet always had plenty of money. Cars, holidays, clothes. We all wondered about it, but Andrew told me not to gossip. None of our business, he said. Well, that was a joke.'

She was silent then, and Lois shifted around to make herself more comfortable. 'Why was that, Mary?' she said gently.

'Because he was the first,' she said and then began to

cry in earnest. 'All those consultations and visits, when she was perfectly well. Nothing wrong with her at all. Perfect excuse!'

'Did you say anything to him?' Lois was aware that there must be so much to tell. They couldn't stay in this wet, cold place much longer. But she dare not interrupt Mary, in case she should think twice about confiding in her.

'He just laughed, then got cross. Said I was a jealous woman and if I wanted to save our marriage I should get things into perspective. It was around the time of my last pregnancy and I'd just lost the baby. I couldn't believe he could be so cruel.'

'Did you ever have any proof that he was carrying on with Gloria?' Lois was trying hard to keep a level head. She knew that anyone who had been in such an emotional turmoil could not be entirely reliable.

Mary stared at her. 'Of course,' she said simply. 'There was the other baby—' Crack! She was interrupted suddenly by a gunshot behind them. Both of them leapt to their feet, and clutching rugs around them, stumbled out of the wood and into Lois's car. Mary Rix's face was white and she was trembling. Lois took several deep breaths and turned the key to start the engine. It spluttered and died. Twice more she tried, with the same result.

'Damn!' she murmured. 'Give it a minute or two and I'll try again.'

She looked into the wood fearfully. How could anybody have known they were there? By her car, of course. She'd made no attempt to conceal it.

'Lois! Look! There's someone coming!' Mary fumbled for the door catch, as if to run.

'Hey, wait,' said Lois. 'Aren't they rabbits?' The man came closer, gun held in the safe position, a pair of limp, dead rabbits in his hand. They sat as if frozen in the car and watched him approach. He glanced at them curiously, then nodded. Lois wound down the window. 'Morning,' she said shakily. 'Just trying to start the car. I think the engine's damp.' He told her to have another go, saying he could help if it wouldn't fire. But this time it did, and Lois backed hastily out on to the road, changed gear and headed back towards Farnden.

'Shall I come in, make you a cup of coffee?' she said, as they drew up outside the Rixs' house.

Mary's face was still pale and drawn. But she shook her head. 'I'll be all right,' she said. She hesitated. 'There's one thing I'll never forget, though,' and added, 'you should know this about Gloria Hathaway. She came to the surgery one morning, and I answered the door. Didn't want to see the doctor, she said, but had a letter for me. She handed me an envelope and went away. I took it into the kitchen and opened it.' Her face darkened at the memory. She was silent for a moment, then turned in her seat to look at Lois. 'It was a photograph,' she said. 'Of the other baby—'

'Oh, Mary . . .' Lois murmured, her heart aching for this poor woman's suffering.

They sat for a minute or two and then Mary said, 'Better go home now, Lois. Forget what I said, dear,' she added. 'Best forgotten, all of it.' And she ran to her front door and disappeared.

Lois had no intention of forgetting. She turned Mary's words over and over in her mind, and thought she understood. If Mary was truthful, and Lois was sure she was, Gloria Hathaway deserved everything she got. Such cruelty was unimaginable. But she had to be sure. It was Gloria's baby in the photograph, that was almost certain. As for its father . . . well, Lois needed confirmation from someone who was sure to know. Tomorrow was Lois's day at Gillian Surfleet's and Lois hoped very much that she would be there, ready for a little conversation. There was quite a lot more to talk about now.

The telephone was ringing as Lois opened her door and she snatched it off the receiver.

'Lois? Janice Britton here. Not sure if you know, but the DI asked me to ring you. They've detained Dr Rix for questioning, in connection with the murder of Gloria Hathaway. He says it's very important for you to be careful. And your family.'

'What! What do you mean?' Lois was shaking.

'Don't be too alarmed. Just be vigilant, that's all. Keith agrees that you are vulnerable, knowing as much as you do. Better go now,' Janice added. 'Bye. Take care.'

Thirty-Six

Later that day, when Lois was back home and trying to keep her mind on her family, the pub in Long Farnden witnessed an unusual event. At first, it was empty, except for an old man half-asleep in the corner by the log fire, a sheep dog dozing at his feet.

Dallas Baer stepped into the gloom and thought it looked like a fine old painting. Dark browns and warm reds reflected in brass and copper, the old man's head sunk on to his chest, the dog – it was so peaceful. Ah well, that would soon be broken when the young ones came in. Tall, powerful young farmers, giggly blonde girlfriends in tight jeans and skimpy jerseys. Not Dallas's cup of tea. All noisy and confident, shouting above each other's heads, monopolising the dart board and shove-halfpenny.

For now, though, it was just the old man and Dallas Baer, who walked to the bar and rang the little brass bell. Don Cutt came through from the back and greeted him.

'Your usual, Mr Baer?' he said, reaching for a half-pint beer glass.

Dallas hesitated, then said, 'No, thanks. I think I need a stronger brew tonight. I'll have a whisky, please.'

Don raised his eyebrows. 'On your own, Mr Baer?' he said. 'How's the missus?'

'Fine, thanks,' said Dallas, wishing the publican would mind his own business. Soon he'll be asking about Dr Rix being questioned. Everyone in the village would know by now that he had been taken to the police station in Tresham. Half a day was more than enough for a piece of news as momentous as that.

The door opened and the Reverend Peter White walked in

and, close behind him, Professor Barratt. Good God, thought Dallas, they might make an effort! They looked as if the end of the world was nigh. But then, perhaps for some of them, it was.

Drinks were bought and then the vicar leaned over the bar and said confidentially to Don Cutt, 'Don, old chap, I wonder if we could use your function room for a little informal meeting. Shouldn't take more than an hour. We'd be most obliged . . . parish council business, a little off the record,' he added hopefully, as if by taking Don into his confidence he would forestall any awkward questions.

'In the absence of the ex-chairman, I suppose,' said Don Cutt meaningly. 'Well,' he added, 'here's your new one, chairwoman Nurse Surfleet herself.'

Gillian positively bounced up to the bar, smiling broadly, nodding a greeting to the old man in the corner and said good evening brightly to them all. Her smile was a reassuring embrace. In her strong arms, on her ample bosom, they could rest their anxious heads and all would be well. At least, that is how Dallas Baer saw it, and in spite of himself, felt cheered.

'So is it OK for us, then?' he asked Don Cutt, who nodded grudgingly.

'I suppose you won't want to pay for hire of the room,' he said, only half-joking. 'I shall have to put the electric fires on . . . no other heating in there,' he added. The others ignored him and, taking their drinks, they headed off for the privacy of the pub's function room, a bleak place smelling strongly of stale beer, and dreary now without the usual balloons or confetti or tables set for cricket teas.

They sat down at the beer-stained table and looked glumly at each other. 'Well, who's going to start?' said Malcolm Barratt.

'I will,' said Nurse Surfleet. 'The rest of you look as if you're incapable of starting a donkey race. Now,' she added briskly, 'what do we know for sure. Andrew has been taken to the police station for help with their enquiries. We know that much from Mary. We also know that he is a true and loyal friend and will give nothing away that isn't forced out of him by the Tresham Gestapo.'

222

'Don't be ridiculous, woman!' said Malcolm sharply. 'This is extremely serious, and we can do without your silly jokes.'

Gillian Surfleet glared at him. 'Very well, Professor,' she said. 'You take over.' She hated them all. Men! Weak, cruel and selfish. They hadn't really cared tuppence for Gloria, not one of them. Andrew Rix had been different. And it had all been so long ago, with him. The others were recent, amoral casuals without a responsible thought between them. Although she had no time for what Andrew had done, at least he had tried to put it right, had stuck by Gloria and supported her as best he could. If she had to eliminate them, one by one, Andrew would be the first to be ruled out.

The Reverend Peter White was trembling. He knew that the rest of his life was at stake here, in this cold, fusty room. The others could probably survive. Barratt was more or less self-employed, comfortably off. The world that Dallas Baer moved in would care little for extra-marital dalliance. In fact, thought the vicar, it would probably enhance his prospects of promotion. Quite a fellow, that Dallas Baer! Whereas he, a supposed man of God, would be out on his ear in the shortest possible time. But first, the scandal, the humiliation. He looked round at the others. The big question, however, was still unanswered. Who killed Gloria? The police had taken Andrew, but the vicar would stake his life on the doctor's innocence. And yet . . .

'Which of us spoke most recently to Andrew?' said Gillian Surfleet in a now icy voice. 'I had a talk with him yesterday. He was confident. Said none of us need worry. The police were no nearer finding Gloria's killer and even when they did, it would turn out to be a passing burglar . . .'

'. . . passing by the village hall kitchen?' said Dallas Baer incredulously. 'Hoping to steal a few mouldy cups and saucers and plastic spoons? Come on, Gillian, he can't have been serious!'

'Well, perhaps he didn't say just that, but what he meant, I'm sure, was that the murder was not necessarily in any way connected with our . . . well, our little business venture. Gloria's and mine.'

There was a silence, as the men took this in. Then Peter

White suddenly got to his feet. He gripped the edge of the table, for all the world as if it were a pulpit. 'Look here,' he said in a harsh voice. 'It'd be better if we called a spade a spade. You, Nurse Surfleet, were not conducting a "little business venture". You were a Madam and Holly Cottage was a brothel . . . and Gloria –' he choked, and the others said nothing, sitting in shocked silence and waiting for him to continue – 'and Gloria,' he finally managed, 'poor little Gloria, was an aging prostitute, a victim of us all.'

Gillian Surfleet looked as if she would explode, but she said nothing. The rest stared at the vicar in silence. At last Dallas Baer, man of the world, broke the spell. 'Hardly a victim,' he said smoothly. 'She was well paid for her services, that I do know.'

He turned and looked at the others, and they slowly nodded. Yes, they had all paid for her time and attentions. But the vicar? This was news to Dallas Baer and Malcolm Barratt. They knew about Andrew Rix, though his involvement had been years in the past. Peter White? They could hardly believe it. He knew about them, certainly, and that was why he was here. But had he . . . ?

It was Dallas again who spoke for the rest. 'Um, Peter, old chap,' he said. 'Didn't think that you'd, well, you know, partaken of Gloria's charms!' He smiled, and then hastily smothered it as he realized that the vicar was near collapse. He had slumped down in his chair and covered his face with his hands. His anguish was answer enough.

Malcolm Barratt, looking at the pathetic figure, felt anger rising. 'Gloria Hathaway was a promiscuous bitch,' he said, and held up his hand to stop Gillian's furious interruption. 'She opened her door and legs to all comers – so long as they'd got the necessary to keep her in cars and holidays. God knows when she started it. But by the time we came to this idyllic little hellhole, she was an experienced pro. She fooled me at first – and sex and *homo sapiens* is my subject! "Do come in, Professor, and have a cup of tea." Oh, that cooing, virginal voice. Honeyed words to trap the unwary.'

Nurse Surfleet could contain herself no longer. 'You hypocritical sod!' she burst out. 'As if you didn't go along with your tongue hanging out! I was there the first time, don't forget! God, you couldn't wait to get your pants down! And it wasn't the first time away from the marriage bed, that was for sure!'

Peter White groaned, and muttered that now he knew where Hell was. It was here, here in this dreadful room. And he deserved to be in it.

'Pull yourself together, Peter,' said Dallas Baer. This was all getting out of hand. A sense of proportion was what was needed. After all, women like Gloria were everywhere and men merely accepted what was offered. And paid for it, too. He didn't believe in divine retribution. At the moment, all he was concerned with was how they could present an acceptable version of events to the world at large and their wives in particular. As for Gillian Surfleet, she was beyond the pale. Whatever she had suffered through Gloria's murder, she definitely had it coming to her. A community nurse, after all! He would rather not think about her motives.

'I wish Andrew was here,' said Peter White, visibly pulling himself together and sitting up straight in his chair. 'He would know what to do.'

'I know what to do,' said Malcolm Barratt. 'We have to find the murderer, and then all attention will be diverted from us and on to him . . . or her.' He could not stop himself glancing at Nurse Surfleet and she glared back at him. 'Now, let's be constructive,' he said. 'How shall we begin? Who would be the best person to help us out?'

The trouble is, thought Dallas Baer, we all suspect each other. Even the vicar could have done it. None of us have convincing alibis, and all of us have motives, however slender, as in my case. And none of us believe that Andrew Rix could have done it. Why, then, had the police taken him? For what he knew? For some reason that none of the rest of them knew?

'I know who'd be the best person,' said Malcolm Barratt suddenly. 'Lois Meade.' He shushed Nurse Surfleet as she began to protest, and continued. 'Lois cleans in all our houses. An objective observer. We are, let's face it, all under sus- picion . . . not yet, thank God, by the police, but here, amongst ourselves. Lois sees everything and hears most things. She could tell us things, if we said we wanted to help solve the murder, and drew up a list of questions agreed by us all.'

Dallas Baer sighed. 'Not a chance,' he said. 'Lois Meade wouldn't give you the time of day, let alone information picked up on her rounds. No, that's a non-starter, Malcolm.'

The room became silent again, as they realized they had got nowhere. Then it was Nurse Surfleet's turn to make a suggestion. 'Suppose we wait a couple of days,' she said. 'Let's see what happens to Andrew Rix and then meet again? He might be home and cleared of any involvement by now. Meantime, Lois is with me tomorrow. I'll see what I can get out of her. She probably does know something, and has more than likely put two and two together. Could be quite awkward, in fact . . .'

There was a touch of menace in her voice that made Peter White shiver. 'I should not want Lois worried in any way,' he said firmly. 'Or harmed. She's had a lot of family problems lately, and it would be most unacceptable for us to bother her in any way.'

A little authority had crept back into his voice and Gillian Surfleet's agression subsided. 'I wouldn't worry her,' she said sulkily. 'Just ask her a few questions. We're good friends, Lois and I,' she added, with a smile that hinted at unpalatable secrets.

Soon after that, with nothing much having been achieved, they broke up the meeting and drifted back into the pub. Dallas Baer and Malcolm Barratt ordered more drinks and began to talk in loud voices about golf, deceiving no one, least of all Don Cutt. Gillian Surfleet and the vicar left straight away and outside Peter White put his hand on the nurse's arm.

'I meant what I said, you know, about Lois,' he cautioned. 'God forgives us most things, but unkindness is, in my view, the eighth deadly sin.'

Gillian Surfleet shook off his hand angrily, and marched off down the street towards her cottage. How dare he! She was smouldering with dissatisfaction at the way the meeting had gone. They thought they knew everything, those men. If they knew what she knew, all of it, they'd be a damn sight more worried than they were now!

*   *   *

Sitting by her window, Mary Rix watched Nurse Surfleet go by, briefly lit up by the street lamp, and wondered whether she should go to the door, call her back and ask her to come in and keep her company. At least Gillian knew the whole story. She had been there, through it all. Mary knew how Gillian had felt about Gloria Hathaway. She had felt so sorry for her. It was still a mystery to Mary how that spinsterish, self-regarding woman could have inspired such love and loyalty. She had led Gillian astray, if you looked at it clearly. How the poor thing must have suffered! A much-loved village mainstay, forced to guard a secret that could destroy everything she had built up since she arrived in Farnden.

It had probably been a kind of blackmail. Once Gloria realized how much Gillian cared for her, she would have used that affection without a qualm. And when the awful blow had struck Mary, when she could not deal with the revelation on her own, Gillian had been wonderful. Practical and understanding. She had handled the whole thing with discretion and tact. It had been made easier, of course, by Gloria Hathaway's ruthless unconcern for anybody but herself. She just wanted things smoothed over and back to normal as soon as possible. Gillian had organized it all, and had comforted Mary, knowing that at that particular time it must have hurt her dreadfully. I wanted my baby more than anything in the world, Mary remembered, watching Gillian's disappearing back, while Gloria, that wicked woman, had cared for nothing.

A loud knock at the door startled her, and she looked out of the window to see who it was. Andrew! She rushed to open it, hugging him in relief, regardless of what had gone before. Questions tumbled out of her, but all he said was, 'Didn't have my keys, Mary. Sorry. Think I'd like to sit down for a few minutes. Bit of a gruelling time . . .'

She led him into the warm kitchen and he sat down at the table. 'I'll make some coffee,' she said.

Andrew shook his head. 'No thanks,' he said.

Mary sat down next to him, and quietly took his hand. She said nothing, because she could think of nothing to say. She'd

227

always waited for him to take the lead. He wouldn't let her down now.

After some minutes staring at the darkened window, he turned to look at her. 'Mary dear,' he said. 'I know now. I know who it was . . . who killed poor Gloria.'

'So do I, dear,' she said. 'I've known for quite a while.'

Thirty-Seven

G illian Surfleet looked at the kitchen clock. Ten past nine. It was very unusual for Lois to be late and Gillian felt nervous, suspicious that someone could have got at Lois and warned her off coming to her house this morning. She shook herself, told herself not to be so stupid. The whole thing was descending into ridiculous melodrama, she thought. That meeting last night had been a good example. Peter White, who should know better, wallowing in self-pity, Malcolm Barratt just out to save his skin at all costs, and Dallas Baer, a cold fish if ever there was one, quite sure that he had done nothing out of the ordinary, merely indulged in a little bit of stuff on the side and no harm done.

But harm had been done. Gloria had been strangled in a dark, steamy kitchen, in a state of silent terror. Gillian was sure of the terror. Gloria had never liked the dark, and left lights burning all night 'to keep the bogies away', as she had said. She would have been steeling herself in that kitchen with its blank, dark windows, hurrying to make tea for the women, desperate to get back to the safety of the brightly lit hall, where that woman had been droning on about milking cows, or whatever it was. If only she had been there that night! Well, she had been there, in a way, and had done nothing. She would never forgive herself. She had been getting ready to go over to Ringford, and had watched the dark shadow go along the footpath past her cottage and up to the village hall, knowing quite well who it was. She had followed a few paces behind, softly, in her nurse's shoes. Then she had stood and waited. And when the screams came, she had turned tail and fled, back along the footpath and into her cottage, shaking from head to foot and gasping with fear at what had been done, and at her own connivance. It *was* connivance, to do nothing. And then she had seen the shadow returning, and still had stood in her dark kitchen, peering through the window, immobile. Had she wanted Gloria dead? She dare not even ask herself that question.

Twenty past nine and still no Lois. Gillian went to the telephone, dialled Lois's number and waited. No reply. Well, perhaps she was on her way, after being held up by one of the children, or a traffic jam in Tresham, or a flat tyre on the road. Or a visit to the police station . . .

'Morning!' It was Lois at the back door, voice cheerful and apologetic. 'Sorry I'm late. Josie again, not feeling well, and deciding to stay at home. So I had to make sure she wasn't lead-swinging and then leave her some food, and by then . . .'

'No bother, Lois. Don't worry. I was just worried that you might be ill.'

Lois pulled off her coat and hung it behind the door as usual. 'Soon catch up, anyway,' she said. 'Are you out this morning . . . how's that old lady in Ringford?'

It was all so normal. How could Gillian begin to find out what Lois knew? It was almost as if Lois had decided to forestall any awkward questions. She kept up a stream of inconsequential remarks until she had all her cleaning things ready and then disappeared upstairs to start on the bathroom. Gillian could hear her singing tunelessly, and shrugged. She could wait. Maybe at coffee time the opportunity would come. She had changed her appointments around so that she could have the whole morning free. Perhaps if she got out some old photographs and left them on the table, that might start some useful conversation. She took out a green, leather-bound album, and opened it. She turned to a page where a young woman half-smiled at the camera, holding a tiny, new-born baby in her arms. It was herself, in better days, and she was smiling at Gloria, who had reluctantly taken the picture.

Josie was not feeling ill at all, of course. In fact, she felt very well, alert and excited. Melvyn had phoned, luckily while

Mum and Dad were out, and arranged to meet her this morning in the shopping centre.

'Best place for a secret assignation,' he'd said, to make her laugh. 'Lose ourselves in the crowds. Never be noticed that way. I'm longing to see you, Josie,' he'd added in a different, softer kind of voice. 'I've missed you a lot.'

'Me too,' Josie had replied, looking at herself in the mirror that hung above the telephone and thinking that she looked a lot older than fourteen, nearly fifteen, specially with her hair this way. 'See you then,' she'd said. 'I can get rid of Mum OK and get the bus. I'll be there.'

Melvyn was already there when she walked up the long street, with its tall palm trees and sparrows flitting in and out. The sun was shining through the glass roof, and it felt warm and springlike. Josie saw him, leaning up against one of the pillars, reading a newspaper. His familiar good looks gave her a happy jolt. There'd never be another like Melvyn, whatever Mum said. He was special. She walked softly up to him and stood close, saying nothing. He looked down at her, smiling.

'There you are, then,' he said. 'Let's go.' He took her hand and led her down the long sunlit boulevard, out into the car park, and up to a car that she recognised as the one they'd taken to Yorkshire. He held the door open for her, laughing and attempting a formal bow. Then he started up the engine and cruised out of the car park and took the road in towards Tresham.

Josie thought she had never felt so happy. Melvyn was driving with one hand, the other stroking her leg, sending thrills of excitement through her. He put in a tape and turned up the thudding music until Josie felt her mind whirling away to the hypnotic beat. It was not until the car slowed down and stopped, that she saw where they were. It was the deserted back road that led down to the canal.

'Come on, Jose,' said Melvyn, grinning at her. 'Time for a surprise.' He took her hand and pulled her out of the car, slamming the door and locking it.

She stood looking at him, her happiness evaporating fast, and a horrible, creeping fear taking its place. 'I don't want to go to that place,' she said, her voice now like a little girl's. 'Take me home, Melvyn. We'll be in trouble if we go there.'

Melvyn still smiled, as if he had not heard. 'I've made some improvements,' he said. 'Wait 'til you see. All mod cons.' He kissed her lightly on the cheek, and drew her along beside him.

When they reached the factory, she stopped, snatched her hand away, and said, 'No, Melvyn. Not in there. *Please!*'

He took no notice, and put his arm around her shoulders. 'Come on, daftie,' he said. 'You gotta trust Melvyn. He'll look after you.' And in spite of her protests and attempts to turn around and run, he manoeuvred her into the warehouse and shut the creaking door behind them, taking a key out of his pocket and locking them in. 'Cosy?' he said, as he led her to that same deserted room. It was indeed transformed. Clean and tidy, with furniture arranged neatly in place. Melvyn had made a home. 'Just for you and me, Josie,' he said. 'Now sit down there, and I'll get us some dinner.' He opened a cupboard and took out paper bags and cans of drink, setting it all out on a table. There were proper plates and glasses, knives and forks, and two chairs ready for them. Josie sat down mechanically, her eyes glazed with terror at being trapped. When she wouldn't eat, Melvyn drew his chair up next to hers and fed her titbits, as if she was a recalcitrant child. Finally, he pulled her to her feet and put his arms around her. 'Our own home, Jose,' he said. 'Nobody can get us here. We're safe here, for as long as we want.'

Josie was shivering now, and Melvyn took her over to a new, garishly covered sofa. 'There,' he whispered close to her ear. 'Have a rest for a bit.' Then he opened another cupboard and took out a bright pink blanket. It was clean and he spread it carefully over her. 'See?' he said. 'Everything we need. Just you and me, Jose.'

She looked at him pleadingly. 'I want my Mum,' she said.

He did not seem to hear and instead walked over to the table in a purposeful way, sat down, and began to read a magazine.

'Who's that, then?' said Lois obediently. She was sitting at

Nurse Surfleet's kitchen table, her coffee still too hot to drink. Just my luck, she thought, to have to look at a load of old snaps. Why do people do it? As if I care. Then she stared harder at the picture on the page Gillian was shoving towards her.

'Guess who?' Gillian said again. 'Come on, Lois! Surely I haven't changed that much?'

'It's you, is it?' Lois looked closer at the faded print. 'Good heavens, so it is. Well,' she said, thinking quickly, 'I think you're much better looking now. That terrible hair style! Blimey!' Her mind was working rapidly now. That baby . . . it was just another new-born, of course. But the way it was wrapped, and the shawl itself, looked identical to those other snaps, the ones in Gloria's cottage and at the Rixs'. 'And the baby?' she said casually.

Gillian's face was pale now. 'I think you know who the baby was, don't you, Lois?' she said, in a cracked voice. 'Especially if I tell you it was Gloria who took the photograph?'

Lois knew that whatever she said now was terrifyingly important. Gillian's response would tell her, she was sure, the answer to the whole sorry puzzle. And then it would be for her to act. Or for Gillian to act. Suddenly Lois was frightened. It was, after all, a matter of life and death. Somebody had felt strongly enough to strangle a defenceless woman, and cover his or her tracks so well that the police were still, as far as she knew, only on the approach road to the solution. She had been warned already. If she became a serious threat, this unknown person would have no hesitation in making sure she kept her knowledge to herself. She might be threatened again, or harmed, this time. Or one of her own family might be hurt. Oh God, not that!

Lois stared at Gillian Surfleet across the table. 'No,' she said, as lightly as she could. 'Looks to me like any other new-born babe.'

Gillian Surfleet frowned. Was Lois really so innocent? Or making a good job of pretending? She was torn between that vow of silence made so long ago and now a desperate need to clear things up, let in light and air, and breathe easily again. After all, Gloria was gone for ever, no longer able to hold her in thrall with her manipulative moods. Those bloody men had no call on her loyalty and here was Lois, who had done her no harm, and who quite possibly was in danger herself.

Gillian turned the album round so that it was facing her again, and peered down at the photograph. 'Poor little soul,' she said. 'He didn't stand much of a chance, really. Gloria didn't want him, you know. She couldn't even be bothered to think of a name for him. The doctor named him. Melvyn, he called him. Said it was the first name that came to him. Gloria said any old name would do. She seemed to have no maternal feelings at all, and when they took him away she just laughed with relief. It was horrible, unnatural. I thought maybe it was just the shock, but she was no different later on, when Melvyn found out and came to see her. She was so cruel to him, rejecting him out of hand. She could be cruel, you know, Lois, very cruel indeed.' Gillian Surfleet paused, remembering the pain inflicted by Gloria Hathaway's cruelty.

Lois felt sick. Melvyn! Josie's Melvyn? Supposing it was? Gloria's son, and rejected out of hand. No wonder she had felt sorry for a lad who seemed a loner, a bit different from the rest. But what had it led to? Where was this conversation going? She was breathless with alarm now, but before she could speak, Gillian Surfleet had started again.

'And the father, Melvyn's real father,' she said. 'Well, he couldn't take him, though I think he wanted to. His wife wouldn't have stood for it, not at that time, anyway.'

Lois stood up suddenly, jerking the chair away from the table. 'Gillian!' she yelled. 'Do you know what you're saying? For God's sake . . . are you talking about Melvyn Hallhouse? Was it Melvyn in the village hall kitchen that night? Was it him who—'

She couldn't say it, but Gillian Surfleet was nodding now, and tears were running down her red cheeks. She began speaking again, her words slurred now by the tears.

'Melvyn wasn't christened, mind, until those people adopted him,' she said, not looking at Lois, talking more to herself. 'I never liked those Hallhouses. Specially him. He was a violent man, it was said, and those kids were frightened of him. Violence breeds violence, they say . . .' She looked up, then, as if waking from a bad dream. 'Hey, Lois, where're you going?' she said. Lois was wrenching her coat off the hook.

'Home!' she shouted and, like a whirlwind, was out of the house and gone.

'Josie?' Lois tore into the sitting room, then upstairs and down again, panic rising sharply. 'Josie! Josie, where the bloody hell are you!' Nothing. The house was deathly quiet. It was half past eleven, and the boys safely at school. Derek wasn't due home for another hour. Oh my God, Melvyn's taken her.

Lois's heart was pounding so hard she could hardly hear the engaged tone when she dialled Keith Simpson. No time for second thoughts; she rang the police station and asked for Inspector Cowgill. 'Tell him it's Mrs Meade and it's bloody urgent.' It seemed hours before the cool, steady voice said, 'Ah yes, Mrs Meade. How can I help you?' And then Lois was shaking so much that it took several minutes before she could get out the whole story. 'Now he's got her and I know exactly where!' she shouted, and then calmed down while Cowgill told her exactly what they would do, and reassured her that they would locate Derek immediately. A police car would be picking her up in a matter of minutes.

Thirty-Eight

When the car came, Lois registered Dr Rix sitting huddled in the back seat. How could he help? Her mind was spinning, but she would not even try to work it out. Josie was all that counted. If she thought hard enough about her, willed with all her strength that nothing bad would happen to her, maybe they'd get there in time? She scarcely noticed that Keith Simpson was sitting in the front, nodding reassuringly at her.

'Where's Derek?' she said, looking round wildly.

It was Keith who answered. 'On his way, Lois. He'll probably be there before we are.' The doctor looked at her blankly, then turned to stare out of the window. She frowned. What the hell *was* he doing here anyway?

'Have you got something to do with . . . ?' Her voice tailed away. She mustn't think of anything but Josie, shut up in that filthy factory with a lunatic. And a lunatic who had killed his own mother.

'I shall be able to talk to him,' the doctor said, turning away from the window and pulling himself together with a visible effort. 'Try not to worry, Lois.'

She stared at him. 'You? Why you? Why should he listen to you?'

'I'm his father,' said Andrew Rix simply.

After that, nobody spoke until they drew up outside the derelict factory. A number of cars were already there and Lois saw Derek shaking his fist at a police officer who was trying to prevent him getting to the door. She rushed over to him and when he saw her he held her tight and stopped shouting.

'Ah, there you are,' Hunter Cowgill stepped forward and spoke to them calmly. 'We are pretty sure he doesn't know

236

we're here. Windows are all boarded up and the room they're in is well away from the road.' He'd had his men check out the old factory some time ago, when they became aware that Melvyn was taking in odd items of furniture. He cursed himself that they hadn't acted sooner, before Josie had been taken. Warning Lois had not been enough. He prided himself on waiting for the right moment. It was one of his intuitive skills, but he doubted if Lois would have much faith in him now. He had been almost there. The doctor had been helpful, of course, but was clearly determined not to incriminate his own son, even supposing he had known that Melvyn was the killer. After all, fathers don't shop their own sons, as a general rule. Families mostly close ranks against the police, and Hunter Cowgill didn't blame them. He was a rational man, and now he hoped to God they were in time.

'This way, then, Doctor,' he said, and they approached the factory door together. He had sent all his men out of sight, leaving only Lois and Derek in view of the door. Lois watched them, noticed the peeling green paint, the dirty ring round the door handle, where hundreds of workmen's hands had opened and shut it in the past. Her mind was out of control now, roaming on its own, noticing stupid things and refusing to concentrate on Josie. Lois clutched Derek's hand tighter. Neither could speak.

Cowgill raised his hand and knocked firmly on the door. Not a sound. Nobody breathed. After a few seconds, he knocked again, louder, and then several times more. Again a pause, and then Lois breathed in sharply. The door opened a crack, and in the eerie silence she heard Melvyn's voice.

Now the Inspector had stepped back, out of sight, and Dr Rix took over. 'Could I have a word, Melvyn?' Lois heard the words, spoken for all the world as if he were asking someone to step into his surgery for a moment, and she felt Derek stiffen beside her. She squeezed his hand.

Melvyn was speaking again, but she couldn't catch the words. Then the doctor turned around and looked straight at her. 'Lois!' he called. 'Over here, my dear, please.' The Inspector, out of sight by the car, nodded and beckoned her forward. She walked forward to where Andrew Rix stood smiling at her. It was a brave, pleading smile. Behind them, Derek stood alone, discouraged from following only by Cowgill's hand held up in restraint.

'Melvyn?' said Lois, in a quavery voice. 'Have you got Josie with you? Is she all right?' She could see only his white face, his dark eyes burning out at her.

'You can come in,' he said, 'and you . . .' He motioned to Andrew Rix. 'And them others can just go on home, because we're not coming out.'

By now Lois was shaking all over. So, he knew the police were there. Somehow this made things much worse. Now there was no hope of talking him and Josie out into the open. Lois shut her eyes, and felt herself whirling.

Then Dr Rix took her hand, and said in a perfectly normal voice, 'Come on, then, my dear. Let's go and see what these two have been up to.' He half-pulled her behind him, into the dark factory, and she heard Melvyn lock the door again.

It was not until they reached the inner room, the little home so carefully set up, that Lois saw Josie, apparently asleep on the sofa. Then she saw the knife. Melvyn held a bright, shiny-bladed knife in his hand, and with it gestured that they should sit down on the two chairs by the table. With his other hand he held his finger to his lips, and then pointed to the sofa in the corner. Lois gasped and made to stand up, but Melvyn was there with his knife, forcing her to sit down.

'She's asleep,' he whispered. 'I don't want her woken. What we got to say won't take long, and we can say it quietly. Then go and tell them that if they don't leave us alone, I'll kill myself, and Josie as well. She's mine now. I love her and she loves me. Where I go, she goes, too.' Then Lois knew he had lost his reason, and felt a greater terror than she had ever known.

But Andrew Rix was nodding, and, still smiling, patted Melvyn on the arm and whispered, 'Try to relax, old boy, nobody's going to hurt you. There'll be no more killing, not for you nor Josie.'

The pain in his face had transformed him into a very old man, but Melvyn had no pity. 'Shut up,' he said shortly. 'You didn't say nor do nothing then, when I needed a father, so it's a bit late now. I want to talk to *her*,' he added, waving the knife at Lois, the blade catching the light like an electric spark.

'What d'you want?' Lois managed. Josie stirred in her sleep, and once more Lois tried to go to her. But Melvyn stood in front of her, holding the knife as if he knew exactly how to use it. Dr Rix sat rigid in his chair, his expression bleak beyond words.

'Josie's mine,' Melvyn repeated. 'I'll look after her until she's old enough to get married and then we'll stay together for ever. I shan't harm her, nor force anythin' on her she don't want. You and Mr Meade can rest easy.'

'How will you live?' Lois's voice was stronger now.

'I got money,' Melvyn said. 'And I know ways of gettin' supplies that your friends out there don't know nothin' about. We'll be fine, Josie and me. And nobody's gonna take her away from me!'

Suddenly Andrew Rix stood up. 'All right,' he said, his face suddenly changed. 'Enough of this nonsense, Melvyn. Put that stupid knife down, and let's go home.'

'Home!' said Melvyn, half-crouching now, on the defensive and brandishing his knife at his father. 'Home!' he said loudly. 'Your home? Is that what you mean? Why didn't you take me there in the beginning, then? Scared of the scandal, was you? Wifie wouldn't hear of it? She must've known.'

His voice had woken Josie, who sat up, staring at Melvyn, then at her mother. 'Don't move, Josie,' said Lois quickly. 'We're just having a chat, then we'll be going.'

Andrew Rix stood unmoving, in spite of Melvyn's threatening gestures. 'I was wrong, son,' he said. That word, spoken awkwardly, jolted Melvyn, and he shook his head, as if to clear it. 'I should have insisted,' his father continued. 'But Mary had just lost her own baby, and I couldn't do it. Gloria didn't care what happened, so long as you were out of the way. So I took the easiest way out.'

'Gloria!' Melvyn spat out the word. 'I hated her. She was a bloody whore!'

'Melvyn!' said Lois, also getting to her feet. 'Not that

language in front of Josie, if you don't mind! I don't call that taking care of her!'

Melvyn backed away from them. 'She was a tart, my mother,' he said. 'And so I got rid of her. Did her customers a service, I reckon.' He laughed mirthlessly. 'Reckon they were all getting fed up with the old bag.'

'You were right,' said Andrew Rix, and Lois stared at him in amazement. 'Gloria was no good, but she had such a way with her when she was in a good mood. And then she could be so cruel. Poor Nurse Surfleet had a terrible time with her.'

'That old dyke!' said Melvyn. 'Deserved all she got.'

'But your mother was sick in the last year or so, Melvyn,' continued the doctor. 'She thought she was very ill, before she . . . um . . .' He coughed, and seemed to search for the right words. 'She was desperate for comfort, you know, in the end, and no one really cared for her . . . except Gillian Surfleet and her affection was thrown back in her face.'

'Ill?' said Melvyn. 'How ill?' His voice was full of suspicion.

Now Josie, in spite of Lois's fierce looks, stood up from the sofa and walked towards Melvyn. 'You didn't tell me about your poor mum, Melv,' she said, and put her hand in his. 'What was wrong with her?' she continued, looking at the doctor.

'She thought it was the worst, I'm afraid,' said Andrew Rix. 'Though it was far from certain. We were still doing tests, but she went completely to pieces.' He took a step towards Melvyn. 'Come on, old son,' he said, but Josie stepped in front of him.

'Get away from him!' she said loudly. 'Watch him, Melvyn,' she added. 'They'll try to trick you.'

'Josie!' said Lois. 'For God's sake!'

Josie took no notice of her. 'Come on, Melvyn,' she said. 'Let's go for a walk, away from this lot. We can go the secret way. And don't try to follow us, Mum!' she added. 'It's very dangerous back there by the canal, unless you know what you're doing.' She pulled Melvyn away, towards a collapsing doorway at the back of the room.

Lois moved towards them, but Andrew Rix caught her hand and held her back. He shook his head. 'Wait,' he mouthed at her. 'Melvyn!' he said then, loudly, so that they could hear him.

'What?'

'Did you ever wonder why I called you that name?'

'No,' Melvyn replied flatly. 'Don't make no difference.' He'd come back into sight now, still holding Josie's hand.

'It's my own name,' the doctor said. 'Andrew is my first, and then Melvyn. I gave you my own name. Such a tiny scrap of life . . . and I loved you then more than anyone before or since. I loved you and I gave you away.' He reached out his hand. 'I'm so sorry, son,' he said. 'So very sorry.'

Melvyn bit his lip and his eyes shut for a second. 'Huh,' he said. Then he retreated again into the darkness.

'I'm going after them!' said Lois desperately. Andrew Rix shook his head. 'Police,' he whispered, and made a circular motion with his hand. 'Surrounded,' he added.

But Lois could not see Josie go without her and she walked quietly after them. It was without air or light, evil-smelling, a cocktail of human detritus and the stagnant canal. She felt her way carefully, so as not to make a noise, aiming for a slit of light up ahead. Another door, and she prised it open slowly. Dazzled by the light, it was seconds before she could see the canal only feet away from her. An overgrown path led along the back of the factory, and she peered out. Josie and Melvyn were there, up by the old brick bridge, a couple of children, hand in hand. In front of them stood the police, two of them, and one of them was Hunter Cowgill. Lois stared, petrified, scared to move a muscle in case she should precipitate something unthinkable.

Melvyn moved sideways suddenly, and before the police could be there, he was on the bridge, holding on to the wooden rail and dragging Josie after him. Lois was frozen to the spot. She saw the rail snap and Melvyn fall backwards, hitting the black water with a yell that cut into her, breaking the spell, and she ran forward. Josie was still on the bridge, her arm held tight by Hunter Cowgill, who had got there just in time.

'Take her,' he said to Lois. 'And wait in the car.' But Josie would not go. She was screaming Melvyn's name, pulling away and trying to go in after him. 'Josie!' said Lois sharply.

'Do as you're bloody well told!' Josie stopped struggling and began to cry.

'Mum, they've got to get him out,' she said.

Cowgill stepped forward. 'We shall, Josie,' he said. 'Look, Simpson's there already.' He strode off down the towpath, and Lois heard him say, 'He's got a knife. Get him . . . but remember the girl's watching.'

Much later, after Josie was in bed and asleep at last, Lois remembered Cowgill's words. 'He can't be such a bad bloke, that Inspector,' she said to Derek, who sat holding her hand. 'To think of Josie watching. Thoughtful of him . . .'

'Don't trust any of 'em,' said Derek. He was still trying to sort out the whole thing, but overriding everything, filling his head, was the fact that his Josie could easily be dead. 'Steer clear of them all in future, Lois, and that's an order,' he said.

Thirty-Nine

L ate summer in Long Farnden, and the village was quiet
at last. The long street with stone houses on either side
had finally seen the last of the gawpers and ghouls. A black
and white cat stalked out of a gateway and crossed the road,
leaping up and lightly touching the top of a stone wall
before disappearing amongst bright flowers and trees that
were beginning to turn to autumn colours.

Two cars cruised slowly into the village from the Tresham
road and came to rest outside a substantial red-brick house.
The *For Sale* notice had slipped to one side and the estate
agent, slamming his car door and aiming his key at it, turned
to straighten up the board.

'Kids!' he said, and smiled at the young couple who had
emerged from the other car. 'Come along, this way,' he
encouraged them. They opened the gate and walked up to
the front door. Blank windows on either side gave the house
a gloomy air, and as the agent unlocked the door and beckoned
the couple into the hallway, they shivered, although the day
was warm and the sun bright.

'It's been on the market some time, I believe?' said the
young man.

'Ah, yes, well,' said the agent, opening a window in the
big, high-ceilinged drawing-room. 'The market has been a
bit depressed.' He pointed out the attractive features, the
elegant marble fireplace, plasterwork on the ceiling, and a
well-polished parquet floor.

'We'd heard something about a scandal in this village,' said
the young wife. 'Didn't this house belong to a doctor?'

The agent looked uncomfortable. 'Yes, quite right,' he said
briskly. 'He's retired now – gone off to the West Country

for a well-earned rest. These GP's, you know,' he chatted on brightly. 'They have a very difficult job. Long hours, night calls, father confessors . . . all that.' He motioned them across the hallway into another room, the twin of the first, but with a hatch through to a large kitchen. 'The dining-room,' he announced, and once more showed them its attractive aspects.

'This doctor,' persisted the wife, and the agent frowned, 'wasn't he involved in that murder case? Some woman strangled in the village hall? Not that long ago, was it, Simon?'

Her husband nodded. 'We were discussing it on the way over,' he explained. 'Remembered the village name from the stories in the paper. Big splash at the time, wasn't it?'

The agent sighed. He realized he would have to come clean. 'Quite right,' he said, and hoped he could make it as brief and unalarming as possible. 'The doctor here had an affair with that woman years ago and she'd had a baby. Got him adopted privately, but the boy found out who his real parents were, and when his mother didn't want to know, he killed her. Then the whole scandal came out: woman had been the village bike – several respectable citizens—'

'Including the vicar,' said the wife with a smile.

'Yes, including the vicar,' continued the agent. 'They'd been her secret lovers. Real goings-on! Police got the lad, didn't they?'

The young couple couldn't remember the details. Something about a cleaning lady and her daughter. 'All water under the bridge, anyway,' said the agent. 'Now, let's go upstairs. Lovely spacious bedrooms, two bathrooms . . .'

The young woman shook her head. 'Don't fancy it, Simon, do you?'

Her husband looked doubtful. 'The price is very good,' he said.

'No, I couldn't live here, knowing all that.' She shook her head firmly and made for the door.

As they emerged once more into the sunshine, another car drew up. It had a battered air, and skidded a little, sending up a cloud of summer dust at the side of the road.

'Ah,' said the estate agent. 'My next client. Good morning,

244

then,' he added, shaking the young man firmly by the hand. 'Sorry we couldn't interest you.' The young couple drove slowly down the street, stopping briefly outside the village hall, the vicarage, a quaint cottage that looked like a tea-cosy, and then accelerated and disappeared.

'Morning!' said the agent, turning on his welcoming smile. 'Mrs Meade, isn't it?'

Lois walked towards him, and behind her Josie trailed, dragging her feet. The long school holidays had been difficult to fill, once the horror and pain had abated. Now she'd agreed to come with her mother because it was better than staying at home on her own. Her friends had pestered her at first, then slowly melted away. She didn't care. They were all just kids. Anyway, she'd never been to Long Farnden, and she was curious.

They followed the agent into the house, and as he began his sales patter, Lois said, 'You can save your breath. I know this house. I used to work in this village, but not any more.'

The agent's eyebrows went up. 'For the doctor?' he said.

Lois nodded. 'And you needn't ask me any questions,' she added quickly, practised now at fending off unwanted attention, 'I don't talk about it. In fact,' she added, 'you could just wait in the car and let me and Josie go round on our own. We'll come and find you when we've finished.' He looked doubtful, but agreed reluctantly and left them to it.

It was an odd experience for Lois, and she was glad that Josie had decided to come with her. She walked slowly from room to room, and remembered snatches of conversation with Mary Rix: the time they'd turned out the baby's room, the days she'd ushered Gloria Hathaway into the doctor's surgery, and Mary's strange reaction. Most of all she felt the doctor's presence.

'What was he like?' said Josie suddenly. Lois caught her breath. It was the first time Josie had asked any kind of question connected with Melvyn. She'd gone through the whole aftermath of that dreadful day in the derelict factory in a kind of mutinous silence, as if she blamed her mother and father, the doctor, the police, the Hallhouses – everyone and anyone – for what had happened to Melvyn.

It was this house, Lois realized, that had suddenly warmed Josie into life. It wasn't chilly, or frightening, for them. And the doctor's presence was so strong and reassuring, just like it had always been.

'Sit here,' she said, putting her arm round Josie and drawing her down to sit on a window seat in the sun. 'He was very nice, the doctor,' she began. 'Kind and thoughtful. Always polite to me. Didn't treat me like dirt, like some of them.'

'What about his wife?' said Josie.

'They'd had sadness,' Lois replied. 'Tried hard for a baby and never made it. But quite recently they'd come out of that, and were happy. For the first time for ages, I reckon.'

'He had it off with that Gloria, though,' said Josie.

'So did several of them,' said Lois. 'A randy professor and the vicar. You remember him when you were in hospital that time. He wasn't bad. And the cool bloke at the gallery. He's still here and his wife must be having her baby now, or soon, anyway. Funny couple, but suited, in a way. The professor's gone, but they were that sort, always moving on.'

'Why didn't the doctor take Melvyn to live with him, if they couldn't have a baby of their own?' Josie couldn't leave the subject, now she'd started. She needed to know what had been so unbearable for Melvyn.

Lois shook her head. 'Don't know,' she said. 'But if you think about it, Mary Rix would've had to have been a saint. Couldn't produce one of her own, and then be expected to bring up a little boy her husband had fathered with his fancy woman! Blimey, Josie, can you imagine it?'

Josie didn't answer. She could only picture a tiny baby, wrapped in a shawl, howling for his mother who didn't want him. She shivered. 'What about the vicar? What happened to him?' she asked.

'Resigned,' said Lois. 'Gone to London. He sent us a card, remember? Working in some boys' club and engaged to be married. Probably the best thing he could do. He certainly wasn't happy here.'

Josie wandered out of the big kitchen and started to climb the wide stairs. 'What about us, then, Mum?' she said. 'Could we be happy here?'

Lois looked down at the sheet of agents' particulars in her hand. The price was ridiculously low, and Derek had said to go ahead, if that's what she wanted. She stood up and followed Josie to the foot of the stairs. She thought of Nurse Surfleet, still living and working in the village, full of bitter memories. Her part in the sordid affair had somehow been hushed up and hadn't come out in the press, though of course the village knew and lost their respect for her as a result. Lois thought it strange that she hadn't moved away.

It was a couple of minutes before Lois answered Josie's question. Would Derek like it here? Plenty of outbuildings and a big garden. He'd like that. And rooms for all the kids to have one each, with a huge attic where they could have their stuff.

'What do *you* think, Josie?' she said. She felt out of her depth still with Josie. They'd had all kinds of counselling, of course, but Josie had maintained a stubborn silence, turned in on herself in a grief she could not share. For hours, it seemed to Lois and Derek, she shut herself in her bedroom, talking quietly to the little ginger cat. Time, the experts said. Give her time, and she'll come out of it. Now she seemed to have begun, and Lois was anxious to get it right.

Josie didn't reply, and carried on up the stairs with Lois following. 'Where's that little room you told me about,' Josie said at last, adding, 'Where they'd set it up for a baby.' Lois showed her. It was bare, except for the curtains left behind, the nursery curtains that Mary Rix had decided to leave there when it became a sewing room, but in the end had abandoned.

'She could've had Melvyn in here,' Josie said, and Lois saw with huge relief that she was crying, large tears streaming down her pale cheeks. It was the first time since Melvyn's arrest, and Lois knew it was a step forward. She stretched out her arms tentatively, and Josie finally returned her hug. 'Got a tissue, Mum?' she said, and after a minute or so walked over to open a window. She pushed back the curtains. 'Nice view,' she said, and the yellow sailing boats danced once more in the breeze.

Lois nodded, her thoughts still with the Rixes. She wondered if Dr Rix *had* ever considered asking Mary to have

Melvyn. Was it just possible that she would have agreed? She had seemed a strong woman. No, she'd never have taken Gloria's baby in, not then, with Gloria still living in the village, watching with a supercilious smirk of triumph.

Lois wandered from room to room, remembering sunny days, thinking she could hear the hum of Mary's sewing-machine. And what about me? she thought. I'd never take up the old jobs again, for those that are still here. The kids wouldn't like it. No, it'll take a bit of thought. She felt a different person from the one who'd come to Farnden as a cleaner. Something to do with Keith Simpson, and Janice and Hunter Cowgill, of course. He'd been in touch, asking her what her plans were. Don't want to lose contact, he'd said in his cool voice. Let us know what you decide to do, he'd said, several times.

She had been talking in a desultory way with Derek, and he'd suggested maybe expanding, setting up a cleaning business. 'Careful Cleaners, you could call it,' he'd said. The idea had been smouldering away in her mind, and she could see its possibilities. Other villages, other houses, with a few cleaners on her books to hire out. She could work well from here, even set up a little office in the doctor's old surgery. She'd think of a better name than Derek's suggestion! And Hunter Cowgill? Well, she could see possibilities there, too.

'Mum?' It was Josie, still in the sewing room, calling to her. She went back and stood with her arm around her.

'All right, love?' she said.

Josie nodded. 'More or less. And anyway, Mum,' she added, 'if we come to live here, can I have this room for my own?'

Lois smiled. 'So is it decided?' she said, and they walked back to the estate agent, arm in arm. He'd been in the job a long time, and as they came out of the front door, he looked at their faces and knew he'd made a sale.